Towers of the Hungry Ghosts

by

Lee Kaiser

Paths Unknown

Towers of the Hungry Ghosts

Cover Art by *The Wild Rose Press, Inc.*

The Wild Rose Press, Inc.
PO Box 708
Adams Basin, NY 14410-0708
Visit us at www.thewildrosepress.com

Publishing History
First Edition, 2023
Trade Paperback ISBN 978-1-5092-4758-5
Digital ISBN 978-1-5092-4759-2

Paths Unknown
Published in the United States of America

Seeming far away inside a memory, Ram rose to kick at a loose piece of plaster on the hearth. "Even if he is alive, it's irrelevant. It's been seven years, for God's sake. If he wanted to contact you, he would have done it by now. Have you thought about that?"

Paula turned her cheek from him and winced. The image of Goran on his final day in India, standing with his surfboard—deciding to throw away everything, including her—was always lurking around the murky fringes of her mind, showing itself at night in bed when she thought of him. She was justified in leaving Goran, but the opposite was like a gut punch.

They stared into each other's pain, slack-jawed. "You can really be mean sometimes," Paula said.

"Guys, guys. Calm down." Julie slid between them, hands raised. "I'm going to Poenari fortress to chant and meditate tomorrow. Anyone else up for it?"

Ram immediately stepped forward. "I am."

Julie turned to her friend. "Paula...? Don't look so shocked. What you saw was a prank. Ram said it happens every year."

Julie moved closer to whisper. "Come and chant with me. It'll ground you."

Get grounded. If the limp bodies weren't a prank, if Dracula's hungry ghost was at work impaling people— then their day trip to release Poenari's frustrated spirits would be anything but grounding.

Dedication

To my dad, Len, whose adventures of the armchair variety inspired my writing.

Chapter One

It had sounded like a long reprieve, those seven years—the average length of a bad marriage—but all too soon, one spring day while Paula knelt in the muggy heat of her greenhouse, her cell buzzed. She dug the phone from her skirt's pocket and groaned.

Her time was up. It was Ram phoning from his house in India. With Goran officially dead and his vast estate dumped into her lap, his best friend would no doubt want her to start promoting the famous painter's legacy.

Of all the crazy stunts Goran had pulled on her, leaving Paula his entire fortune was the lowest. Before Goran, her predictable backwoods life in Western Canada had waxed and waned with the seasons: plant the garden, eat it, chop the wood, burn it, give the tests, mark them, stock the pantry, shovel the snow.

Life held no dead ends, no blind corners.

So when Goran disappeared in 2006, it didn't occur to her it was anything but a publicity grab. As one year stretched into another, only then did she admit it—her former lover was gone for good.

Still, of the two burdens, she expected his money to be the lesser evil. His habit of ignoring his millions was one thing she approved of during their three years together. What Paula dreaded most was her relationship with his collection of prized paintings.

Combative was the word Goran had used.

Not easily flustered, as she rose to take the call today, she stepped on her hem and staggered sideways.

Yes, Paula was that woman who could garden with grace in ankle-length skirts. She preferred coarse denim. Had a closet full of it hanging above clunky desert boots. But unlike those other gardeners, with scant effort six-foot-tall Paula, tiny of waist and narrow of hip, always appeared as turned out as the Eiffel Tower on New Year's.

"Ram. Look." The greeting came out with more rancor than intended. "Goran's most valuable paintings are in commercial galleries. The rest can gather dust in vaults like the ugly Cabbage Patch dolls my students abandoned in—"

"I'm not calling about the paintings," Ram said. "You've never been to Goran's castle in Romania. Let's go see it. It'll be fun."

No, Paula thought, fun was harvesting her berry patch in a sunny southern valley of British Columbia or watching her deaf students begin to play with classmates in the schoolyard. Measurable results.

"I can't abandon my students before the end of the school year. They'll be traumatized."

"Oh, brother. Paula, you're a multi-millionaire now. Live a little."

"I am. Quite happily."

A wheezing sigh at Ram's end. "There must be a young teacher who could use the work and money. Don't be so selfish."

"What?" Ram had always been good at manipulation, or what he called *the power of persuasion.* Her friend Julie said Ram had been practicing nonstop on her ahead of his run to be a chief minister in India.

"Aren't you in the middle of a political campaign or something?"

"That's not for months. You know, this could be your and Julie's last chance to visit before she moves."

"Moves?"

"To India…Uh-oh. She didn't tell you yet?"

"What about her meditation hermitage north of Vancouver?"

"She closed it. I'm really pumped about us this time."

"Oh dear. Just make sure you stay pumped this time. As for Romania, I wasn't interested in Goran's stuff when he disappeared, so why would I want to see his abandoned castle?"

"Because a cousin found paintings inside one of the towers. Goran must have done them when he was a teenager."

Her heart jumped. Could one of these early works be what she'd always hoped for—something other than the abstract, mangled darkness which made Goran famous? She knew of only one other bright star so far.

"Whatever you felt about Goran and his art and how it damaged both of you," Ram continued—*Goran and his art, indeed. It ruined his health, yet he still refused to give it up*—"it's never too late to forgive. Anger is a pretty heavy thing to carry around year after—"

"I wasn't angry. Just disappointed." Silence at the other end. She'd been caught. Ram knew way more about toxic anger than she ever would. "I'll think about it."

At noon, Paula went inside for lunch but found herself pacing at the door of her bedroom. Rarely shut

3

since she needed the heat from the woodstove in winter and breezes in summer, behind it, blocked from view, was Goran's portrait of her in a sunhat. Aqua green was the color he'd chosen to match her eyes and bring out the red hair which fell across her shoulders in sheets.

She hadn't so much as glimpsed the painting in years. Paula swept back the door before she could change her mind and lifted the portrait from its lonely spot.

Not quite sobs nor anything like grief, her breath quickened in jittery bursts. Ram was right. This frameless canvas, balanced edge-on between her palms, would never feel as light as it truly was. *How* Goran had died—that memory had staying power.

Guilt was no featherweight.

Would it kill her to go to Transylvania and retrieve the new paintings? Just this once.

Of course not.

****

Two weeks later, Paula found herself in the back of a motorhome, travelling on a ragged road in a strange country at bone-cold twilight, looking for her castle.

The highway north from Bucharest's airport narrowed, the traffic thinned, and suddenly the motorhome was like an insect skirting the monumental retaining walls of the Varges River's hydro dam.

Seated at a fold-away table behind the driver, Paula craned her neck out the slider window, her gaze running with the highway up and across the dam. In that moment, the wind lifted the crown from her head and dashed it into the ditch. *Good riddance to the silly paper charade.*

She ducked inside. "Umm…Ram?" she said over his shoulder. "That cardboard crown you bought in Bucharest is in the ditch back there. I don't want you to think I threw it away. The wind took it."

When Ram chuckled, he hissed and jiggled like an oversized inner tube filling with air. "Three hours. That's how long you reigned over the family castle."

Paula ground her teeth into the overstuffed word; she wasn't in Romania to *reign* over anything—especially not Goran's millions or his depressing paintings. She was here to forget about them.

She leaned forward to dig her fingers into one of his shoulders. "Can't you see what he's doing?"

He flinched and glanced back. "What who's doing?"

"Goran. He wants to get the last laugh in."

Ram exchanged wild-eyed glances with Julie, sitting in the bucket seat beside him. "I'm trying to picture how a man who's been dead for seven years can laugh at anything at all."

"Don't be a snark." Paula thumped her fists against the scratchy cross-stitch of the motorhome's bench seat, unleashing the dreaded faux pine scent and a fit of sneezes. "Why do they always have to…?" She reached to open the slider window at her back only to see a reflection of her hideously pouty lips.

"I'd be happier as a—a truck driver on the Trans-Canada Highway than a multi-millionaire, much less the *la-dy* of his castle."

"Breathe, Paula," Julie said.

"Think about it. We weren't even together anymore. You should have the money, Ram."

"Not me. I haven't even touched the money my father left to me. Anyway, I made more than enough before I hung up my geologist hat for politics. Or have you forgotten? Big Oil blood money. Isn't that what you called it?"

At the word *politics*, Paula's mind began to churn. "That's what you could use it for." About to thump her fist in triumph, she remembered the last chemical-infused dust cloud. "Your campaign in India."

"My opponents would sure love it. 'Executor of Will Siphons Money from Dead Friend's Estate.' " He glanced at her in the rearview mirror. "Geez, Paula, if you're that stressed, leave the lot of it with the estate planner."

"Oh. Him." Paula gave the guy the thumbs down. "See." She shuffled to the edge of the bench seat to shove her disgust at each friend in turn. "This is exactly what's wrong with too much money. It's like Goran's paintings—an unnecessary disturbance to the mind. I'd rather bury it somewhere than prop up child sweatshops or genetically modified food inside that high-yield portfolio of his.

"Julie." Paula reached for her friend with all the gravitas she could muster. "I trust you. Why don't you take it for something?"

Paula's lifelong buddy twisted in her bucket seat, screwed up her face, and blinked. "Because I made a vow of frugality to my Buddhist mentor, maybe? I mean, how much is it? Ten? Twenty million American dollars?"

"More," Ram said.

"Anyway, Goran hated me. His ghost would strangle me in the night if he knew I had his money."

Imagine that, after years of creeping around each other in their shared grief, Ram's timid chuckles washed over Paula like a milky balm and trickled into a still-raw corner she didn't know was there.

Minutes later, Ram swung the vehicle into a turnout probably meant for snapping photos. He shut off the motor. In the shadowed dusk, the only evidence of the dam was the dull roar of water and a misty film on the windows. Maybe Ram was tired and wanted to change drivers.

"Julie, switch places with Paula…Please."

As soon as Paula settled in, he pivoted until they were face to face and close enough for him to cup one of her hands between his. "There's something you must remember."

What in the world…? Paula caught Julie's eye, but her friend seemed as surprised.

"Goran loved *you*, not me. Or…not in the same way. He loved you right to the end."

Damn him. Anxiety knifed through her; her bottom lip began to quiver. "You're saying I shouldn't have left him?"

"You know I'm not. I won't pretend to speculate why you're the sole recipient in his will, but I imagine he left it with me because he knew I'd treat it as sacred."

He released her hand and sat with his thoughts a minute before starting the vehicle. "This is what he wanted."

"My friend," Julie said, resting her hand on Paula's shoulder as they pulled away. "Don't rush into any decisions on your inheritance. Be patient, and let the answer come to you."

The Varges Dam, Romania's pride, imprinted itself on Paula's memory, then blinked out as the motorhome plunged through a concrete tunnel and emerged on a mountain track jammed against an endless rock face. Any slower would bring them to a complete halt. Like great knobby claws, the ancient oaks overhanging the vehicle scraped and squealed across the metallic roof, as if to swallow them whole.

Somewhere in the valley below was her castle. Unless they were lost.

"You know, I can't find that tunnel back there on the map." She raised her eyes from her lap to find Ram white-knuckling both sides of the steering wheel. Not his usual cavalier style, but she soon realized why.

The last bend into shadow cast the drop-off into a confusion of milky edges, the valley bottom obliterated by the lingering mist kicked up from the dam.

"You're doing fine." She squeezed his upper arm, the sticky dampness hot against her fingertips. He wore a synthetic dress shirt of all things—a resilient habit from his wealthy Indian upbringing, and the worst garment to hide the beginnings of a paunch, six foot two or not.

"I know, I know," he had said that morning when Paula cast her evil eye on the bulge at Bucharest's airport.

Paula checked the map one final time and announced: "We're lost."

"Why do you think I've been looking for a damn place to turn around for the past half hour?" Ram said.

The sentence was no sooner out than the cliffside ended. They piled in behind a horse-drawn trailer of hogs swaying and rattling into a village straight from serfdom. "Gross." Julie was the first to draw her window tight against the pigs' dung. The stench seemed to congeal on the tip of Paula's tongue.

Old men with broad-brimmed felt hats and beards of spun glass swung their ox-carts aside as the motorhome sped past. In a field beside a soot-blackened clapboard house, a round-faced woman swathed in scarves and bent over a hand plough flicked her hand up the road when she saw Ram stopped and leaning from his window.

"There. Across the road," Paula said. "That looks like a hotel." She pointed over his shoulder at a weathered timber veranda where a rusty sign of a giant perogy squealed a seesaw tune in the breeze.

Three nubile women in fishnet stockings and vinyl mini-skirts lounged atop the railing like drowsy tropical parrots but came alive at the sight of Ram striding through the dust. Oscillating hips gave way to hand gestures before he returned.

What in the world would hookers be doing in a remote village, Paula wondered, just as Ram voiced the same question.

"I guess it's a job. Either that or starve," Paula said.

Julie turned up her nose. "Did they offer you a three-for-one deal?"

"Something like that."

Paula smirked to herself. Built like a long-legged brick of ice-cream going soft around the edges, Ram had more than enough terrain to keep all three busy.

He sucked on his front teeth. "This is Poenari village all right, but they don't know how much farther the castle is."

Across the street, the trio of hookers erupted into frantic bellowing at something beyond the motorhome. A bare-armed butcher in a bloody apron stepped from his stoop, stubbed out his cigarette, and shuffled to Ram's window.

"You ask about the castle? Not far, but the old mine road, she is a wild ride. Falling down and going like this." He chopped his hands in a pattern of spastic switchbacks.

How much wilder could it get? Paula thought.

The butcher squinted into the setting sun. "Sleep at the village pension."

Ram had tackled his fair share of dodgy roads, both day and night, he told the man. The sallow butcher gave him an offhand shrug that begged to be taken more seriously.

Minutes later, Paula sighed as a Tourist Rooms sign swinging from a gabled adobe went by in a blur. Instead of the prolific colors of popsicle orange or sky blue, this particular cottage was painted pastel pink.

The so-called mine road was no worse, but also no better. Paula had her nose in the map again when she looked up in time to see a bold, red sign caught in the headlights. "Whoa. Stop the vehicle…Ram? I said stop." When he ignored her, Paula reached over and rapped her knuckles against his skull.

"Ow-uch." The motorhome skidded to a halt.

"Did you not see the sign back there? It said 'Beware.' " Here was not the amenable thirty-four-year-old she knew so well, but a squirmy little boy with a secret.

"It was a warning about wolves in the area," Julie crowed from behind them. "And something else I couldn't make out."

Paula armed her naturally raspy voice with an edge. "I want to see it for myself. It can't be any more than four meters back. Pass me the flashlight, Julie."

"I'll come, too." Julie barely had her bottom off the bench seat when Ram cut in.

"No. No." His words slid out as if the forced silence had left him exhausted. "We're not lost. The sign points uphill to Poenari Fortress."

Silence until Julie said: "Are we supposed to know

what that is?"

"Vlad Tepes?" Ram hinted. "Of the House of Draculesti."

Paula sighed, tired of his tedious game. "What's this about?"

"At the top of those stairs we passed is the citadel of Vlad the Impaler. Also known by readers as Count Dracula."

"What?"

He raised his hands in defense as Paula bolted from her seat. Was it not common courtesy to tell potential homeowners about their new neighborhood *before* handing them the key to the front door?

"There's not much left of it, anyway," he said. "I always thought it was kinda cool. Goran and I used to go up there as kids and scare the knackers off each other. Dracula's just a made-up story, but the real Vlad Tepes was a nasty dude. He had a fierce hate on for the invading Turks. Used to impale them through the arse on poles and leave them to a slow, agonizing death. The stories about him eating his victims could easily—"

"Oh, for God's sake. Stop." Paula's stomach dropped at the idea of such horrific energies lingering nearby. Within the white noise of the running motor, she pressed her fingers to her lips in prayer, closed her eyes, and murmured: "May all beings be at peace," over and over until the cutting edge of Julie and Ram's argument broke in.

"Ram says you wouldn't have come here had you known about this Vlad guy and what he did up there." Julie poked her thumb above her head. "That's not true, is it?"

"Well...I—" Surprises of all varieties, good or bad,

were terrible things. This went far beyond that. "I need to know what's ahead and prepare for it. It's hard to say what I would have done."

Ram turned his head and wrinkled his nose at Julie.

Before the vehicle rolled onward, her limbs began to tingle in a swirl of vertigo. Reflected in the passenger's side mirror, the fog swallowed the sign. Was it really all child's play for Goran to grow up next door to a place with such a blood-soaked past?

The motorhome began a steep, snaking descent which Paula assumed would end at the entrance to the castle.

"We should see water any minute," Ram said.

"You mean it's on a river feeding into the reservoir?"

"No. Even better. The castle is right at the edge. Waterfront property now. I wanted it to be a surprise."

"Not again."

"Just wait, you'll see."

The dirt road dead-ended at a flat clearing where dregs of daylight fell on a gravel boat launch. They were deep inside the forested pit which was the Varges Valley, staring at all that remained of her castle.

"What the hell happened here?" Ram jumped down and trudged like a wooden soldier to the water's edge. He raked his fingers through his hair, not uttering a word before turning to the two women at his side. "The place is hardly recognizable. They told me the hydroelectric dam flooded the grounds, but I didn't think the entire castle would be under water."

From the inky stillness of the reservoir jutted a solitary stone citadel. In the fading light, it seemed as shapeless and forgettable as a village water-tower riding a hump of land. The scene washed over Paula like chilly rain; the final spark of anticipation she'd felt on the countryside byway went out.

"Geez, I'm sorry," Ram said. "They left a boat for us. It's got to be around here somewhere, but we'll have to stay in the motorhome or go back to the village. It's your call, Paula."

"It isn't what I thought." She burned with an entangled mess of embarrassment and anger that choked off words—she'd set herself up only to be let down. Not since Goran had she played that pathetic song. *Get the paintings and get out.*

"I'm sure it'll look better in daylight." Ram could never hold his tongue on an important choice, whether his to decide or not. "Look. There's even a dock."

Although well-built, it couldn't have held more than a single boat, Paula thought.

"The reservoir eventually feeds into the Danube. Cool, right?"

Tune him out.

"You can't see it from this angle, but there's a courtyard and a chaplain's cottage a few yards from the citadel's entrance. That's where Goran and I always stayed straight from our boarding school in England. I'll bet it's all above water. God, have…what…more than twenty years already passed?"

Julie crept closer to ask if Paula needed a hug. "Not right now." What was this place? A musty smell of branches blackened by frost drifted from a steep embankment beside the road—the aroma of villagers' roast pork and smokey hearths just a memory.

She stared at the impersonal monstrosity which had been Goran's childhood home. How could she have been so cruel as to leave him when he needed her most?

"I shouldn't have come." She turned decisively from the shoreline. "I'm headed for an appointment with a dead man. I can't believe there was a time I thought we might live here. Instead of my cabin." Her face collapsed into a grimace. "Such a pathetic romantic."

"After all the work you did," Julie said, catching up to her before she reached the motorhome, "you actually want to go there again? Plunge that knife in? No one I know is more devoted to living in the present moment than you. Give yourself some space."

"Your man is right beside you." Paula jabbed a finger in Ram's direction. "Mine is submerged at the bottom of the Indian Ocean. Dead in the water." In the creeping mist, her fleece poncho lay damp and heavy across her shoulders. "I don't feel a bit of warmth from anything here."

Julie grasped Paula's shoulders. "Come back to us, friend. Goran is gone, but we're still here…and so is the castle he gave you. As soon as we find the paintings, we can leave if that's what you want."

This time, Paula easily fell into Julie's arms. They no longer felt cold and twitchy as they once had. Despite Julie's spiritual path she would never be Paula, the woman their town called the Hermit Priestess.

"I don't think we should go any farther tonight." Julie arched onto the balls of her feet to announce this over Paula's shoulder. "Bears can swim. Damn good." She pointed to the water. "We'll need an early start to check every corner of that thing before we stay there.

"First, I'm going to boil water for tea inside. We've got the leftover cold cuts and bread in the mini-fridge. Paula, you need to relax while I help Ram find the boat if that's what he wants. Okay?"

Paula nodded, then straightened to look at Ram.

"Amazing. That's exactly what I was going to suggest." Ram came to kiss the top of Julie's head. "Love you."

This wasn't getting any easier, Paula thought. Since her friends had reignited their romance months earlier in India, she was the uneven third leg of a drop-leaf table, the one better left out of sight. Every show of affection added to her own well of unfinished business. During their years together, Goran could never say these words because he didn't yet love *himself.*

****

In the passenger seat of the motorhome, Paula cupped her tea, the steam warm against her cheeks and weary eyes.

Ram appeared at the open door. "Feeling better?"

She smiled and nodded but reared back as he fished a pistol from the glove compartment and shoved it inside the back of his waistband.

"Don't worry. It's not real," he said immediately. "Bought it in the same toy store where I got the crown. It shoots harmless blanks but makes one hell of a *bang*." He turned to join Julie in a search for the boat trailer a Vlakia relative had delivered from the village earlier that day.

Soon after, there were faint shouts within the roadside bushes and bobbing beams. A band of clouds rolled by, plunging the world outside her window into blackness. She reached under the dash and patted around for the headlight switch. As light illuminated the cab, she sat up. On the outside of the windshield, inches from her face, shone the piercing amber eyes of a wolf, its paws propped against the vehicle's hood.

Paula froze, her eyes wide and shining at the natural magnificence before her. It was a regal, well-fed animal with long, tawny fur. She felt safe inside the enclosed cab until a menacing snarl raised one corner of its mouth. It thumped one massive paw against the windshield, turned to a phantom sound, and bounded from sight. The sheer momentum left the motorhome rocking under her.

"Over here," Ram said. A metronome of light swept the dark. "We found it."

The body does not lie. Her hands trembled while she revved the engine and pumped the horn a few times in case the wolf was still around.

As Paula stepped from the driver's seat, Julie turned to her. "The whole neighborhood must be awake by now."

Paula scanned the hood for paw prints but, seeing no trace, glanced up. "Just getting used to the rental." Talk of wolves and tired eyes could play tricks.

"Our only neighbors would be vampires already awake. *Ah—woooo—*" Ram arched back with a howl cut short by Julie's fist bump.

"Is this how you plan to carry on in India during your campaign?"

"Nope. I reckon this is my last chance to be a perfect wanker without anyone knowing." After eschewing his roots for almost two decades, Ram had turned tail on the world's oil complex to take on corruption in the northern Indian state of his birth. The politician with the black kinky ponytail planned to milk his environmental epiphany for all it was worth, even though the credit lay with his Julie.

"Save the jokes for the morning, Musahar. Let's

hook up the boat trailer and get some sleep."

"Yes. No more talk of vampires." Paula spoke in the defeated tone of a weary mother with raucous children.

A moment later, Ram's muscular arms pulled her into him. "I'm sorry. I'm so ramped up about being back here. I'll take some blankets and sleep in the boat tonight. You ladies can have another cuppa and catch up—"

Paula tore herself from his embrace. "No. Don't sleep outside. I'm fine. See? I'm fine." From her friends' frowns, Paula realized she was shouting. She rarely raised her voice.

****

Paula woke in the dark, the sliding window beside her laden with condensation from the coldest part of the night—what the superstitious called the third watch between midnight and three in the morning.

Of course, Ram had insisted on spreading his sleeping roll on the floor in the galley kitchen to give the women the double foam bed at the table. She cracked the window open, pulled the heavy quilt she shared with Julie tight over the light T-shirt she wore, and lay back to enjoy the refreshing puffs of night air grazing her cheeks.

A far-off, elongated howl reached her, and for a moment, she reveled in the tremulous sound so often heard from coyotes in the hills outside her cabin—until an equally mournful reply erupted from directly below her window. Julie stirred in her sleep and turned away, and Paula gingerly slid the window shut.

At the sound of sharp scuffling noises on the gravel outside, she propped herself on one elbow and caught the back end of the giant, red wolf trotting out of view into the fringe of underbrush alongside the water.

****

"Stop. It's going wide again."

That was Julie's voice. Paula broke into a jog along the hillside horse trail she'd discovered at dawn. Her friends were not only awake but were already launching the rowboat. They would have to forgive her wanderings once she told them about the grand woodland of aged oaks she'd stumbled upon. Not the measly oak centerpiece common in parks back home, but an entire forest of them.

A vehicle door slammed, followed by shoes crunching through gravel. "It's just a rowboat. How hard can it be?" Ram's voice said. "Claudia's message said she hauled it out here behind her scooter."

"A scooter around those corners? Doesn't she have a car?"

"Probably broken down. Of all the cousins I've met, she's the most like Goran. When you see her, you'll know why."

Already buoyed by the morning sun playing on her back, the idea of meeting Goran's relatives, people who knew him long before she did, brought a smile to Paula's face. She broke from the shoulder-high bush. "Then I'd definitely like to meet Claudia."

Her friends turned and stared at Paula, then at each other. "See," Ram said to Julie.

"I didn't want to wake you." Paula came alongside them. "You weren't worried, I hope."

"We just finished that argument," Ram said. "I won. I said you were a grown woman out for a walk."

"I'm dying for coffee." Paula reached for Julie's car-cup. "May I?"

"Sorry about the sugar." Julie handed it over, and

Paula took a couple of deep swigs while her friend turned to Ram. "I know you want to get the job done, but we should let Paula try now that she's here. She has the most experience with launching fishing boats back home."

Paula had known what to do from the start. To be fair, although he was an engineer Ram had likely never launched any kind of watercraft before. During her winter in India, only once did she see a sport boat on the beach where she spent much of her time while Goran and Ram surfed. The fishermen pushed out and pulled in their bulky wooden skiffs with help from many hands.

"Get in and give it a try, then." He held out the key.

Best to make it sound like she'd just thought of it. "Hey. The three of us could probably carry it in, don't you think?"

Julie immediately guffawed at their short-sighted stupidity, but Ram kept up his skeptical pout even after they'd loaded their overnight gear and were underway.

"When did the hydro plant flood the valley?" Paula couldn't care less. It was an icebreaker.

"Goran and I had just graduated from uni, so..." His oars sliced the flat surface. "Must have been three years before I met you and Julie in India."

She marveled at the narrow strip of water. "You could easily swim it, couldn't you?"

"I can't imagine what that dock back there is for," Ram said. "The hospital predated the reservoir by decades, so it wasn't for that."

"What hospital?" *This* was interesting.

"He never told you? The Soviets occupied Romania after the war. Since the castle was more like a palace, they confiscated it. Turned it into a mental hospital. Sold off everything and pocketed the money." Ram pulled with the gusto of an Olympic sculler even though the current was negligible. "Goran was born into the midst of a bunch of nutters. His grandfather and grandmother, the old count and countess, were put to work as manual laborers."

"That must have been a shocker," Julie said.

"The medieval citadel up ahead was here first, on a hill. Goran's ancestors moved in three hundred years later and built the palace below. Imagine the sheer size of it. Fifty bedrooms. There was a banquet hall with a marble rotunda and indoor fountain. The chapel had flying buttresses and a vaulted ceiling Goran said was neo-Gothic. He was the art guy. I wouldn't know. We're floating over the former recital hall right now."

At this, both women peered over the side in synch, but Paula noted the water was shot through with a fine silt.

"At one time, his ancestors owned all the woods and farmland for one hundred square kilometers, including the village we passed through."

"How did they afford Goran's boarding school? They must have got it back at some point," Paula said.

"Not the land. And the palace was gutted except for a secret cache of paintings. I have this memory of his mother standing in the cottage's kitchen, crying." Ram paused, the image seeming to run through him. "The place became a chain around their necks. They had no farm rents coming in. Hell, they were growing food where the lawns used to be. His parents died in poverty long before the hydro-electric windfall."

"Goran never returned after university?" Paula asked.

Ram hesitated, grinding out a couple of strokes

before answering. "Nope. He was here for his mother's funeral when he was sixteen. He had issues with relatives. You know."

"No. I don't." How often had Paula heard from friends about these unutterable *issues*? Hers was a loving family unit of two adults, one child. No relatives, annoying or otherwise, closer than a three-day drive. Paula's issues had been with the ten-year-old kid next door with the double chin, and just about every classmate, grades one through three. That included the school terror, Julie Paglia, who got away with swearing—in Italian—and sat beside Paula this very moment.

"Then you'll have to ask Goran's oddball cousin what happened. I'm not one to gossip."

"Bullshit." Julie leaned forward and slapped his leg.

Precisely, Paula thought. Hard to know whether the problems Goran had with relatives were simply not juicy enough for Ram—or too explosive to repeat. Snooping into sensitive family history wouldn't endear her to Claudia, a virtual stranger. Best to let anything important surface naturally as their friendship grew.

Was this the end of Ram's surprises—or just the beginning?

The citadel's stone base loomed, menacing as a midnight iceberg—more massive than it looked from afar. This was not just a tower but an entire conical fortress the width of a football field. Where the rocky escarpment ended and the gray fortress started was so seamless the structure appeared to rise from the reservoir.

Ram glanced over his shoulder and swept one oar wide. "Here we are at the citadel already."

Chapter Two

The unseen side of Paula's island held a gentle slope of treed ledges covered with brilliant yellow weeds. This was more like it.

Ram ran the boat aground on a pebbled strip of beach where a zigzagging set of stone stairs led to the top. Paula, the best prepared with her usual calf-length denim skirt and waterproof boots, offered to haul the boat up so the other two didn't have to get their runners and pants wet.

The place was hers, yet stepping onto the lifeless promontory felt somehow intrusive.

"Come." With the boat safely ashore, Paula held out her hands to the other two. "A moment of silence to remember Goran." A breeze rustled the ropey limbs of a solitary dying oak where Paula imagined baby Goran had lain sleeping in the arms of his mother on hot afternoons.

They clasped hands in a circle; Paula tilted her head skyward, eyes closed, while Ram and Julie bowed their heads. He choked off a sob, no doubt overwhelmed with memories of the days before water invaded every cranny of the palace Goran's ancestors had occupied for centuries.

They'd brought backpacks, bedrolls, the cooler of food, gallon cans of kerosene, the Coleman stove, gas lanterns, and jugs of water. Hauling it up stone steps worn from brutal winters, and with no banister, would take most of the morning. After they emptied the boat on shore and flipped it over their gear, Ram led the way up.

"Slow down and wait for us," Julie yelled to him.

"You gotta see the view from here." Already at the last stair, he bounced on the balls of his feet, then stepped aside for Paula.

Bent double from the climb, she raised her eyes to distant peaks and valleys. They reminded her of green velvet throws tossed over sofas, rumpled and crimped beside cascades of white water. Definitely old-growth forests, as were the dignified white beech trees lining the edge of the citadel's expansive but overgrown courtyard.

Their feathery limbs cast a shadow through the low morning mist where she stood among a chaos of purple groundcover. It lent a splash of color to the citadel's unwelcoming gray stone, but nothing could redeem the weathered double doors at the center of it all. The battered oak and rusted trim looked threatening enough without the two towers blackened with age to each side.

"No dawdling." Ram handed the industrial flashlight to Paula. A few strides of his long legs took him to where one of the hulking doors was ajar, propped open by stray stones. He squeezed past, bear spray in hand.

Inside the threshold, the two women entered a short corridor so tight and dingy her friend's hand shot out to grab Paula's shoulder. Beyond, Ram's voice gamboled: "*Waa—waa—waa*," followed by staccato footfalls on stone.

Once inside the lofty central core, patches of waxy light from an overhead cupola of stained glass reached the dreary flagstones they stood on, but otherwise, a suffocating stillness pressed in.

Julie called Ram's name. No response. As they crossed the rotunda, Paula spun around at the hollow tap of footsteps, sure someone was there, only to realize it was an echo of her own heels.

She shone the flashlight into a horseshoe-shaped arcade of doorways, before running the beam up a grand staircase at the far end leading to an overhead mezzanine.

Julie raised her voice. "Don't think you're going to jump out and scare the hell out of us. We know your game." She leaned toward Paula. "Come on. Let's make him wait and check out one of these other rooms."

Pushing the wedge of cool fluorescent light before them, they skirted the staircase and crossed under the arched arcade where a mouse scuttled into a dark corner.

"Now this is what I call a hearth," Julie said, as they entered a spacious oblong room with a mammoth fireplace. Slender windows along one wall overlooked the reservoir and motorhome in the distance. "You could fit an entire roasting pig in there."

Paula had read everything she could find on the internet about Romanian castles and the early medieval fortresses. It was the educator in her. She spied brick ovens through the doorway of an adjoining room. "This has to be the banquet hall because…" She ducked into the next room and raised her arms in triumph. "Here we have the kitchen."

Much squatter, but brighter, the kitchen formed an L-shape with the banquet hall. In front of a sooty fireplace, an expansive stone counter dominated mid-room. Even more telling was the sprawling iron slab atop the four red-brick ovens.

"My gosh, is this an industrial kitchen, or what?"

Paula said. When fired up, the stovetop could have heated at least a dozen large pots or kettles at a time.

The main light came from a row of shallow smudged panes near the ceiling and a porthole-sized window above a porcelain laundry tub, which overlooked the water. Paula opened a set of shabby french doors reduced to a checkerboard of broken and whole panes, and stepped into a walled kitchen courtyard. At its center stood a water well, overrun with pine cones and broken branches.

"Well." Julie motioned toward the kitchen. "Looks like we can set up camp here, if the chaplain's cottage isn't—"

Paula gripped her friend's arm. "Shhh...Do you hear voices?"

Julie shook her head, but both of them retraced their steps to the entrance rotunda where they heard, "You come at me with that ax"—Paula spun the light beam into dark corners, searching as the words ricocheted into the cupola and back down—"and you'll get a faceful of bear spray."

Ting. Ting. Cr—aak. A grating collision of metal on stone. Then a gruesome scream.

Julie tore up two stairs at a time but faltered at the top.

"This way." Paula turned on her heel, and the corridor went jet black. She slammed into what felt like a rubber wall; the impact flung her backward. Someone latched onto one wrist as she stumbled.

"Whoa there." Her captor stepped into the light, gripping a scrap of chair leg with a protruding nail, and grinning like an imbecile. *Ram.*

"You utter asshole." Seeming to use her last morsel

of air to yell this, Julie bent over into a wheezing fit.

"Hey. Aren't you glad I haven't been ax murdered?"

"No. And if I had one, I'd make sure the job was complete."

Paula couldn't recall seeing this juvenile spontaneity in Ram before. She still tingled; her voice caught in her throat. "Please don't do that again. It's not funny at all."

"Yeah, I guess," Ram murmured. "Another childish game I played with Goran after the staff moved out." His shoulders slumped; he knew he'd gone too far. "I think Goran spent more time here than in the cottage with his family. Strange, because this is where all his troubles started."

Downcast, Paula glanced up at the cryptic comment in time to see Julie scowl and shake her head at Ram. Over Ram's shoulder, she could see the open doorway of one room and the gloomy interior within. "It's way too dark to be up here until the afternoon sun comes around. Let's go."

From their spot at the top of the grand staircase, they stood before a race-track-shaped mezzanine. "There's the entrance to one of the towers." Ram pointed to an arched doorway at the far end, directly above the citadel's main entrance. Dim slivers of morning sun escaped from it. "It could be where Claudia said she saw the paintings. Let's go up while we have the light."

Inside the murky tower, they climbed the stone staircase, barely wider than a man's shoulders, and ridiculously steep. Scooped from the walls, the steps had worn into washboards from a millennium of soldier's feet tramping to the battlements at the top.

"Ram? Wait up for me."

Barely begun, he stopped while Paula hustled to the step below him. "What did you mean about Goran's troubles starting inside the citadel?"

"Oh. Um…Just that his father and mother died in here only three years apart. That's all."

She let it sink in. "But…Goran said they all lived in the cottage. Right?" He had disappeared around the next bend, the click of his heels fading.

Long minutes later, with Julie and Paula almost clawing their way on hands and knees, a whistled tune drifted from above. They rounded a bend where Ram leaned in a shaft of sunlight from one of the battlement slits.

"How the hell…" Julie sagged and gulped in air. "…can you see where you're going without the light?"

"It's not my first time up these."

"That's got to be a hundred steps so far." Paula tilted her gaping jaw to the razor-thin breeze from the slit.

"Not nearly," Ram said. "It's too dark in here for speed."

"And too stinky." Julie pressed the back of her wrist to her mouth. "Were these towers the precursor of the modern urinal?"

Paula grinned to herself in the gloom. "Probably rodent pee." She squinted through the narrow opening. "Judging by what I see of the twin tower, we're almost at the top."

The final turn dumped them into a tight cubbyhole of a landing streaked with black mildew.

Plop. Plop.

They faced a modern metal door like one used for an industrial utility room, the keyed deadbolt locked tight.

Plop.

"What was that?" Julie raked her fingernails in a fury across the top of her head.

"Hold still." Paula pulled at her friend's hands. "Let me see." Paula smirked. The arachnophobic scalp-scrubbing had untangled Julie's madhouse hair. "It's just drips off the ceiling."

Immersed in his own drama, Ram was giving the impregnable stainless steel a thorough thrashing. "Why in hell didn't Claudia say the door was locked? Sorry, guys. I'll message her when I catch a signal on my satellite phone."

The two women began the painstaking shuffle to the bottom, leaving Ram behind. "If I remember right," he called down, "the chapel on the ground floor has morning sun. Unless it's in ruins, it's an amazing place."

"What would a chapel be doing in a citadel?" Paula groped her way along the stone wall.

"Every medieval fortress had one. The safest place to be in a siege. Back then, no God-fearing man would dare attack a holy house."

After exiting the tower, Ram raced ahead back to the grand staircase leading to the ground floor. "Down here, this way." With the two women on his heels, when he reached the bottom, he turned left to march along the colonnaded arcade and stop before carved gilt doors more massive yet than those at the entrance.

Parting the double doors revealed the chapel floor to be a wasteland of toppled pews and bird droppings from a bevy of doves cooing and roosting along overhead crossbeams. A few of the oak benches in the front row still clung to their former life, slumped against the pillaged pulpit, stripped bare of what Paula speculated had been gold leaf trim.

Lording over everything, as if challenging one to ignore the sacrilegious decimation inside, an ethereal light streaked through the east wall of ceiling-to-floor stained glass. It drew them forward and under the threshold in silence, so they didn't at first see what hovered above.

At the first circle of the room, Paula stumbled back and pointed above the doors. "Who in their right mind would paint *this* for a chapel?" She stared at the freakish mural of a wolf's head skewered on a spike, its sinister toothy snarl dripping with bloody sinew and conjoined with a scaly serpent's body.

"I don't know." Julie tilted her head, an expression both pensive and sour. "Is it any worse than spikes through hands and feet? When I was a kid, I couldn't look at the crucifixion statues on Sundays. The sheer size of this easily commands the entire chapel."

Ram sidled alongside Paula, his voice a tentative whisper. "It's the family's battle standard. I'd bet you anything it's Goran's work. Just from the scope and innate violence."

Paula stepped back to glare at him. "It is *not* his. How could it be if you've never seen it before?"

"Because the last time I came here we were only fifteen. I was getting a sense of the dark places Goran's mind went, but there's no way he could have painted something of this complexity at that age."

"There's nothing grand about this."

"Come on, Paula. This is art, or are you idealizing his work?"

During their circle on the beach, Paula had decided romanticizing Goran would be the best way to get through the island's unsettling overwhelm. "I'm not into this right now. Let's get a look at the cottage, if that's where we'll stay."

Ram hesitated. "Julie, give me the light. I want to make a quick visit to the crypt to honor Goran's parents. I doubt I'll be inside here again. Not into religion." Ram took the flashlight and turned. "See you guys at the cottage in ten. Cross over the knoll in the yard. It should be right there at the edge of a drop-off to the water.

The women had taken no more than two steps when Paula called to him. "Wait. I'll go with you." When she caught up and slipped her hand into his, he brightened, their bond restored in an instant.

"Together again, I guess," Ram said, giving it a squeeze.

There was a time after Goran's death when she and Ram were as intimate as friends could be, thrown into a mutual trauma where surviving it called for them to drop all pretense and agree to start their lives anew, no matter how painful the letting go. For a time, it had felt like she was closer to Ram than her childhood friend, Julie, and eventually Ram surprised her by admitting he felt the same way.

Rightly so, her friends' fresh start returned Paula to the background, but occasionally, like today, she caught a glimmer of their old bond in Ram's eyes. That gift would never die.

The crypt staircase was no more than ten steps down and broad enough to descend abreast. "Keep your eyes on your feet. No telling how worn these stairs have become," Ram said.

The remarkably intimate space forced him to slouch. Graffiti covered the walls and exterior of two concrete tombs rising from the center. Carved in script on the metal plate of one, bent and broken as if someone had tried to pry it loose, was *Tiberius Count Vlakia, 4th Count of Varges. Died November 4, 1990, Aged 88.* The smaller tomb was conspicuously bare of any name.

Ram squeezed between them. "That's the grandfather, old Count Vlakia. Goran's parents are over here in this corner," he said.

"And the tomb with no name?"

Ram raised the flashlight to it and squinted. "Probably was meant for his grandmother, the countess, but she escaped to England when the Soviets moved in. Never returned. Left her son behind with the old count, but took her teenage daughter with her. That would be Claudia's mum."

"Claudia's mother? The one you call Aunt Lisbet went to England as a girl?"

"Correct. She lives here now, but she's as British as they come."

In a dingy, low-slung corner, she grasped the hand he offered, and they stood on the ancient flagstones in silence, their toes touching the beveled edges of the metal floor plaques marking the ashes of Goran's parents.

Tibor Vlakia, one inscription said. *Beloved Husband, Died August 13, 1991, Aged 53.* The other bore *Sophie Vlakia, Beloved Wife, Aged 52,* who Paula noted died exactly three years later to the day.

The resolve in Ram's grip and the serenity which envelopes all places where the dead lie, quickly dissolved any desire she had to mar it with questions about Goran's parents.

Suddenly, he let go of her hand, bent down, and lay

the flashlight at his feet, crossing himself and joining his palms in prayer. Ram had spent his childhood in a Catholic orphanage in India, but this display of faith surprised her. Was this behind his ambivalence about her following him into the crypt?

His prayers hung in the dead air like a droning swarm. As she turned away to give him a moment of privacy, Paula froze in her tracks at an image on the dark wall behind them. There, illuminated within the flashlight's cameo was a mural; its unmistakable meaning twisted her insides tight as a garotte. She gasped at the life-size fresco of herself and stumbled from it at first, then drew near and dropped to her knees, mesmerized.

Now that Goran was *officially* dead, why not go to Romania, her friends had said. Tidy up a few loose ends at the old ancestral castle. She'd relented, descended into this gloomy crypt to pull on one of those dangling threads.

Now her whole damn life was about to unravel.

Seven years since he'd disappeared—was this mural not proof Goran was still alive?

In the depths of a medieval chapel gutted of anything holy, Paula palmed the cold, smooth plaster. She trailed fingertips across a jagged row of freckles at her hairline before moving to the sprinkles of sand on her cheek and lips—here was the day on the Bay of Bengal when she fell asleep while Goran surfed. She woke to the sun-warmed press of his lips on hers. When she'd propped herself on one elbow and laughed, he snapped this image with his cell phone's camera. How proud he'd been to own the cutting-edge technology in 2002.

If there was any doubt as to the time and place, one

corner of Suni's guesthouse had nudged its way into the background. At the mural's lower end, beads of perspiration bisected the deep well of her cleavage. What yearning and sorrow he must have felt with each dip of his brush. She squeezed her eyes shut against his pain.

Was it possible he loved her so deeply?

That day on the beach had been long before the first episode hit, and she'd admonished Ram for not warning her off Goran. "What are you talking about?" he'd shrieked. "You were already in too deep the first night. You would have told me to get lost."

So true.

Ram stirred and scooped the flashlight from the stone floor, sinking the mural into obscurity. No way was she leaving without confirming what she'd seen.

"I'll carry the flashlight." Ram let go of it, but before he could turn to climb the stone steps into the chapel she said, "Look at this, and tell me what you think." The painting jumped to life under the cool rays rippling across the crypt's ceiling.

He inched forward, speechless, no doubt already running possible scenarios as to how his friend could have kept this painting a secret from both of them.

"I'll tell you what it means to *me*." She thrust the beam into his startled eyes. "Goran is still alive."

"Paula. Sweetheart." He palmed the flashlight aside, and she felt the warmth of his hand on her shoulder, but there was little sweetness in his tone. "Goran died in India seven years ago. We looked on the beach for weeks. Way longer than Julie and I should have."

"And did you find a body?" *No body meant no death.* Goran's painting of her put the theory back in play.

"How many times do we have to go through this? The only way to identify him would have been by his swim trunks. Maybe not even that, knowing how much he liked to surf naked."

"Then, how did this get here?" She spun the light to the wall. "From the time Goran met me, he never returned to Romania. Other than his last eight weeks, we were always together, give or take a day."

"Obviously, he painted this between the time you'd left him and when he disappeared in India."

"You can't be serious." Knowing Ram, in the minutes since the discovery, the logistics engineer in him would have thought through the timelines and arrived at the only reasonable conclusion: Goran couldn't have come to such a remote location without them knowing. He must have painted this after he'd disappeared.

"Okay." Paula slapped the flashlight into his clammy palm. "Let's count. We know for sure after I left him he spent the first month with you in Stockholm." She pinched off an index finger. "And the last three weeks in India at your father's house." She pulled on the finger beside it.

"So that leaves a week," she said, yanking on a third finger. "Which might be enough time to visit the family castle except...he had called you in Brazil from your own Stockholm landline three days before he flew to India."

Paula pumped her pinkie in his face. "We're down to four days, Ram. Since there's no record of him flying out of Stockholm, you're telling me he crossed Europe by train, drove up here from Bucharest, painted this wall mural, and returned to your penthouse all in four days."

"Probably."

"Ra-am. Stop yanking my ponytail."

"Look. I don't know, but this doesn't mean Goran's alive. There's a piece of information we don't have. It's as simple as that."

Ram drew conclusions from data, not speculation, and until a moment ago she hadn't thought him capable of a single unreasonable belief.

"None of the village relatives saw him. How did he cross the reservoir to this island so quickly?"

"Swam?" Ram shrugged.

"This isn't a joke. Not to me." Still panting and dizzy, it certainly wasn't.

"You asked a question. I answered it." He snagged his satellite phone from his right hip and aimed its light at the steep flight of stone steps. "I'm heading up. Take whatever time you need. I'll be outside the citadel."

To pace and think in private, Ram?

With his foot on the first step, he called over his shoulder. "Seven years, Paula. That's a long time to be out there with no contact whatsoever." There were ten plodding thumps to the top before his footfalls faded inside the chapel.

Paula scanned the crypt's floor. At least this part of the chapel was completely free of the tang of bird droppings and rodent pee. Too cold even for them? She imagined Goran on a low stool, the edged scent of his oil paints pushing against the dank sadness of loss and human remains nearby.

How all things abandoned and decayed could inspire him so, she would never understand. The least whiff of linseed oil in arts and crafts stores still turned her stomach because it reminded her of the chaos inside him. Would that nausea ever go away?

Paula lowered herself cross-legged to the floor. Ten years had passed, but what a natural beauty she'd been at twenty-eight. An impossibly flawless harmony between her ivory complexion and the thick ponytail she always gathered at the crown of her head in the heat—the strands exploding like a fountain of pink champagne.

Yet, back then, it mattered not one iota to her she'd been blessed with long shapely legs and teardrop eyes, spaced a touch wide to give the illusion of a rare pedigree.

It was for this reason she accused Goran of idealizing her in his drawings. "I look like an anemic Raphael poser," she used to say, until one day he marched her and the finished portrait to the broad mirror beside their bed. He *had* captured her enchantments and not what she herself imagined—such an invisible blight for people like her with a disability.

Did he leave this painting inside his childhood home knowing she would see it? Was it a peace offering from him, a suggestion that they try again? Perhaps, harder.

****

Outside, after the crypt's utter darkness, Paula and Ram blinked against the midmorning sun; he scuttled up the knoll like an escaping spider.

"The chaplain's cottage is this way."

"Julie should see that painting of me down there," Paula shouted ahead.

"It's your island. Do as you like."

"And I want the cousin's number. Hear what she thinks."

Just before he dropped from view, he yelled, "I expect Claudia will show up on the weekend. Believe me, she's just as curious about you as you are of her."

Although the climb wasn't enough to take her breath, she paused under a plum tree to inhale the fragrance of pink blossoms hanging sweet as candy canes. From this shallow rise, the rocky knob which held her citadel and cottage looked to be at least an acre. The reservoir made it easy to imagine a moat.

Only now, outlined under morning shadows, did she notice the towers at each side of the entrance were crowned. Clearly added in later centuries, the turquoise balconies of an arched Turkish design dotted the citadel's second story. As pretty as it was, except for the mural, Paula still didn't see much she'd want to claim as her own.

"Isn't this the most amazing place you've ever seen?" Ram said when she caught up with her friends on the stone steps of the cottage.

"This house has had better days." She raised her face to the pigeons and doves flying in and out of a patchwork of red tiles missing from the steep-pitched roof. The cottage, more gray than white, was not unlike the other village homes they'd passed: relaxed edges soft as wax, and gabled windows sunk into thick walls of mud brick.

Ram let loose and jumped down, backstepping to the plum tree. "We should get married," he said to Julie. "Right here, under this tree."

In the gaping silence, Ram struck a ridiculously rigid pose and flung an accusing finger at her. "*Ahhhh*," he hissed, and both women chortled at the gravitas. "This is the third time I've asked. You can't turn me down again."

"Whaddya mean?" From Julie sprang mock incredulity. "I said *yes* the first time, but your job got in the way. Remember? The second time, I convinced you to skip the wedding and spend our honeymoon at a Himalayan monastery. By the time that train wreck was over, your baby was on the way."

His grin collapsed. Ram crept forward and grasped Julie's hands. "Are you in?"

She didn't waste a beat. "I'm in." She drew close, squeezed her eyelids tight, and whispered, "I've always been *in*. You must know that."

Ram bent down, not on one knee, but both. He lowered his face into the hands he held and kept it there. The two women exchanged knowing smiles. For Ram, this was not just a proposal but heart-felt gratitude.

Where other women could not or would not have forgiven Ram his misdeeds, Julie had dug deep from a place inside her newfound Buddhist beliefs. *To err is human*...If that sounded too simplistic, Paula had told nonbelievers, consider this: Julie no longer needed Ram in her world to be fulfilled. When Ram cut her loose over six years earlier, she ran with it.

Yet, how was Goran to redeem himself when the root of his problems had been his very existence?

Of course, she was better off without him. She'd cut Goran loose, and he ran with it, too. He simply opted out. Or so she thought until today.

****

Inside the cottage were three squat spaces: a sitting room, a kitchen, and an adjoining bathroom. Neither animals nor weather had penetrated thanks to the intact casement windows and shutters. But above, someone had already boarded off the stairs to the second story's invasion of roosting birds. To Paula, this stopgap and the wooden table and chairs left behind hinted at squatters.

The built-in ceiling-to-floor bookcases would do for

their gear. Oak benches scarred by time extended from each side of an expansive bay window of the kind depicted in paintings of ringleted girls in pinafores reading in the afternoon sun. Julie and Ram threw their sleeping mats there. The perfect length for Julie, by the time Ram left, he said he wasn't sure whether to appreciate the ad hoc bed or despise what it may have done to his spine.

"That pantry off the kitchen is so big I can sleep there and give you lovers some privacy. I'll use the back door to come and go." No one disagreed with Paula's idea.

In the bathroom, the three of them hovered over the sink and clawfoot tub, and poked at the capped-off piping and drains for a way to syphon waste water to the outside. As if this wasn't perplexing enough, Ram was adamant they use water from the ancient well inside the citadel courtyard.

"Go ahead. Drink brackish water. But we better set up a toilet first since you'll be on it most of the time," Julie said.

Paula gestured across the toilet bowl. "Here's a perfectly good seat. Put a bucket in there. Cover your business with sawdust and *voilà*—a toilet. I used one at my cabin the year I had to dig a new septic field. Empty it in the bush, and nature takes it from there."

"What bush?" Ram said. "I'm not into rowing a bucket of crap to shore. Just dump it into the reservoir from a window in the citadel."

Paula stepped forward, aghast. "We can't throw untreated waste into a water source."

Before Ram's head had stopped its loll, he was arguing. "Look. There isn't anyone onshore between us and the dam ten kilometers downstream. Whatever we put in will be totally dissipated by then. I'll buy three buckets in town. I'm dumping my crap on the downstream side of the citadel near the beach. We can row out and collect water upstream from that."

"God." Julie clutched the crown of her head. "This is totally medieval."

"Isn't that what we're here for? To experience the romance of castle life. Right, Paula?"

Paula laid her arm across Julie's shoulder. "Sorry, sweetie. He's right this time. We're going to have to go with the flow." Although humor didn't come naturally to Paula, it came occasionally by accident.

"We should get the woodstove in the sitting room going. Into gathering scrap along the shore?"

Rather than return to the dock, they rowed to the closer shoreline behind their island.

While they gathered fallen branches and driftwood, Ram's satellite phone rang. "Ram here…Hey, I'm great…What the—? Are you sure? That makes no sense. Does it? Hang on while I try for a better connection along the shore." *Claudia*, he mouthed to Paula and walked out of earshot.

She continued in the opposite direction, drawn to what looked like a low-lying spit of land branching from the island.

"I can see another part of the island back there," she said when she returned to dump her armload of branches into the boat. "The end of it is close to this side. Why don't we leave the boat there instead of the beach?"

Ram pushed some of the firewood aside and sat down inside the boat. "If you're talking below the cottage, then there's a bloody steep hill down to it and no stairs. Goran told me that was his toboggan run. Before this reservoir, of course.

"Hmm…Better crappy stairs to the beach than no stairs at all, I guess."

As soon as they were underway, Ram announced, "Claudia says she doesn't know anything about the locked tower. And get this. That email telling me Goran's early paintings are here in a tower—she didn't send it. Her email is *countessclaudia*—the one I got was from *cvlakia*."

"Are you kidding?" Julie said.

"I know. She's been in contact with me as the executor of Goran's will, but only by phone. I didn't mention the paintings to her, so she assumed Paula was coming to check out the castle."

"Was it one of the other Vlakia relatives, initial *C*?" Paula said. "They're everywhere, aren't they?"

"Yup. But she can't think of anyone."

"Someone lured us here for paintings," Paula said. "I'm not leaving without checking every corner of this monster. As for tonight, we're going to end up in the motorhome again unless we get that woodstove going."

****

The temperature inside the cabin had plummeted, but this time they couldn't crank up the propane. In the kitchen, Paula added long underwear to a wool-blend skirt and slipped on dry runners. Around her lay her backpack and everything from the beach except the bedding.

A rust-stained porcelain sink sat in one corner. Stripped of its piping, it drained into a bucket where she noted a shallow scum of water. *Squatters?*

Paula carried her wet desert boots and linen skirt. A

trail of dribbles snaked along the route from a bubbling pot of canned stew in the kitchen to the chairs at the woodstove which were serving as a drying rack.

Ram was stacking wood beside the potbelly stove, located dead center of the room. He still wore his jeans, wet to the knees, his feet a violet shade inside his damp sandals.

"Good grief," she said. "Get out of those clothes and put on some warm socks. I'll get the fire going."

The minute she reached into the firebox with the first stick of kindling, she could feel it and see it: the ashes warmed her outstretched palm; a tiny ember still glowed—someone had definitely been here the previous evening.

Ram stripped off his jeans while Julie rifled through his backpack, likely looking for dry pants and heavy socks. All the damp clothing, including the wet cargo pants she'd traded for heavy leggings, was flung across the back of the four wooden chairs.

"If we find the paintings tomorrow…" Julie broke a twig in two, tossed it into the stove, and fanned the nascent flame with gusto. "I say throw them into the motorhome and get out of here."

"*Throw* might be too strong a word," Ram said. "If they *are* Goran's, now that he's dead, there'll be a stampede of collectors wanting to buy them."

"I'm okay to hang around a few more days but not in a freezing cabin," Paula said. "We'd best haul the chainsaw out of the motorhome and collect something other than branches." In Romania, it seemed one could preorder all sorts of add-ons to an RV rental. For the right price, of course.

Paula spread her palms atop the table, letting the

earthy, unvarnished feel of the wood comfort her. She gazed at the tiny flame which had begun to sizzle and spit and wondered: had Goran sat here only hours before?

Chapter Three

It had been a miserable night in the cabin, the drizzle and splat of cold rain off the eaves still going at daybreak. Paula rose from her air mattress on the floor, fed more spindly branches into the fire, and slipped back into her sleeping bag with a vague memory of Ram or Julie doing the same during the night.

She pulled the bag over her head at the sight of icy rivulets on the window by the front door. Soon, the room warmed, and she rose to slip on a skirt and heavy sweater over her long underwear. The others wouldn't be up for another hour or two.

While she waited for her tea water to boil on the kitchen camp stove, she stepped outside into a frosty world of honeyed crystal, sunniest at the top of the knoll where icy plum blossoms sparkled like a pink chandelier. That would be her spot.

Chair in one hand, tea in the other, she eyed the blank gun on the countertop before tucking it into her skirt pocket and heading up the knoll. Bears were most active during early mornings in spring and summer.

If only Ram and Julie could see this wonderland. Ground mist swirled outside, but nothing stirred within the dark cottage. Settled under the tree, she squinted against the rising sun, and in that instant, a black mass darted from view near the front door. She jumped to her feet, her hand on the gun in her pocket.

Nothing else moved until a breeze kicked up and parted the fog. Below, prowling around the outside of the cottage was a pack of wolves. Or—She blinked against the mist. Could wolves possibly get onto the island? How foolish she'd feel setting off the gun and waking her friends needlessly.

She stood for a better look, immediately bringing the intense eyes of one of the animals on her. It sprinted forward. Desperate, she glanced over her shoulder at the citadel. Too far. Then the plum tree—robust enough to hold but slippery with frost.

Frantic, she slammed the chair against the trunk and hauled herself to the crook of a branch just as the animal's snout appeared at her boot. She raised the blank gun. *Boom!* The shock wave reverberated within her like scattershot, sending the wolf thundering down the knoll.

Low and menacing, a woman's voice pierced the mist. A ragged stranger seemed to float within it. Tossing her twisted snake pit of black hair, she raised her arms, palms up, high overhead, scattering the wolves over a nearby embankment.

Tall and bone-thin, a face cut with age, she wore a billowing white blouse over a torn burlap skirt which flapped about her ankles. Her embroidered vest and the red bandana capping her head snatched her from the ranks of a common tramp and into the realm of a nomadic fortune-teller.

The cottage door banged open; out burst Ram, swinging a charred piece of firewood and naked except for his jockey shorts.

Hyper-alert, Paula slid from the tree and advanced, the gun at her side. If the wolves returned, a lot of good it would be, never mind Ram's piece of brittle charcoal.

He stopped in his tracks as the strange woman wheeled around.

"Well." Her head swept up and down his body. "You've filled out nicely."

Ram lunged to embrace her. "I honestly didn't have a clue it was you," he said, holding her at arm's length.

Paula kept her distance. While they'd sat on their water-bound rock, had a new fashion craze swept the globe? Instead of shredded denim, threadbare, soiled burlap?

"We seem to be picking up right where we left off. No?" She homed in on Ram's hands, hovering in front of his crotch. "I don't believe you wore any pants that time, either."

With Ram's virility diluted to a lopsided smile, he glanced back at Julie, standing on the steps and clutching a blanket, then said to Paula, "Uh—you can put the gun away, now."

"I was sure I saw some kind of wild animal."

"Naw, Claudia's fairly tame, aren't you?" The two of them guffawed into the wind, locked in a weird private moment until Ram's eyes strayed to Julie once more and the grin fell right off his face.

"Okay, then. Claudia, this is my *fi-an-cée*, Julie, and over there is my dearest friend, Paula. That's not a real gun by the way. I'm going in to throw some clothes on." Without a glance back, he shouted, "Goran's cousin."

The woman's enthusiasm evaporated at the click of the door. She looked down her nose at Paula.

There was no mistake. Paula had clearly seen this bizarre woman among the wolves. "I've been sitting on that chair up there, but I didn't see you come up from the beach. How did you get here?"

The cousin frowned and shifted to a superior tone. "I wouldn't climb those stone stairs if I were you. To be honest, which is what I always am." Claudia aimed an acerbic eye at Paula. "This rock has never been more treacherous than now." Without warning, she wheeled around as if challenging Julie's sour stance, and the two of them studied each other with the shiftiness of thieves divvying up a bag of money.

"Cat got your tongue?" Julie finally said, stepping forward to close their jagged circle.

Claudia descended on her. "Don't use those words with me. I despise idioms. They're gauche and the sign of a stagnant mind."

A wicked glee spread over Julie's face. If only Paula had Julie's courage to put this high-bred vagabond in her place.

"You good?" Julie asked Paula. She crooked a finger in her friend's direction, never taking her eyes off the cousin. "I'll meet you in the citadel. No more than ten minutes."

"Oh, take your time," Claudia said to Julie. "In fact, go back to bed if you like. I can find my own way around. Although…now that there's a new owner, it would be bad manners. Perhaps worse. Trespassing."

Paula couldn't imagine a more disastrous start for Ram's future wife and Claudia. What to make of the tasteless *no pants* quip? How dare she insult and embarrass her friends that way? And were those not gray hairs in that tangle of braids? The woman must be well over fifty.

Poor Julie. Not that Claudia had given Paula any reason to like her so far, either. Black marks were piling up against this relative—the cousin was a rough

47

character with base morals, someone Paula was thinking might even be a thief.

Why else would Claudia turn up on their remote island so early in the day without notice if not to steal the paintings before Paula found them? She certainly had the leathery face of a desperado in need of a meal. Not only that, but how did she cross over if they already had her boat? Paula was of a mind to let the cousin go ahead while she checked the beach for any cohorts.

The two women were wandering the main floor of the citadel in utter silence, their barren companionship a perfect match for the hollow venue, when Ram appeared, flashlight in hand, and said, "We can see if the paintings are in the other tower."

Perhaps Claudia would lose her hard edge with him around. Paula tagged along up the grand staircase to the same hall at the far end of the mezzanine which held both entrances to the towers.

She remembered the view from the knoll: two identical towers, one to each side of the citadel's entrance.

It took a couple of yanks from Ram's powerful arms before the warped iron door released and creaked open. "FYI, Paula." He ducked through the cramped opening. "The only way up these towers is from the second floor. And if the paintings aren't here, well…"

"I won't be able to help," Claudia said. "Good grief. I haven't been up these since that last time with you."

Ram missed the first step; the flashlight tumbled from his grip.

These two were tight all right.

The stairwell up the second tower, no less gloomy, exited at the top into a cozy round room streaked with sunlight. Spaced evenly, the slim windows were just wide enough to drop the deadly boulders and hot oil Paula had seen in the medieval battle scenes of old movies.

"Not much of a panorama," Claudia said. "But there are our paintings."

Our paintings? Since when were Goran's paintings Claudia's? Paula estimated as many as a dozen portrait-sized, unframed canvases leaned askew along the far wall.

Before Claudia took another step, Ram caught her arm. "Careful, that subfloor may be rotten in places. It's a long way down."

"I doubt this tower has a hollow core," she said, stepping in to stamp her foot twice. The vinyl tiles didn't budge. "Wouldn't be much good against battering rams if it was."

"You have a background in the architecture of antiquity, do you?" Paula asked.

With the arrogance to hear it as a compliment, Claudia's knuckles rapped out a dull beat. "These walls are at least six feet thick. Perfect to muffle the screams of mental patients. Ram." Claudia turned to him. "Do you remember my mum telling us how the psychiatrist used the top of one tower as his office?"

Ram shrugged.

"Sure you do. He wanted to keep an eye on the isolation cell." She pointed out the window slit to where the twin tower was visible beyond the citadel's main entrance.

Without knowing why, Paula reached out and wrapped her fingers around the black bars of the window she stood at. She was thinking of the prisoners and mental patients whose screams, as Claudia said, went unheard. As she uncurled her fingers, she noticed the ledge strangely dust-free.

"Looks like the maid has already come and gone," Paula said. *This sarcasm thing is starting to be fun.* She circled the room to halt directly in front of Claudia, arms crossed, head cocked, but imagined she looked no more threatening than a hungry pigeon on a park bench. Her legs were going soft. "You're sure you never brought the paintings up here?"

Claudia opened her mouth and frowned. "No. But it's a good place for them." She stepped around Paula to the nearest window. "The towers are the driest and warmest part of the fortress. They get sun all day, narrow as the windows are."

Genuinely curious, Paula asked, "Does the other tower have bars?"

"I don't know. Does it, Ram?"

He shrugged again and squirmed under her sultry eyes, as intense and shadowed as Goran's had been.

So, the towers were where this temptress had lured in an adolescent Ram, perhaps indulging in a bit of prisoner and jailor kink at the same time.

"What was your mother doing in here when it was an asylum…if you don't mind me asking?"

Unbelievable. Claudia alone mistook the question for a joke about mental illness and hooted.

"Goran's father worked the gardens; my mum was in housekeeping. Brother and sister. Thirteen and fifteen when they started. My mother's memories are all that's left of the original palace."

"And boy," Ram said, "does she have some stories to tell."

He seemed so oblivious to the tension between the two women Paula wondered if she was spinning drama from nothing.

"My favorite," Ram said, "is when the palace was a hospital and the young future count took the garden's front-end loader for a joy ride. Drove around the palace, giving the victory fist. Wouldn't you know…" Ram bent into wheezing guffaws. "Peeking from the bucket is a ransacked marble statue of the esteemed Vlakia ancestor who built the place."

"Is that what you call funny?"

Even Ram couldn't escape Claudia the Mirth-Slayer. Paula wouldn't have been surprised to see her pull a dagger from within her rags. Her passive-aggression had more traction than a Humvee in a bog.

"The communists were carving slabs of marble from the Great Hall of Honor as if it was a round of Dutch cheese. All that valuable stone craft. Gone."

"Still," Ram said. "Goran's father was supposed to inherit the palace. Not the brightest kid, was he?"

"No, but Uncle Tibor is the one the village still admires. The potatoes he grew for the Soviets were so abundant he started giving them away. Old peasants still stop my mother and thank our family for saving them from starvation during communism."

Always curious about Goran's parents, Paula soaked in every bit of this impromptu family history. Yet, village lore of this magnitude didn't easily fade. Might other locals resent her as much as Claudia appeared to?

Ram marched to the jumble of paintings. "Whaddya say we each grab a couple of canvases and get these downstairs now?"

"Don't—"

"They—" Claudia added over Paula's words. "Forgive me, Ram. They should be protected before they're moved."

Not a chance she'd give Claudia access to the paintings. "No one's going to touch the paintings but me."

"Whatever you wish." Claudia waved off Paula's confrontational tone. "By the way, my mum wants you to have the only surviving photograph of the palace. If you'll take it."

Of course, Paula would.

"Everyone in the village knows who the countess is. Mum's eccentric but can still laugh at her change of fortune. Anyway…" Claudia swatted the space between them. "You'll understand when you see how she lives."

Like the old woman who lived in a shoe, Paula wondered, overrun not with children but wolves?

Whatever familial spark the aunt had generated was short-lived. As soon as Ram headed down, Claudia's sinister tone returned. "But don't ask her about Goran or even mention his name. Ever."

"Really? She's still grieving? I knew you and your mum lived in England during his boarding school days, but Goran said he only ever got together with you."

"Did you not hear me? It upsets her terribly."

The woman's rigid smile sent a wave of nausea rolling through Paula. Confrontation often upset her, but never before had anyone generated such intense aversion in her. Claudia was brash, inconsiderate, and lascivious. But so could Ram be, someone she would do anything for. Paula trusted him, and therein lay the difference.

After the others left, she sifted through the puerile

efforts of the master Goran would become, turning them over in her hands, searching for the weary ghoulish faces he liked to insert into his chaos of swirls. She could imagine his voice so clearly, as if Goran himself had stepped into the light beside her: *Not this one. Yes. Hang that one. It's better.*

These early paintings didn't seem so burdensome as the others. They were vulnerable, as if they had a history and feelings. And now they were homeless. Goran had entrusted her alone with cherishing and protecting his art, at least until she found it a new place to live.

Paula was on her knees, setting aside a semicircle of paintings from the stack when Julie entered.

"What do you think that Claudia's up to?"

Despite her friend's question, Paula kept sorting the collection.

"Didn't send the email, so she says, and didn't bring these paintings up here. Who else would have?" Julie asked. "I think she's after the hydro dough. You have to wonder if she used the paintings as bait to check you out, and now she'll go after the money."

Finally, Paula looked over her shoulder and Julie's eyes settled on her. "I'm even thinking she might have hired someone to kill Goran."

It brought Paula to her feet. "She might be a petty thief—but murder? Do you really think so?"

Had Claudia contacted her a year ago, or even a month ago, before Paula knew how conniving she was, she would have gladly given up the money, the citadel, and even some of Goran's minor works. *Don't even mention his name...ever.* What was *that* about? Claudia had put a crack in Paula's open-handed, safe life. Instead of fleeing, she owed it to Goran to stay and fight for his legacy.

"Watch yourself, girl. There's something off about her, and I'm not saying that just because she did the dirty with the man I'm about to marry."

The memory of Claudia's chilling smile inserted a kernel of dread in Paula she couldn't ignore. Was Goran dead after all—at Claudia's bidding? It was entirely possible this down-on-her-luck cousin would feel the palace and land it stood on should have come to her mother after Goran's parents were both gone. Claudia would be the recipient of the million-dollar compensation instead of this girlfriend who appeared out of nowhere. After all, the last aristocrats to live at the palace, the old Count and Countess Vlakia, were grandparents to both Goran and Claudia.

Was Claudia here to decide which might be easier: vanquish Paula in court—or have her meet the same fate as Goran?

Since it was understood they were far from done with the topic of Claudia, the two friends moved on to what was at hand. Paula hoisted one particular painting chest-high and turned to Julie. "What hits you first about this one?"

"Uh. It's depressing. Horrific. Like those black and white photos of bombed-out cities."

"The setting?"

"A castle. Here, I guess, or the one underwater."

"And this one?"

"Same. But this can't be how the palace looked."

Paula set it aside with the other paintings. "When Goran was thirteen, his father died in an accident. Three years later to the day, his mother dies. You heard Ram; Goran never returned. He stayed with Ram's family during school holidays, and apparently, they even paid for his entire university expenses."

Marching to another painting, she pointed to a ghostlike face in a window. "Look at this. It shows up in every one of these. Here…here…and here. Whatever happened at this castle is at the heart of the tortured images he created as a painter. He's back here to put it to rest. That's who painted me in the crypt. Goran's ghost."

Julie's face contorted. "Goran's ghost did not paint that mural."

"Of course not. Goran himself did." Paula looked on as her friend's chin collapsed to her chest. "It's got to be one or the other. Admit it."

Paula strode to the center of the room and dropped to the floor, cross-legged, regal as a chieftain. "I've been up here thinking this citadel could be home for all of Goran's paintings. A kind of castle gallery."

Slack-jawed, Julie sank down beside her. "That's nuts. Crazy's supposed to be my turf. Why bring Goran's work from galleries and safe storage to this crumbling bunker of a building in the middle of nowhere?"

"Across from Dracula's castle isn't nowhere." She rose to peer from the battlement window with a partial view of the reservoir. "It could be a living gallery of Goran's most terrifying images. Why settle for a boring white wedding?" She spun and parted her outstretched palms as if unveiling a marquee. "When you can have a medieval feast inside a haunted Transylvanian castle."

"Okay, good. It's only a joke."

"Maybe not. I rarely joke."

****

Paula wasn't fussy when it came to her living space, but she always agreed to protocol, what Ram called *best practices*. Of course, he would want to insure the paintings before they moved an inch out of the citadel.

Since the insurance appraiser couldn't come up from Bucharest for a week, Paula spent the day inside the tower room wrapping each painting in blocks of Styrofoam to guard against dust and their trip down the stairs. That none of them had the added weight of frames was fortunate but not surprising since Goran had no income in his school days.

Where she'd been cutting the blocks to size, the tiled floor was a carpet of white bits. They stuck to the broom's bristles like fridge magnets, turning the circular room into a swirling snow globe.

They'd even settled along the high ledge that served as a place for her lantern. Throughout the citadel, dead electrical outlets remained, but for now, its new residents were back to candles and oil lanterns.

Paula, while tall, still had to raise herself to the tips of her toes to flick the broom across the ledge.

Splat. She jumped back until she realized what had tumbled to the tiles: a ruled scribbler like one used in primary school. Scrawled across the card-stock cover, in tiny print, was *Dr. Haller's Journal, 1950-1951*.

A timely distraction from her frustrating task. Paula shifted the lantern to the floor, sat down, and opened to the first page.

Dr. Albert Von Haller's Journal

August 3, 1950, Arges County Criminal Lunatic Asylum

This journal has come about on the advice of my favorite professor in Moscow, who, seeing me off this spring on a train bound for Romania, said it was his last and possibly most crucial directive for my future as a psychiatrist.

"In this post-war world," he told me, "you are bound to end up on a ward with no other medical colleagues to confer with except inexperienced nurses. Keeping a journal will ground you." His eyebrows twitched in a way I'd often seen in classes. "It might save your life."

I was overcome with warmth toward the old man, who had not only delayed a comfortable retirement in order to bolster the Republic's stock of doctors, but had also made wry attempts to humor our sorry lot while he did so.

I have decided to journal in English, the international language of science, which will prove more difficult to understand should another employee attempt to read it. My communist comrades in Bucharest have assigned me to this rather isolated and, need I say, palatial madhouse originally built as an aristocratic pleasure palace. Yet I find tragic signs everywhere. In the palace's chapel where I go for solace, all the stained-glass windows have been excised in favor of thick leaded glass and unsightly iron bars.

What I hear from some of the old servants who find their circumstances elevated into administrative positions within security, horticulture, housekeeping, and kitchens, is that the former count and countess were roused from their bedchambers and detained more than a year ago. They now sleep in the former stables. They must make do as they are not allowed even the most basic access to the citadel cafeteria. Seeing as the children's draft ponies are not yet confiscated, the stables must be a malodorous place to sleep indeed.

Vlakia Palace has been sold off, carried away, and siphoned into the homes and offices of the Romanian cadres in Bucharest. Missing chandeliers, dismantled marble fountains, and open sky where stained glass once kept out the rain, remind me daily what was here short months ago. Ironically, the gargoyle sconces and medieval suits of armor left behind make a morbid but fitting backdrop for lunatics.

Paula closed the journal and gazed around the circular room. This had to be the psychiatrist's office that Claudia had mentioned. *The count and countess...* The count must be the one laid out inside the crypt's tomb. Goran's grandfather. The children would be...*good grief*...his father, Tibor, and Aunt Lisbet.

How was it possible this journal hadn't moved from this room in sixty-two years? That she was the first person to hold it since Goran's father was young enough to have a pony? And the family was living in their horse stables? Even if they were still there when the hospital closed, it was possible Goran himself was too young to remember.

The past history of the palace and citadel was valuable. At the very least, the old aunt might want the journal. She slipped it into a large pocket of her skirt and headed to her new room above the citadel's main doors.

Days earlier, when Paula's dawn risings in the cottage began to collide with her friends' late nights, she'd gone in search of a comfortable room on the second floor of the citadel and found out—castles didn't do comfortable. Of the eight ringing the mezzanine, she chose one with a functioning fireplace and morning sun that could take the chill off its stone walls.

Just as grungy as all the others, she'd had to scrub it raw to rid it of mouse droppings, chimney soot, and mildew. The offensive trio conjured up memories of the pickled pigs' feet her father used to burn on their barbecue.

Together, this room and the one beside it spanned the entire front facade of the citadel, from one tower to the other. Yet, it felt cozy. She could easily reach the ceiling beams by simply raising her arm. Notoriously inefficient, at least this medieval hearth gave off enough heat in the spring temperatures to place her air mattress directly on the plank flooring. She kept her sawdust toilet in there, too, and began cooking on the citadel kitchen's wood-fired stovetop.

Paula was living in the medieval fortress—perhaps the first person to do so since the hospital staff had left over thirty years earlier.

Chapter Four

For most anyone, living in a castle in 2013 would be mind-bending. A woman like Paula, however, didn't want her mind changed—let alone bent.

Then Goran walked into her life and here she was years later in Transylvania, inside Poenari's brow-beaten hardware store at the edge of Romania's version of the Wild West. Held together with rough-hewn logs and mortar, the store was a catch-all for every staple from flour to chainsaws and even had a hitching post for horses.

The three friends were in town to gather their survival gear when she heard a string of Italian curses rolling off Julie's tongue at the end of the farm implements aisle. The only trigger which could awaken this lost art of hers was Ram's obsession with men's apparel. Paula was sure if only it paid enough, he'd be a clerk in a Manhattan clothing boutique. Julie's shopping style: *grab 'n' go*.

Ram was up to his elbows in a bin of clear-out snow boots, and there were two problems with that: winter was six months away, and snow boots were nowhere on their shopping list of kerosene, propane, plastic pails, and sawdust.

A gnarled farmer with his head in the opposite end of the bin popped up and responded in Italian. Who knew Romanians often did migrant farm labor in Italy?

According to this local, Poenari village had started as a silver mine above the Varges River.

Boom and bust, Paula thought, when Julie translated. No wonder the place had so many boarded-up churches and inns—ornate three-story timber buildings with nothing inside but stray dogs.

Ram wasn't the only one with roaming eyes, though. Near the bags of sawdust, Paula found herself looking into the maw of a gas-powered generator she knew could send her on even more unimagined tangents.

She ran her fingertips along the canary yellow curves of its 208 cc engine. "This one could light up the cottage nicely, couldn't it?"

Ram laughed and continued hoisting the sawdust onto their wheeled cart. "It's got the juice all right, but way too big for your suitcase."

"I meant…"

"Theoretically?" Ram said.

Julie dropped her burlap bag with a *thud*, her lips frozen in an incredulous *Oh*.

"Didn't you tell Ram about my gallery idea?"

"You said it was a joke."

"I said it might be."

"What are you guys talking about?"

"I'm thinking of making the citadel into a gallery for Goran's paintings."

As soon as it was out, Julie's shoulders sagged. She brushed past Paula, the peevish *flip-flop* of her sandals fading along the worn boards of the store.

"It would only be open in summer," Paula said.

"*Hmpf.* You're serious about this?"

"I think I *am*," she said after a long pause. "I'd still go home to my deaf students in winter, of course."

"Of course."

Silence. "Do you think it's a good idea?"

"It's a damn good idea. I love it." A startled curiosity spread across his face. "I never would have thought you capable of something so—so radical." He pulled his satellite phone from its holster. "Here. You better phone your estate planner. It's going to take a whack of change to renovate that dilapidated fortress."

****

At the dock, the battered aluminum rowboat, while nothing special, was the center of attention now that it was missing. It was their only way to get home.

Paula stumbled out from the dense underbrush above the shoreline. "No sign of it up there either." She motioned to the flattened patch of dry grass where Ram and Julie stood. "Why would it be, when this is where we beached it and hid it before driving into Poenari?"

Ram pumped a fist into one palm. "Looks like some jackass stole it."

"Oh, calm down," Julie said, hooking one arm around his waist in a hypnotic sway. "Easily replaced. Just think, we can stay in the motorhome tonight and take a hot shower with the hand-held nozzle. *Ahhh.*" That seemed to soften Ram's irritation.

The pails and five-gallon water jugs they'd bought in town were safe enough, but Paula couldn't see sleeping with their refilled propane tanks jammed to the ceiling.

She refused to believe the boat had been stolen. At least, not from them. More likely Claudia had handed them a stolen boat to begin with, and the owners heard it was abandoned near the dock. Her theory wouldn't go over well with Ram, so she merely said, "It might show up before dark. Maybe someone borrowed it to go fishing and feed their hungry children."

"That's about as likely as finding it in a pawn shop," Ram said. "I'm phoning Claudia. She won't be happy, but what do you bet she'll find another boat by morning."

By the time they'd trudged back to the dock and motorhome, it was dark. They moved the vehicle to a flatter spot closer to the road. As Ram wandered, trying for a signal, and the women transferred the propane to the outside of the vehicle, Paula spotted two dots of light advancing through the dense bush near the cab. With a predator on her mind, in three quick steps she was at the switch for the headlights, flooding the bush with light.

Two draft horses clomped to a standstill, their heavy breath curling across the headlights' beams. The riders raised their forearms against the brilliance; their other hands went to their sidearms.

A blast from headlights would startle anyone but to the point of them drawing guns? Before they could yank their horses' reins to turn back, Paula leapt into view.

"Wait. Good evening." Her forced cheerfulness couldn't make up for her lack of Romanian or the strange night-time encounter. "We're looking for our boat. Did you see a rowboat anywhere?"

Both men wore English riding breeches and boots, and one man's face was hidden within the shadow of a sort of Amish hat. They turned to each other but said nothing.

Ram stepped from the dock into the ring of light. Ever alert for any chance to show off his boarding-school French, he said, "Let me try. *Excusez-moi.*"

He didn't get any further when a stiff Northern European accent betrayed panic. "Good God. You must be lost."

"No. We're staying here," Paula said.

The man with the hat nudged his horse forward, and now she could see, despite the grand riding gear, he was splattered with mud from his boots up to his thick beard. "Camping here is forbidden." This one sounded Romanian. "If you are tourists going to Poenari fortress for a thrill, they closed it due to a wolf attack."

"Wolves don't attack unprovoked. They're terrified of people," Julie said. "It must have been wild dogs."

Ready to agree, Paula stopped herself, remembering the giant wolf in this exact spot.

The man smoothed his untidy beard a few times. "Bears, too, stalk the fortress, and vultures circle its towers."

Julie muttered, "Oh boy. Cue the pipe organ and release the birds."

"There is nothing out here to see." The drama dandy swiped his arm across his chest with the force of a traffic cop. "You must leave immediately to the safety of the village."

"Yeah, we'd love to get the hell out of here, but some boat thief scuppered that plan." Ram pointed in the direction of the reservoir, then nodded at Paula. "That lucky woman inherited the island out there."

The men glanced at each other again as if they hadn't understood, then their palms flew to their mouths, one hiding his guffaws behind a feigned coughing fit.

With an abrupt pivot, Ram wished them a pleasant moonlight jaunt and stomped toward the motorhome. The horses faded from view along the road to the village; the *clip-clop* of cantering soon accelerated into a gallop. Paula opened her mouth to say she no longer felt safe sleeping at the boat launch, but Julie spoke first. "That was way too weird."

Ram had already started to hoist the propane tanks back into the motorhome. "Nutters, I'd say. Between the boat thieves and those guys, I hope that's the end of the unfriendly locals. If the rooms at the pension don't have hot showers, I'll throttle the desk clerk."

"Phone Claudia and get her started on another boat," Paula said, handing Ram her cell phone. "It'll grab the tower closer to the pension. I want to get home as soon as possible and start cleaning out the debris inside the citadel." Did she just call the island *home*? Even Ram stopped punching in Claudia's number and raised his eyebrows.

****

Well-scrubbed, well-fed, and rested from real beds, the trio headed back to the dock midmorning. Ram claimed Claudia was resourceful, and Paula had to admit he was right. A replacement boat was there for them.

It wasn't until they were loaded and on the water that Paula figured out what was bugging her. "This is the same boat."

"What?" Julie said.

Ram stopped rowing.

Paula patted the aluminum seat she sat on. "Right here beside me. This dent is in the exact same place. I remember it because I had to avoid it. I'm not as padded in the butt as you two."

From the middle seat, Ram raised the left oar out of the water. "Oh, crap. This paddle has the same crack."

The two of them stared at each other in silence for a moment until Julie squeezed past the boxes of groceries between her and Ram and placed a palm on the shaft of one oar. "I'll row. Phone Claudia while we still have contact through your satellite phone."

After they traded seats, he tried her number once again, bringing the handset to his ear. "Hey, Claudia. Ram…Yeah, we found it. We're on the water now. Listen, I don't know why, but this is the same boat, the one you originally lent us…Yeah, we're sure…" A series of grunts came out of him, a feigned chortle, then he ended the call and sat staring between his feet.

"What's so funny?" Paula asked.

"This boat belongs to Claudia. She thought it was hilarious that her cousin so generously volunteered the boat he stole, not knowing it was coming right back to us."

"What? Someone in her own family took it, and she's not going to confront him?"

"I guess not."

Not a single excuse for this woman's disregard came to mind. "Why *would* she care, I suppose?" Paula said. "Since she's not the one inconvenienced or stranded in the middle of the night."

"She assured me the joke will be all over town, and no one will try to steal it again. Look. I'll admit she can be self-centered. It doesn't mean she's a write-off. That she can't be trusted. Seems to me you've got the same problems with her that you had with Goran, minus the infatuation phase."

That hit the pit of her stomach square-on.

Julie jabbed her foot into Ram's back. He started and twisted around. "Paula doesn't need to hear that," she said.

No, Paula didn't need to be reminded she'd written Goran off. His painting of her in the crypt was piling on more than enough regret.

****

The next week seemed to be evaporating before Paula's eyes. Soon she would turn her life upside down to transform a mildew-maligned fortress into an art gallery.

For the other two, no doubt time ground on. By the third day of thunderstorms, they were like castaway contestants scanning for the helicopter which would whisk them from their misery. All three of them paced at the cottage's rain-splashed bay window, tracking the lightning strikes exploding along the reservoir, and longing for a glimpse of the beloved motorhome with its foam bed, on-demand hot water, propane furnace, and bar fridge.

Cabin fever took on new meaning when the only furniture one had was a table and four unbalanced chairs.

Their first day back at the beach to gather firewood, Ram kicked the stiffness out of his legs. "I'm so done with sleeping scrunched up inside that bay window."

Julie stepped back from the log round she was splitting, the sledgehammer poised like a golf putter. "What was that?"

"I should float one of those pines over here and build a four-poster bed frame from it."

"In your dreams." Julie punctuated her caustic tone with an eye-roll, but Paula turned from it, the crack of her ax echoing across the reservoir.

"The plums will be ready in eight weeks," Julie added. "Why not start with a packing box?"

The topic died on the high-strung *tings* from the maul and wedge. Ram tugged on his earmuffs, clambered into the boat, and rowed to the spot where he'd been chain-sawing deadfalls.

Paula laid down her ax. "When you came back from the Himalayas four years ago, you were so much calmer and happier within yourself. Something has happened now that you're back with Ram."

"Like what?"

"You told me to call you out if I saw any of the old negativity. So, I am. Did you not see how hurt Ram was by your sarcasm just now?"

"But he sounded so foolish. I've watched you mill trees on your property and build your own bed. It's crazy hard."

"Oh, heavens." Paula shook her head at the compliment. "He was strutting his feathers for you. If any man vowed to chop down a tree for me and build our matrimonial bed from scratch with his bare hands, I would think that's the sexiest thing in the world."

"And if you built it for him?"

"Ah. That's different. And something I've had to accept to make peace with life. Yet…you never saw anyone more excited than Goran when I told him I'd built every piece of furniture in my place."

A spark of warmth let go deep inside her. She'd forgotten how special Goran could be.

"You can't be saying his art counts for nothing," a rabid and very drunk fan once told her. During her first months with Goran on the beach in India, Paula had been so out-of-her-head in love she never asked him what he did for a living, nor did she care. Professional surfer? Out of work actor? Or her favorite—gigolo.

He'd had an outrageous number of middle-aged female friends whom she suspected were drawn to him for the same reasons she was. Where Paula was sensible to the point of stodgy, Goran was spontaneous to the edge of infantile; where she was reclusive, pensive, to Goran, every day was to be lived like the Friday of a long weekend. The nights with free-flowing cocaine were "just business."

She'd tolerated his sex romps with women almost twice her age because they tailed off the longer she was with him. While Paula had been relaxed and timid in bed, Goran had the erratic, tightly-coiled moves of a metallic Slinky. It never got old for her, but it wasn't enough of a wash against the other chaos.

At the pebbled beach, Julie seemed to be rethinking the Ram incident. "I want peace," she said, "but I won't ever settle like you for being treated as less than."

"Then at least let him love you. Don't shut down again."

Her words finally hit home. Julie threw back her head, her eyes clouding with tears. "I have been slipping into old patterns, haven't I?" Her fingertips dabbed at her lids. "I can't seem to find anywhere warm and quiet enough to meditate. The cottage is where we cook."

"What about using the chapel inside the citadel?"

She sucked in her bottom lip. "I don't mind the wolf's head, but the place is too big and dusty. I need a space I can clear out and call my own."

Paula followed her friend's gaze skyward. "The tower with the paintings?"

"It's worth a try," Julie said.

Chapter Five

Paris, 2004

Paris wasn't New York or Hong Kong, where hanging around a hotel for a month could seem like a year. Still, Paula was forced to endure it like any major city where sirens wailed all day and night while Goran finished his commission—this one covering a wall inside the home of a telecommunications magnate.

"Go home to your cabin." Knowing she'd stay, his suggestion always came at the end of the second week.

Tramping through Paris's public gardens and museums was pleasant and tiring enough to give Paula a sense of accomplishment. While Goran painted throughout the night, she rose early and went out. Perhaps that was the reason she didn't see the usual warning signs until it was too late.

"Get up. We have to go." Paula woke to Goran's voice, his hands pulling her from their hotel bed. She let herself slip to the carpet and noticed someone had thrown the hotel's terry bathrobe on top of her.

Fully dressed, Goran was pacing and repeating, "I knew it. I knew the minute I saw them in the elevator."

Four in the morning, according to the clock, meant he'd probably just got home. "Who are you talking about? You must be exhausted." She struggled up and started to peel his paint-splattered vest from his shoulders, but he pushed her away and darted to the balcony.

"I can smell smoke," he said, leaning over the railing to see the upper stories. "Come on. This place is going up any minute." On the way to the door, he yanked her arm enough to make her yelp.

If there was fire, surely someone would have pulled the alarm by now. "All right. Okay. Let me put on this robe, and we can go down to the lobby to find out what's happening."

"No lobby. That's where the terrorists will be. I parked the car outside the underground when I saw the flames."

"Goran, my love. Why do you think there are terrorists inside the hotel?"

"I heard them in the elevator. 'I say we tear up this place tonight.' That's what they said. They were laughing as if it was funny."

"Are you into the coke again?" There was no reasoning with him when he was inside one of his psychotic episodes, but sometimes if she kept up a dialogue long enough, he would tire himself out. "Let's get in the car then and go to another hotel." She could drive around until he fell asleep.

She opened the door into the hallway, and someone on a surfboard cruised by. The wall of water stayed put, like a river of Jell-o.

"Hey." The guy gave Goran a thumbs-up when he saw him. "Lookin' good, Slinky." That's what the coke-addled crowd in Madagascar called Goran. Strong and thin as a wire brush.

The surfer continued to the exit and tipped from view down a swirling eddy. They rode the same waterfall into the street—thankfully deserted, since she was now outside in a terry bathrobe.

As always, Goran crouched to check under the car for bombs. When he popped the hood, a man with a pen and paper sat up inside. Goran cursed and slammed it, crushing the fan's head.

She pulled away and steered into a residential neighborhood with little traffic. Within minutes, they were descending a steep laneway.

"There they are. Stop them," Goran said.

The steering wheel left her hands and flew out the window. The lights of a car coming up the hill blinded her and entered the cab head-on. Someone was calling her name. "*Paula? Mademoiselle? Paula? Paula?*"

"Goran," she cried out and woke, flinching at full moonlight in her eyes, the hair at her forehead limp with sweat. Her skin crawled and tingled with the terror that she was dying. Before her, feet away, the outline of a man dropped from view outside her bedroom window on the second floor of the citadel.

"Goran. Wait." She struggled out of her sleeping bag and bolted to the open window. Spears of white bark glowed and shifted in the wind, but nothing else stirred in the courtyard below. No longer snuggled in the warmth of her bedroll, she shivered as the chilly mist from outside tumbled about her. The dream, the dark outline, and her cries to Goran seesawed in a fuzzy jumble.

She latched the panes and shutters tight but lay awake, unable to ignore a flame of excitement inside her belly. All through the night, the wind whistled off the Carpathian peaks, knocking at the shutters so insistently she rose at one point and flung them aside, convinced Goran had returned. But no one was there.

The next morning, Paula fetched Ram to the mammoth doors of the citadel and pointed at her bedroom window directly overhead.

"I was thinking rodents, not intruders, when I told you to throw the bolt across your door," he said at the end of her account.

"Do you think I was dreaming? Even if someone was here on the island, how would they have survived the fall from my window?"

"They probably climbed in and out from the balcony next door. That's how we used to get at the old man's hooch." Ram made a sour face. "Plum wine isn't the greatest drunk when you're thirteen, though.

"Too bad there aren't any bars on the windows," he said. "But I guess that's because the staff stayed here, not the inmates."

Paula remembered the water in the bucket and embers inside the firebox of the cottage. "Do you think it might be squatters? When they saw the cottage occupied, maybe they came in here and thought there was something of value in a locked room."

Ram stepped back and scanned the window once more. "Or it might be someone with altogether more odious intentions. I'd feel better if you moved back into the cottage."

"That's not necessary. I don't want to disturb you guys every morning."

Ram's wrinkled brow told her he was remembering Paula rattling around before sunrise.

With so many places to sleep, there had to be an easy solution. "Hey. No one could possibly climb in from the reservoir side. I should clean out one of those rooms. I can move there today and put up with the mildew smell for one night before I wash it down."

Minutes later, bent over one of the kitchen ovens to start a cooking fire, Paula heard footsteps behind her.

"Here." Ram laid the blank gun on top of the stone sideboard. "Any more trouble, fire it, and believe me, we'll hear it."

She straightened to stare at the gun, her eyes glassy.

He pulled back and studied her. "You're sure you want to do this gallery thing? Maybe hold off until the paintings are appraised."

"No. No. I'm determined." Using the ends of her kaftan, she dabbed at her tear-smeared lips where a glimmer of a smile flashed. "I was back in Paris reliving the accident. It gets crazier every time." Paula bent down and poked randomly at a tiny flame. "I haven't dreamt about Goran in years." She settled onto her haunches. "Something about this place. Not just the paintings in the tower…"

"Well, this *is* where he was raised." At her back, Ram's voice drew near. "It's like our childhood home is the background music we take with us—whether we like the tune or not."

Paula rose to look Ram in the eye as he said, "I have my memories of our good times here, but now that I'm an adult, the place strikes me as rather brooding and intense."

"So…" Paula rubbed her chin, taking in the entire space and feeling the room receive her. "This island *is* Goran."

In the silence, they glanced at each other from the corners of their eyes.

"But why do I dream about the Paris episode when there were so many others?"

Ram paused. "Paris could have been a turning point. Maybe that's why. His first hospitalization."

Paula's frustrated sigh emptied her to the core. "Couldn't take the medication," she chirped. "Made his hands shake…There was so much more to Goran than painting."

Ram patted her shoulder the way she imagined he might at Goran's Celebration of Life. "Yeah, but he couldn't see it."

At this, her insides tightened. "Was that my fault, I wonder?"

With a wan shake of his head, Ram gave her shoulder a squeeze and left without comment.

Chapter Six

When sunrise bleached the reservoir a pale yellow,
Paula took her morning tea at the alcove window of her
new room to plan her day. Before the afternoon sun crept
around, this seat overlooking the water had the best light
for reading and writing.

Most importantly, the only home invader on this
side of the citadel would be a curious pigeon.

Her eyes lighted on the useless radiator sitting next
to the stone fireplace—no different than the last one. *Oh,
a king's ransom for hot water and a steaming bath in the
cottage's clawfoot tub.*

Duty of the day was to draw up a list of construction
supplies Ram would need before borrowing Claudia's
truck. *Humidity* Paula jotted down, adding an
exclamation mark and his name to indicate he'd
volunteered to come up with a way to protect the
paintings. If she let him, Ram would gladly and
competently take over the entire gallery project.

Red clay tiles for the cottage roof were next on the
list, followed by the yellow generator she'd picked out
in the village. Industrial acid would save them from
having to scrub the mildew off fireplaces and stone
walls. Lumber for a dock. Piping for the septic they had
yet to dig. Oh yes, a pump to bring reservoir water into
an insulated storage tank behind the cottage. Surely that
should be number one on the list? Solar panels,

eventually…Paula flopped against the alcove's plaster wall, overwhelmed a split second until she reminded herself that she'd lived off-grid in Canada her entire life. She could do this.

Out on the reservoir, a bird squawked. She glanced up to see an eagle plummeting to scoop fish from the placid surface. This same bird had come so frequently she thought its nest might be atop the crowned roof of one tower.

While she took in the spectacle, a ripple fanned out across the dark water below her window. Something in the shape of a dolphin seemed to skim the water's surface, headed for the boat launch. She suspected this was the eagle's mate, but when the sun topped the mountains, she could see it was some other creature—swimming, not flying.

She sat cross-legged on the stone bench beside the window the next two mornings, keeping one eye on the reservoir while reading the journal.

Oct 13, 1950

An interesting episode occurred yesterday within view of my bedchamber on the second floor of the citadel. One of the janitors, a former servant, bowed as he encountered the old count struggling to carry a mop and bucket up the citadel's grand staircase. He relieved him of his load, and I heard the janitor was severely reprimanded and dismissed by our administrator, who, like me, has been sent here from Moscow. The old hierarchy is a hard habit to break.

I fear the countess fares no better in the kitchen scullery. Years younger than her husband, she is an exotic and fragile bird with delicate, bone-white fingers of the kind one flashes about at the drawing room card table. Eschewing the no-nonsense post-war armor that other women insist on wrapping their feet in these days, the countess carries on in the scullery with pointy Italian-leather flats, the cleavage between her toes and the curve of her instep almost entirely naked except for a strap high on the ankle and a tiny triangle of leather across the big toe.

But the heir-in-waiting at thirteen years old appears happy enough joking with his fellow gardeners. On a whim, I stopped him one day as he wheeled a load of soil and asked why his family, unlike other aristocrats, had not fled Romania. He said his father assured him their present circumstances would soon be reversed by the Western powers.

When Paula looked up from this passage, with the sun higher in the sky, she spotted the dolphin-like creature between breaks in low-lying fog. She blinked and squinted, then jumped down from her seat to peer out the window. Clearly, it was someone paddling a surfboard to the far shore.

Two days later, the surfboard silhouette reappeared against the opaque predawn water, and she gave in to the urge to call to him.

"Goran. Gor-an." She didn't have to shout. As powerful as a boombox, the fortress wall bounced her voice to the water and back again. "I'm up here. Come back."

Prone against the board, he stopped paddling and pulled his arms tight to his torso. She almost expected him to stand up and catch a wave.

Long after he was out of earshot, she continued

calling until the bobbing object slipped from sight under the mist.

****

"I've seen him three times so far. It must be Goran. Who else could it be?"

In the cottage sitting room, Ram pranced from one bare foot to another while he chucked wood into the stove and fanned the embers with a book. "I'm not ignoring you. Just gotta get this thing going. Goddamn, is this island ever going to get warm?"

Just up, he wore only sweatpants when he'd answered the door. "I agree," he said. "If someone, for whatever crazy reason, was out there on a surfboard, he'd be the most likely candidate."

Julie padded in from the kitchen in flannel pajamas, gray wool socks swimming around her ankles; her down jacket hung haphazardly off her shoulders. She handed him a steaming cup from one hand, and a hoodie from the other, then slouched with her back to the stove's heat, kneading the knots from her neck.

Hoodie on, Ram scrambled into their makeshift alcove bed and pulled the rumpled quilt up to his chin. His back against the wall, he took a gulp of the steaming liquid and set it aside to take up his phone. "If you told me it was some kind of boat, even a canoe, I'd say they were fishing at sunrise." Ram punched the keys on his satellite phone and brought it to his ear. "It's just that the empirical data is too weak to support a surfboard. It was dark, right? And foggy…Hey, hey, guys." He slid the phone to his chest. "Message from Claudia. She'll bring the appraiser here tomorrow afternoon. Finally."

"Stop trying to change the topic," Paula said. "I called Goran's name, and he stopped paddling—then continued."

"I'm not chang—Oh, geez." He threw the handset onto the bedding. "Isn't this what we came here for? Let's get the damn paintings and go home then. And as far as Goran out there on his surfboard, I can't see anyone swimming around this time of year, never mind a man who died on another continent."

Ram eyed Julie as if begging her to take it from there.

"I'm up early these days anyway to meditate in the tower," she said to Paula.

Had it been Ram's arm encircling her, not Julie's, she would have brushed it off.

"I can come sit with you at sunrise if you like."

"Sounds good. Tomorrow, then." Paula swaggered towards the door. "You can find me in the kitchen if not in the room. He seems to appear every three days or so." Obviously, Julie wasn't expecting to see anything, so the surfboard would surprise her all the more.

The next morning, journal across her lap, Paula tucked her legs up under her and waited by her window with Julie. She'd read these stone alcoves were the only spots with enough natural light for reading in a medieval castle's gloom. Still a half hour before dawn, the pages of the journal glowed yellow in the light cast by the kerosene lamp.

November 14, 1950

The new patient Lasorov arrived today. Known as the Bucharest Ripper after strangling twelve women over a five-year period, his is a typical case in that most of them were prostitutes. The challenge I am relishing with this fellow is getting to the source of his pathological cannibalism and particularly whether there is a connection to paraphilia, the unnatural sexual excitement derived from extreme and dangerous behavior.

A psychiatrist rarely has an opportunity to add to the forensic record of such a confounding affliction. What, I wonder, could be at the root of him removing some of the women's hands and feet and, when safely back home, roasting the parts in an oven before devouring them?

My conversation with the young Vlakia boy a month ago seems to be prophetic. The staff gossip is that the countess intends to flee with her fifteen-year-old daughter to relatives in England. I am sworn to secrecy and intend to keep my word. No doubt the count and countess tremble for such a nubile young woman in a setting of rapists and murderers.

On the opposite bench, it was Julie's turn to keep watch for Goran. "What's that you're reading?" she asked.

"A journal I found in the tower. It's really interesting. Describes this citadel when it housed the criminally insane after the war. There was this one patient called the Bucharest Ripper. He liked to eat women's hands and feet after he strangled them."

"Oh, Jesus. Gross." Julie shoved aside her coffee as if it had gone off. "You know, I've been thinking about the history here, too. Wondering how many hungry ghosts this place might have. Goran's ancestors, or even his parents, may still be clinging to their palace. The patients themselves had uncontrollable addictions. Obviously, that's what landed them here."

"What?" Paula cast the journal aside. "Here I sit with you accusing me of being delusional because I think Goran might be alive. But it's okay for you to say this island is full of ghosts?"

"I didn't say you're delusional...Not yet."

Paula stood and took a shallow bow.

"Will you sit down and relax? I've never seen you so jumpy."

"I've never had men climbing through my bedroom windows before. Or weird relatives showing up with their hands in my pockets."

"Then you've led a charmed life."

"What about the mural in the crypt? I suppose one of your hungry ghosts painted it?"

"No. They're not those kinds of angry spirits. They don't try to scare people. They're frustrated."

Paula sat, her arms folded tight to her chest.

"They have mouths the size of a pea, but enormous bellies. Nothing can ever satisfy them."

"If these hungry ghosts are hanging around, why wouldn't they take over someone's body and act out their addictions? That would explain the mural in the crypt."

Julie rose and squinted out the window. "In past centuries, people in Buddhist countries thought hungry ghosts could cause gluttony or drug addiction or..."

"Serial murder?"

"I guess, in theory. But no sensible Buddhist believes that now. The point is, cravings and past actions come and go. We get tangled up in them because they *feel* permanent, but we're all much more than that. It's my job to send hungry ghosts loving kindness so they can let go of their cravings and pass into their next incarnation."

The loving kindness part made sense. Paula had to admit, how was sitting at this window going to change anything? Whether Goran was alive or dead, in the end she wanted him to be at peace. "Do you think Goran is one of these hungry ghosts and I'm tapping into his unhappiness?"

"That is absolutely possible. He didn't seek after much except his painting. It had a hold on him, though. As did his mental illness." Julie touched her friend's knee. "I wasn't very kind to him when he was alive, but it's not too late. If you have a photo, I can add it to my altar in the tower while I chant."

"I had to stop carrying it so I could move on."

"Didn't work, did it?"

Paula shook her head.

"The only prop we torture ourselves with is up here," Julie said, drumming fingertips against her temple.

****

Immersed in an animated conversation with the appraiser and looking like she owned the place, that afternoon Claudia floated past the open doorway of Paula's bedroom. She saw it for what it was—another lame excuse to snoop around. Why else would Claudia be wandering upstairs when the feast hall was where the paintings stood propped in a corner?

Claudia said nothing as Paula stepped from her room. Determined not to give the woman anything she could use to challenge Goran's will, Paula padded behind them in a strained silence down the grand staircase. Let her think they would be leaving shortly with the paintings.

Outside the room tagged to become the medieval

tavern, Ram appeared at Claudia's elbow. "What we envision here is some kind of pub with food and drink. A big fire blazing in the hearth."

Oh, damn you, Ram.

"What's this?" Claudia said.

Ram turned to Paula. "You didn't tell Claudia about the gallery?"

"No. I-I was just getting to that."

"We're going to feed off the traffic up to Dracula's castle," Ram said, baring and gnashing his teeth.

Paula trailed the group into the feast hall while Ram gushed about their plans, even pointing out which walls were high enough to accommodate the pieces presently in London galleries. "The ground-floor rotunda will be last. No paintings in there until we repair the leaks in those skylight panels."

"And what will you do with the paintings in winter? Have you thought about it?"

From her bag of tricks, Claudia had pulled feigned concern. With no one at the citadel, wouldn't she love to make off with millions in artwork?

Paula piped up and smiled sweetly. "Most will go into secure vaults in Bucharest. Elite security forces will guard the rest." Such a load of bull—with an impressive ring.

Chapter Seven

The next time Ram returned from a shopping trip to town, their rowboat pitched like a drunken water-snake tied to the rear end of a motorboat. From the citadel kitchen's only window overlooking the water, Paula grimaced each time a rogue wave splashed across the gunwales, no doubt weighed down with the clay roofing tiles Ram had tried to talk her out of.

Except for the cramped square of space where Ram sat steering the mystery boat's outboard, he'd piled both boats from stem to stern with her wish list. But where was the water pump and hoses they would need to jerry-rig water up into the citadel kitchen's defunct laundry sink?

She watched this odd parade while heating water for a bucket shower. The discovery of a functioning drain and outflow pipe in the kitchen courtyard the day before was a gift from the God of Waterworks. Paula didn't see a need for anything more elaborate than a steaming bucket of water and a ladle, but Ram had to turn it into another project—sink a metal rod across a corner of the stone wall and hang a shower curtain.

Concentrate on the cottage, she'd told him, where the installation of an all-weather water line and septic wouldn't be nearly as simple.

She headed to the beach to help unload and from her vantage point on the stone steps could see the boats coming in perilously fast—especially if they held the four propane tanks. She waved and sliced her palm across her throat, over and over, but only got hooting and hollering in return.

The motorboat was coming in full throttle in a direct line to the beach. It was already too late to prevent it crashing and exploding on shore. A nauseous sinking inside her, Paula began inching her way backward up the steps, never taking her eyes off the shoreline.

At the last minute, Ram swung the outboard sharply from the shore; the towline separated, sending their rowboat gliding effortlessly onto the pebbled beach. He circled back, cut the motor with impeccable timing and drew up the propeller so that the aluminum bow snagged the shoreline, too.

"Not bad for my first time in a motorboat?" he said, after a grand two-footed leap to the beach.

"Phenomenal, actually. But you scared the…" There was a lanky adolescent sitting almost hidden among the building material at the bow she held steady. "Heck out of me."

"Another cousin." Ram stopped coiling the towline around his forearm to point his elbow at the kid. The teen tried to straddle the gunwale but flipped sideways into the water, stumbled to his feet, flicked the wet hair from his eyes, and waved at her.

"He's come to help me and make some money."

Paula wondered how much help this uncoordinated boy could be. Would he be worth whatever generous sum Ram was going to pay?

With the boats so loaded down, she took off her boots, hiked up her skirt, and waded in to lift out one of the propane tanks from the rowboat. "Leave the generator and everything else for us," Ram said, but she continued.

The motorboat belonged to the kid's father. The teen's job would be to ferry Ram to the motorhome and back in it and help re-roof the cottage. As the kid climbed the stone steps, she found herself lost in the past until she felt an arm wrap around her shoulder. "He's got those hazelnut ringlets like Goran, doesn't he?" Ram said.

Her lips twitched with melancholy. "And the intense eyes. It could easily be him at sixteen."

"Except Goran was never a buffoon. An immature asshole at times, yeah, but most people in a lot of pain are. He got that way after his father died." Ram paused at the sound of Julie's afternoon chants starting in the tower. "There she goes. The kid's father will be picking him up at the dock any minute."

"Let me take him. You've had a long day. I can try out the outboard, too." Something else entirely was on her mind. Instead of her window vigil, she could get directly on the water.

On the return journey, she cut the motor mid-reservoir and drifted to the lilt and pulse of a solitary, hypnotic voice, rising and falling on sundown's violet ripples. Julie sometimes sang the "Metta Sutra" in the serene tones of the ancient Pali language for which it was created. Today, her friend sang in English. *Contented and easily satisfied…and frugal in their ways.*

The first time she'd heard this melody, it floated over the rainforest canopy of Julie's treehouse hermitage in Canada. How fitting to chant it above a palace graveyard to the disgusting excess which once existed in the midst of mass starvation.

Dotted within the citadel's silhouette, patches of

yellow glowed here and there—a feeling of being pulled home: to the steaming kettles atop the kitchen's brick ovens, to the warm hearth beside her bed on the second floor, and to the flame from Julie's lantern, winking in the tower like an ocean beacon. Inside the cottage, Ram would be dropping fat dumplings into a pot of goulash, the air clammy with wet jeans and skirts hanging askew on chairs encircling the woodstove.

It wasn't until she was already home and lifting the outboard's bow onto the dark beach that she recalled her plan to search for Goran.

****

Paula turned up the flame on the kerosene lantern beside one of the citadel's brick ovens, already sizzling with heat. Now that evenings were warmer, she preferred to sit here after dark. Besides, she never took food upstairs in case of attracting rodents, but here she could read the journal while stirring her beetroot borscht.

February 15, 1951

To my surprise, I'm finding Lasorov courteous and an exceedingly spirited conversationalist. Of course, he is always strait-jacketed, his ankles restrained while he sits on the only furniture he has, an iron bed anchored to the stone wall. During these counterfeit chit-chats, I am always on guard to the furtive motivations of a psychopath and that this one is of such elevated IQ he often yawns and smiles, making a show of himself.

He has vast knowledge, likely self-taught, of the most esoteric fields, and I wouldn't be surprised if he knew more about psychiatry than I myself. He can talk for hours about the injustices of Europe's feudal systems, and the grandest castles of that time. Yet, he didn't bite at my sadly manipulative query of their horrific medieval weapons and instruments of torture. Becoming haughty, he diverted to praise the exquisite chamber music of Bach and paintings of the Dutch masters.

"Dungeons were not yet a concept, Dr. Haller," he said as I was leaving his cell. "When this fortress was built, entrapping your fellow knight was not a noble venture. Adversaries fought to the death. I am likely the first prisoner to be held here." His face then drained of all color and emotion, and I had my first glimpse of the vile pit of hatred which is his true nature. Filling in the blank slate of his past would not be as easy as I thought.

She flipped to the next page of the journal, thinking how attached she'd become to the doctor who was such a free thinker within the constraints of the Soviet Union.

April 8, 1951
Lasorov asked some days ago if he could have a flashlight in order to read after dark. During my leave in Bucharest, I visited a military surplus to find an old hand-crank one which fits into the palm of one's hand. The nurses carry battery-powered industrial flashlights to go back and forth from their citadel dormitory to the palace wards. Those could easily kill anyone with a blow to the head, but I didn't see the harm in this one for my patient.

The guard who sits at the top of the stairs and can look in through the observation trap tells me Lasorov switches it off precisely at nine when he is supposed to. Yet, I take this lightly as more than once I've found this new employee asleep in his chair with alcohol on his breath. Since the war, good men of sound body and mind are in short supply.

Today the police visited and asked if I could accompany them to the village and assess a young unmarried mother suspected of murdering her baby. I took offense to their description of her as wayward and told them so. Has our world not suffered enough prejudice and blame this past decade? Tonight, as I write this in my bedchambers, I am doubly glad to have spoken out as I ponder Lasorov's daily routine and how grateful and excited he was with the tiny flashlight.

I almost pity him.

Chapter Eight

"Do you want...?" Ram appeared in the window of Paula's respirator hood as she sprayed the inside of the future tavern's fireplace. The safety device was great at blocking fumes and sound alike. She waved him from the room, stepped into the arcade, and removed the hood.

"Don't get too close to this stuff." A sour-smelling whiff forced her to back up farther yet. "Unless you've got lots of brain cells to spare."

"We're heading into town. We can wait for you to change though."

"Thanks, but you've got my grocery list."

"We're going to meet Claudia for drinks at that pension's dining room and grab something to eat."

"Then definitely not."

"You've always been such a hermit."

"That, and...I don't enjoy Claudia's company much."

He slumped, punctuating it with a frustrated moan.

"You've known her so long you probably can't see it. I think she's after the money from the hydro company."

"There's no way she wants that."

"No? If I didn't exist, who's next...? She is. Am I right?

"Yes, but Claudia lives exactly as you do. She has not a single want or need in this world. Other than you, she's one of the most frugal people I know."

It was time for the wild card. Ram could take it.

"There's something…creepy…about her. You hooked up with Claudia years ago. You're not seeing what I am."

"Yeah." Ram bit his lip as if ready to finally agree. "Claudia *can* be catty. I wasn't very happy with the way she popped that on Julie. I was fifteen. She was twenty-three, but it's not like I was a virgin. Besides, no one thinks anything of Julie being four years older than me."

"Your teenage sex life doesn't interest me." She pushed this past history out of the way. "Claudia's preparing for a money grab. She's trying to scare me into giving up rights to the Vlakia lands so the million-dollar payout goes to her, not me. I only qualify as Goran's common-law; it wouldn't be that hard."

"You're not thinking of relinquishing your inheritance, are you?"

"Not a chance. Goran needs me. His paintings do."

"Good. Because I want this gallery to happen as much as you do. Listen, enjoy your time here and don't stress. It's not like you." He pecked the crown of Paula's head. "We'll take the kid with us, but don't worry about bringing the outboard back. I'll lock its motor in the vehicle, and if it gets too late, we may stay at the pension." He called over his shoulder on the way out. "Still got the gun and bear spray in your room? Sure you'll be okay alone?"

"Listen to you after saying not to worry. I'm better than okay. And tell Julie I'll keep up the chanting for her hungry ghosts."

****

It didn't take long to realize this would be a special

night, her first of many alone in her new home. Paula had made her residency application in Bucharest as a Romanian homeowner and part-time businesswoman.

By the end of the afternoon, the future tavern walls were ready for Goran's paintings and her arms and legs were sticky with sweat from the day's heat. With a change of seasons was a sense of forward motion, a small accomplishment in a bigger vision.

She had the cottage to herself—especially the clawfoot tub. She brought the bear spray and Doctor Haller's journal in from the citadel and started heating buckets of water in both kitchens. With three over-sized kettles boiling on the citadel stovetop, there would be more than enough hot water.

Spread out on the cottage table was everything she needed for her impromptu inaugural dinner—cheese, crackers, antipasto, and the bread she'd baked in the citadel's brick ovens. Only one thing more. A bottle of dry red from the cases of wine stored in the citadel kitchen for their open house.

One bottle wouldn't make a dent, but—*aha*—when she got there someone had beaten her to it. Likely Ram or Julie grabbed one to drink with their meal.

The pool of water beside the wooden crate was more puzzling. It seemed to come out of nowhere; a set of wet footprints led to the rotunda and up the grand staircase. She tracked them past her bedroom door, then down the mezzanine in the direction of the chanting tower. Everyone seemed to be wet from jumping in and out of the boats. Perhaps, so as not to forget it, Julie had taken the bottle with her while chanting.

Paula halted at the doorway to the chanting tower. A stab of worry hit the pit of her stomach as she realized the prints were too wet to be those of her friends. They'd left hours ago. Not only that—Paula squinted into the dark corridor ahead—the footprints continued, then faded into obscurity. Damned if she was without the flashlight. She'd have to practically be on top of them to see where they went.

She wavered as it dawned on her. Why in the world was she following suspicious footprints through the dark citadel? Alone. She squeezed her eyelids to relax her clenched jaw. *Whoosh.* Out came all the dead air she'd been holding for—who knows how long?

A thought began crowding out the fear. Was it finally Goran?

Up ahead to her left was the door to her old room. A return visit from the intruder? No way. If the prints led in there, she'd get to hell out, and quick. Maybe barricade herself inside her bedroom and wait for a phone signal.

She crept forward, constantly glancing behind and to each side, until she reached the door. It was shut—as it should be. Or not. Hadn't she left it open to let the room dry out after mopping?

It didn't matter. The wet marks trailed across a patch of light coming from the open doorway of the locked tower they'd climbed their first day on the island. *Why would someone go in there? Unless…crap, of course. It had to be the kid.*

Perhaps he'd opted to continue roofing the cottage while she ran the spray gun. He'd cleaned himself at the beach and instead of taking the rowboat straight home came in here to explore the tower, not knowing the door at the top was locked. Yes, lanky teenage boys sometimes had humongous feet. Maybe he was still stumbling his way up or down the tower and could use her help.

Paula poked her head into the stairwell. "Hey. Kid. Yoo-hoo. Are you up there?" Would help if she'd learned his name. He was from a side of the family with a ridiculous number of consonants in their names. They'd settled on *kid*, and he didn't seem to mind. She kept up the yoo-hooing as she climbed.

For some reason, the stench on these stairs clung to her nostrils more than the ones leading up the chanting tower. It was like breathing inside a plastic bag. She couldn't get any oxygen into her lungs. The gloom, too, was thick as pitch; a putrid air of something rotten pressed in on her from all sides the closer she got to the top landing.

She looked down for exit prints but realized it was too dark to see any prints at all.

To calm herself, she tried to imagine the kid at the top, stretched out in one of his daydreams, or maybe even asleep. Before the last twisting turn, she stopped and bellowed, "Kid. Hey, kid. Answer me."

Her entire body was quaking, as if alive with army ants shuttling up and down her limbs. In just two meters, she would be at the locked door, face to face with the owner of the footprints.

And they weren't answering.

Paula side-stepped up the final turn and froze. Confusion prickled her scalp. The metal door, locked during their previous exploration, was open. Visible in the light from the battlement windows, the footprints stopped cold at the center of the planked floor. Not backtracking anywhere. No one seemed to be inside.

She stepped into the room. Something came at her

head. She shrieked and ducked as it veered off and flew out a broken window. On the sill lay the nest of a bird of prey, judging from its size.

Paula moved to the broken pane, surprised she could see their entire beach below—including the rowboat.

A choking silence settled in—the kid had left long ago in the motorboat with the others. The prints weren't his.

This had barely sunk in when the setting sun blinded her for a split second. As she raised her hand to it, she caught sight of another disturbing scene high above the reservoir on the opposite shore.

Against a heavy purple sky, at the top of a zigzagging pattern of stairs, hung two limp bodies, impaled through the torso. They swayed and flapped in the wind, skewered on long spindly poles.

She rubbed her eyes and squinted.

The grisly figures remained.

Adrenaline ran riot while she pumped down through stair after stair of the tower, the images rearing up before her eyes: dangling arms, flapping hair.

She flung aside the citadel's heavy oak doors, not even stopping to collect the final kettle of bath water. Paula burst into the cottage, bolted the doors and windows, then stood with her back against one wall, scanning for movement beyond the panes. The faltering light outside revealed nothing.

Only then did she remember the wine in her hand. At least she had that.

It took more than one shaky jab to get the corkscrew into the bottle. She set the bear spray, wine, and journal near the tub and...remembered the blank gun in her room. Nothing could get her back in there. Anyway, pointing a mock gun at someone might be worse than no gun at all.

Soothing steam rolled up her arms and legs, the day's dirt chafing off in clouds as she slid out of her shorts and T-shirt. It wouldn't be the evening she'd imagined, but with the wine added in she could at least wind down a notch. Paula inched in up to her neck and raised the doctor's journal to her eyes.

April 10, 1951

I feel quite foolish pulling this journal out again so soon, but my mentor's advice to stay grounded is ringing in my ears. Something odd has happened just now in my bedchamber.

First to remind myself why I asked for the bedchamber closest to the door leading up to the isolation cell. This large room on the second floor is equidistant between the isolation cell and my office tower where I expected to spend most of my days. The isolation tower, which serves as an intake, is virtually impregnable and guarded at both the upper door of the cell and at the entrance door into the stairwell. I observe new patients such as Lasorov until I determine whether they are ready to transfer to a locked room in the palace or must leave entirely to a more secure facility.

Tonight, the moment I switched off my bedside lamp, a sack-like object passed my window from above. Curious, I was forced to finally pry open the rusted clasp on my centuries-old pane and push it open for a clearer view below. Of course, there was nothing on the ground, so I concluded it was a bat diving at a rodent or possibly mad with rabies.

April 13, 1951

The asylum finds itself in the midst of a maelstrom of angry villagers. Another toddler is missing, and they cannot blame the so-called deranged young mother again since she is locked up in Bucharest, awaiting trial. Our patients are the first suspects. However, even if someone managed to get past the hospital's guards and orderlies, they could never breach the high wall and wires which ring the entire property. Nevertheless, we have doubled our security in every building and posted patrols on both sides of the wall.

Paula threw the scribbler on the bathroom floor. Enough of that. Especially tonight. Julie had apparently found some ancient *National Geographic* at a used bookstore in Bucharest. *Why didn't I hunt those down before getting in this water?*

She took a deep swig of the wine, and soon she was drifting, intoxicated, forgetting where she was even. Dreaming she was in the clawfoot at her cabin in Canada and someone was knocking and calling her name. There was the sound of Goran's hyena-like laugh, which always got her going, too. He did love life.

She ran her palms up and down her thighs, thinking of how she used to thread her fingers through the thick matted hair of his chest, then slipped below the surface, into utter silence, her long hair unfolding like a Japanese fan.

Goran, too, in his youth, had lain here. A spark of memory: naked and drifting. Euphoria flashed, but died when she came up for air.

Chapter Nine

Paula woke on the cold hardwood in front of the cottage's woodstove, naked in a cocoon of her friends' bedclothes and swimming in the raw lethargy of a hangover. The food from her celebration was all eaten, the wine bottle empty. Julie and Ram would be here any minute, so she threw on one of Ram's T-shirts and whatever she could find of her own clothes.

There was no hiding the revelry. She stuck whatever she could find under the tub's drain and pulled the plug. Never again would she trust her calculations on how fast a frying pan could fill with bath water. No sooner had she tossed the water out the bathroom window, than the empty one was overflowing onto the plank flooring.

Her plan to clean up the place and enjoy a relaxing morning tea was out the window, too. She reheated and chugged her friends' days-old coffee, amazed at how well it dissolved her hangover.

As she opened the kitchen door, a pattern of striped sunbeams fell across her face, making the terror of the previous night feel remote. Still, she had lived alone far too long to be naive. She tucked the bear spray under her waistband before grabbing three empty water jugs to fill on the reservoir.

At the citadel's main doors—the ones she'd left open—she halted, disquiet gnawing at her upbeat mood. No way had the wind blown the mammoth things shut.

Did this not prove her suspicions of an intruder even more than the wet footprints?

The rowboat was her safest spot until the rest arrived. They passed each other on the water, and when Ram and the kid came down to help carry the full jugs up, Ram smirked and said, "I see you had a fine time last night in the cottage."

"That was the plan, anyway." Reaching the top stair, Paula let the jug drop from her hand and turned to Ram. "I think we had another break-in. A lot of bizarre stuff was happening."

The kid came up last and also set down his jug, staring at Paula in earnest. Was his English better than he let on?

"Take it to the cottage." Ram pointed in that direction. "More roof today. Okay?" The kid trudged on, and Ram turned to her. "Tell me."

"Did any of you guys go up the other tower yesterday?"

"I didn't, and neither did the kid because he was with me all day."

"All right. That's scary, then, because the wet footprints I saw were too large to be Julie's. Someone *was* here. I followed the prints from the kitchen to the top of the other tower."

"Jesus." He hoisted up both jugs and started walking. "Julie needs to hear about this, too. Let's get these to the cottage."

"I'm okay." Paula trotted beside him to keep up. "I did what I was supposed to. Locked myself in the cottage with the bear spray."

He halted with his hand on the cottage door handle and grinned at her. "And got loaded on some of the wine,

I see."

She stumbled in after him. "You guys dipped into it, too. So don't talk."

"Dipped into what?" Julie was at the alcove window, shaking out the blankets and sleeping bags Paula had slept in.

"Another intruder," Ram said. "That's why she slept in here." He stopped short and stared at Paula. "Wait. Is there another bottle missing?"

"You didn't take it to town?"

"No. But this makes sense. Booze and money is what they're after. Petty thieves. We'll lock up the wine in the cottage pantry from now on. No more leaving you here alone."

"I'll be alone every summer."

"Then we'll get Claudia to set you up with a couple of wolfhounds for protection."

The last thing she wanted was to give Claudia and her wolves another reason to prowl around. "No Claudia. And no wolves." Paula's arms chopped out the words, as if cutting his solution off at the knees. "Go on and laugh, Ram, but you won't find what's happening at Poenari fortress very funny. Something's weird over there, too, or I'm going mad."

"I don't doubt you're having nightmares if you're using this thing for bedtime reading," Julie said. She held up Dr. Haller's journal. "I found it on a chair beside the tub." She flipped through. "Have you read this part yet?" She passed the journal to Paula.

April 28, 1951
I am quite exhausted since these disappearances from the village. The warden has ordered me to interview

every pedophile within our walls while also helping him choose from a meager and discouraging list of security applicants. I go through their resumes in my office when I should be sleeping. I know only too well hallucinations can occur from sleep deprivation, and I want desperately to convince myself this is what I experienced last night.

As Lasarov's cell is at precisely the same elevation as my office, I have a clear view of his windows in the distance. At midnight, while slogging through the extra paperwork, I saw something in the shape and size of a French loaf being jettisoned from between the bars of his window. Within seconds, another one flew and then another. I tried desperately to peer from my narrow battlement window for a better view, but finally, cursing, I dashed down the tower steps to the window in my bedchamber. I will forever wish I had remained at my desk.

Tumbling over and over through space as I stared up was a larger square-shaped object which landed heavily below. I had seen the bloodied torsos of young children in autopsies, so at first my mind didn't budge until a far greater horror entered. Three or four creatures crawled from the shadows, their teeth bared, each snapping and growling as one and then another ripped pieces from the tiny body.

Then, the one thing which could interrupt this grisly feeding frenzy soon hurtled down and smashed into pieces like an overripe squash. More wolves dashed forward from all sides, grabbing at pieces of the skull and torso and retreating until all was quiet, the ground picked clean.

I didn't think to go and investigate Lasorov's isolation cell. Not right away. What to tell the warden? I decided not to say anything for now as, without evidence, I could end up a patient in my own institution. To my shock, this meant I had unequivocally decided that what I had witnessed was real. I studied myself in the mirror of my chest of drawers, for it felt like I had suddenly stepped over an invisible line into another dimension.

At the stairs to the isolation cell, I found the bottom guard smoking a cigarette and flipping through a girlie magazine, which was strictly forbidden inside the facility. He quickly shoved it into the large inner pocket of his uniform, but I secretly welcomed this normalcy as it calmed my nerves. I asked him to unholster his gun and precede me up the tower in order to enter the cell. He went up at a good clip ahead of me, no doubt spurred on at the thought he might be dismissed. Soon I heard him hiss to his fellow guard, "Wake up."

When I rounded the last steps, both guards had their guns out. The upstairs one shone his flashlight through the peephole and nodded, which meant Lasorov appeared to be sleeping. One could never know. I didn't smell alcohol on this fellow, but I still requested the downstairs guard be the one to unlock the door. They positioned themselves strategically, and I tried my best to step to one side of the claustrophobic landing. It dawned on me this narrow stairwell would be my last choice for escaping a rampaging cannibal.

The heavy metal door squealed open. Both men trained their flashlights on the bed. Lasorov faced us, eyes shut. I took out my own small flashlight, which was standard employee issue to compensate for the flickering lights of this ancient structure, and scanned the window from which the body parts fell. It appeared pristine, not a speck of blood on the plank flooring below it, either. I *beckoned for the guards to follow me out. One locked the door while the other checked it.*

Needless to say, I didn't sleep all night. I approached the administrator this morning as he entered his office and told him to dismiss the drunken guard. Then I asked for the day off with the qualifier that I couldn't continue to function under the weight of added duties.

"Oh, bugger those village idiots," he said. "Take the rest of the week off. I refuse to disrupt my facility any longer every time a child gets lost."

I will need my wits about me for my next therapy session with Lasorov. Still, I find myself studying my countenance in every mirror I pass for evidence of madness.

"None of that is real. It can't be," Julie said after Paula looked up from the journal. Ram pinched the school scribbler from Paula's grasp and began reading it himself.

"The psychiatrist wrote it when he worked here," Paula said.

"Then he was more whacko than his patients. Another trapped soul to chant for." Julie strode out, no doubt headed to her altar.

"Claudia's mother was working here when it was a hospital," Ram said. "I say we show it to her."

Paula waited patiently until he had finished reading and handed the journal back to her. Trying on her most caustic tone, she said, "Still think I should get a couple of wolfdogs?"

****

Julie transferred the lit match from candle to candle

on her altar. The rhythmic vibrations inside the chanting tower were quickly becoming Paula's only escape from the relentless duties and disturbances on the island. Once the paintings were up, she could take a longer break, meditate, enjoy the place a bit.

On their way out, they passed Ram on the grand staircase to the second floor. "I'm going up there now." He pointed across the mezzanine at the entrance to the locked tower. "Anything in particular I should look for?"

"You'll see," Paula said.

Minutes later, from inside the kitchen where she was cooking her dinner, she heard him pounding down the staircase, but he didn't enter screaming murder and mayhem. Perhaps the impaled figures *were* nothing more than the sun in her eyes.

It was only much later, after dark, that Julie and Ram knocked at her bedroom door with mugs of tea and the layered lemon cake they'd brought from town. She shared the stone alcove bench with Julie and gave Ram the folding lawn chair which squeaked and shook under his weight.

Dessert plate cupped under her chin to catch wayward crumbs, Paula forked a piece of the flaky pastry into her mouth and asked between chews: "Did you see the people impaled on poles at Poenari fortress?" She couldn't have sounded more casual than asking if he ran into someone on the street.

"No. Because I couldn't get in. The door at the top was locked. And I knew it would be."

"Sweetie…" Julie leaned across and patted her hand, forcing Paula to rear back with the realization her friends were going through a script worked out at the cottage beforehand.

She sprang from the bench. "Well. It was open last night. There's a bird's nest on a window sill, and the beach and Poenari fortress are both visible from there. Am I right?"

"It's been so long since I've seen it, I really can't remember." For a moment, Ram stood like a sentry to his thoughts until, "They blocked it off after Goran's mother jumped from its parapet. That's all I know."

"She killed herself? But…I thought…He never—"

"Don't feel so left out. He never told me, either. Claudia did. She grew up in England, so of course she didn't get to know Goran's mother very well, not like I did, but the woman was her aunt. She heard the real story. What gets me is how Goran kept that secret inside himself for so many years."

What Ram had said in the boat rang in Paula's head: *I have this memory of his mother inside the kitchen, crying…They were growing food where the lawns used to be.* Goran and his mother had food, shelter, and freedom from torture. Not exactly fodder for suicide. What happened inside the citadel to make his mother lose her will to live?

Someone with wet feet had climbed to the top of the tower and relocked the door after Paula left. But why would they hide themselves?

"I want back in," Paula said. "Who would have a key? Claudia?"

"She's family, so probably. But she was with us. So was the kid."

"The kooky aunt?"

"She walks with a cane, for God's sake."

"But she could have given the key to someone. Like…Goran."

"Now you think Goran is alive and living in the tower?" Ram pressed himself into the lawn chair, painfully slow, and sighed. "I would love for Goran to be alive." His voice ratcheted up a notch, and all the torment in his words fell on Paula. "Rip into town on our scooters for drinks. Hike to the glacier."

Seeming far away, inside a memory, Ram rose to kick at a loose piece of plaster on the hearth. "Even if he is alive, it's irrelevant. It's been seven years, for God's sake. If he wanted to contact you, he would have done it by now. Have you thought about that?"

Paula turned her cheek from him and winced. The image of Goran on his final day in India, standing with his surfboard—deciding to throw away everything, including her—was always lurking around the murky fringes of her mind, showing itself at night in bed when she thought of him. She was justified in leaving Goran, but the opposite was like a gut punch.

They stared into each other's pain, slack-jawed. "You can really be mean sometimes," Paula said.

"Guys, guys. Calm down." Julie slid between them, hands raised. "I'm going to Poenari fortress to chant and meditate tomorrow. Anyone else up for it?"

Ram immediately stepped forward. "*I* am."

Julie turned to her friend. "Paula…? Don't look so shocked. What you saw was a prank. Ram said it happens every year." Julie moved closer to whisper. "Come and chant with me. It'll ground you."

Get grounded. If the limp bodies weren't a prank, if Dracula's hungry ghost was at work impaling people—then their day trip to release Poenari's frustrated spirits would be anything but grounding.

Chapter Ten

As soon as the kid understood where the three of them were going, he was adamant about staying behind to split firewood.

"Impressive."

"Naw," Ram said to Julie. "Doesn't surprise me he'd rather puff around here. Wait till you climb the stairs. There's fifteen hundred of them."

At the last moment, the kid dashed down the steps to the beach and waded to where Ram stood ready to push the bow out. Instead of jumping in, he slipped his backpack from his shoulder and fished out a handgun, using his palm like a tray.

Ram hesitated, eyeing the kid, then the gun, before gently lifting it, barrel down, and sliding the magazine out. "It's loaded all right," he said to the two women behind him.

"What the hell is a kid doing with a loaded handgun?" Julie said.

"They start hunting here pretty young."

"Gee." Paula arched one eyebrow. "I've never heard of anyone hunting with a handgun." Manning the stern's outboard, her head wobbled like a dashboard doll. "Back home in Canada, I keep a rifle for predators."

Julie twisted around with an emphatic nod at this rare flurry of sarcasm, then poked Ram's back. "Since when do you know how to handle guns?"

"The last summer I was here, there were guns everywhere," he said over his shoulder. "Goran took me into the hills and taught me. This is good, though. If there's a bear with cubs up there, then, ladies—I'm your man."

The kid's attention ping-ponged comment to comment but finally settled on Ram's tough thumbs-up. At that, the teen slogged to shore and climbed the stairs without a backward glance.

****

Ram all but sprinted up the fifteen hundred steps to Dracula's fortress.

Climbing in tandem with Julie, Paula raised her face to his receding figure pumping side to side above them.

"He's showing off again," Julie said.

"I think a game of chess would've impressed us as easily." Paula sucked in a ragged breath. "He wants to protect us from whatever might be up there. We all saw the Dangerous Wildlife sign at the bottom."

"That means nothing," Julie said. "Wild animals hate loud. Obnoxious. Voices. LIKE MINE." The bellowing crescendo left her slumped against the railing and smiling. "And stop scaring yourself with that doctor's wolf diary…C'mon. Let's go."

They plodded on until Paula said, "I admire the psychiatrist, actually. He's smart and…determined to help his patients."

Julie scoffed while they pulled themselves hand over hand up the railing. "As if you don't do that."

"My students *want* to be helped. The only mountain I've ever had to conquer was Goran. I didn't get far."

"You made it here, didn't you?"

Paula brushed off the compliment, more interested

in Ram who suddenly appeared at the lip of the flight, arms folded in mock impatience.

From here, Paula could clearly see the two impaled female figures above them, their loose clothing and long hair soaked red and whipping in the strong crosswinds. Thick rope, threaded at the armpits and crotch and looped over notches in the pole, held them aloft.

Paula stopped dead, her gaze darting between Ram's smile and the bloodied bodies. Had he not seen them?

"Why are they tied to their poles?" Julie seemed as bored as Ram. "I thought the idea was to have the body slip down through the spike." She clamped a palm on Paula's shoulder and broke into an ugly, wheezing chuckle. "Come on. I want a closer look at this handiwork."

"What the hell?" Paula shrugged off her friend's palm. "Ram. Get back here. We're leaving."

"Calm down and look at the delicate hands. Can't you see they're mannequins?" Julie plodded upward. "But I can totally understand why you were fooled."

A few tentative steps up, Paula squinted, then reeled as the first pulse of nauseous energy hit. *What kind of sickness of the soul created this?*

They continued. The more they climbed, the steeper the cliffside became, until sturdy concrete and steel girders propped the stairs high off the ground.

"Don't expect much of the fortress to be left," Ram said as the stairs exited directly into the ruins. "Maybe the top of a wall to chant from. They built them thick back then."

Although there was nothing left but a series of walls, one had iron loops as an ad hoc ladder to the top. *Use At Own Risk*, a sign stated in several languages.

"If I remember right, this is the only way up top. I'm going to release the poled ladies." Ram stepped from the stairs but not before Paula pulled the bear spray from a deep pocket of her flowing skirt.

"Keep it. I've got the handgun."

"And I've got the other gun." Julie brandished the blank gun from her backpack. "There's something I've never said before sitting down to meditate."

Ram called over his shoulder, "Shout when you want to leave."

They found a flat section of the wall, and Julie asked which chant Paula wanted to start with.

"Can we sit in silence for ten minutes," Paula said, "and send loving kindness to all which exists and has existed in this place? I'm feeling agitated. Maybe it's the climb."

No news, movies, or any other media had gripped and invaded her mind quite like the depraved deeds of the Bucharest Ripper, written firsthand by the witness himself, Dr. Haller. She imagined him in his tower office, putting a sweaty, trembling pen to paper. Recording the life and death of a psychopath with an unquenchable desire to kill—straight from Dr. Haller's mind and memory into Paula's. How could such a monster be anything but a hungry ghost left behind to creep along the subterranean passages of her citadel?

Their chant to honor the Buddha, the Dharma, and the Sangha whistled through the eroded remains of Vlad Dracula's castle. They sat atop one of the remaining walls of the dining hall where so many had suffered more than five hundred years ago while he feasted on the corpses of his enemies.

She wished the Ripper well and silently dedicated

the merit of her meditation to his release from the world. Today, in this moment, Dracula's former home felt a measure of serenity and peace.

A jarring rattle forced her eyes open in time to see a majestic horned chamois perched on a section of railing below. It bounded clear with some kind of predator darting under the stairs in pursuit. Leaving Julie to her chanting, Paula peered over the side in Ram's direction.

From a dense stand of trees and underbrush came a shot, then two more blasts in quick succession.

Ram!

She bolted to the ladder with the bear spray. Only two rungs from the bottom, she caught Ram backstepping into a clearing, sweeping the gun to each flank.

"Ram."

"Get back." He sliced his free arm through the air in a panic. "They're everywhere. Go."

"Who are?"

He didn't answer. She climbed, and seconds later the rails under her shuddered with his weight, his ragged breaths right on her heels. "Go. Go. Go," he said, when she glanced down at his wild eyes. A cacophony of snarls and low growls erupted near the base of the wall where she soon saw a half dozen wolves pacing.

As soon as Ram and Paula cleared the stairs, Julie pointed the blank gun at the pack below and fired. The retort scattered them for mere minutes before they skulked back, just as fierce.

"What the hell is this? They're not one bit afraid of us or the guns." She reached for Ram, who was still bent double and gasping from the frantic climb.

Paula clutched the crown of her head, her face a

pained grimace.

Ram finally straightened to take Julie in a tight embrace. "They're determined to drive us out of here," he said over the top of her head.

"I wouldn't be so sure they'll stop at that," Julie said. "Look at their ears. They're challenging us. There's something here they want to protect."

"A den of pups?" Paula said.

"Not *this* close to civilization." Julie wagged her chin. "It's like we're another pack invading their territory."

Ram pulled the gun from the inside pocket of his jacket and released the magazine. "Five shots left against six wolves." He slammed it back into place. "Not that it matters much. I don't think I hit a single one with those first shots. Bought me time, was all."

Julie, the one with the most knowledge about wildlife through her travel writing, eyed the stairs out. "If they're as hopeless going down stairs as dogs are, they might not be able to catch us."

"That's not going to stop them from running alongside and jumping over the guardrails," Paula said.

"Oh yes it will. Eight feet is all wolves can manage from the ground. The stairs are higher than that."

"For a while, anyway," Ram said. "We're going to need both guns and the bear spray to get back to the road."

Julie pulled her cell phone from her backpack. "No signal. Try your satellite phone."

"Wish I could," Ram said. "I never take it hiking in case I lose it."

She sighed. "Oh, dammit all. But once we're headed out, they'll lose interest, don't you think?"

No one answered.

****

Two hours later, Paula and Ram had migrated into their separate miseries along the wall. Julie sat in utter stillness, meditating.

A theory was forming in Paula's mind while she listened to the snarly infighting below; the wolf at the dock the first night, the ones in the mist the morning of Claudia's first visit, and now here—Paula wouldn't be surprised if this shifty woman appeared on the stairs and dispersed the pack with a wave of her hand.

"I'm not sure I want to sit here all night," Ram muttered, rising for the umpteenth time to pace. He hadn't spoken in over an hour, degenerating from an erect cross-legged posture to flat out supine.

"I really expected the police to show up by now. The kid would have been picked up at the dock an hour ago. He must have heard the shots."

Half listening, Paula was busy counting off days of the week on her fingers. "It's the solstice tonight." Ram stopped pacing and looked up. "The shortest night of the year," she added.

"And? Is that somehow relevant? Like maybe these wolves have an all-night bash planned and need something for the menu? Because I noticed one left a while back to get the party started."

"You're losing it, Ram. Three wolves left. There's a pattern. Only half of them are down there at any one time. This—" She pulled the bear spray from a pocket of her skirt. "Could put three of them out of action long enough for us to get a good start."

"Or wait for rescue." Ram was once again mumbling to himself.

"I have no faith in the kid putting the pieces together. Do you?" she asked. "He might show up in the morning, see no one around, and flake off."

"Julie." In response to Ram's shout, the wolves sprang up, pacing and snarling again. He motioned her over. "We've come up with a plan."

Okay. Giving me half the credit is better than none at all.

"From the ladder, I give the bastards down there a snoutful of bear spray," Ram said. "They'll scatter while we run for the stairs."

Julie kept up a lively nod while he spoke but said, "A few things to think about. The other three will be back in no time if they hear their pack members in distress."

"That's where this comes in." Ram pulled the handgun from the pocket of his jacket. "Six bullets against three is better odds."

"I've had a faceful of pepper spray at protests." Julie grimaced. "It's a good plan."

Ram traded his handgun for Paula's bear spray, admitting she was probably a better shot than he was. "I'll hang onto the bear spray. Julie, a *bang* from the blank gun could buy us time, too. The minute the three wolves are gone, go like hell down the stairs. I'll stay at the rear because that's where the others will come from."

But it wasn't. Not at first.

A quarter of the way down the fifteen hundred steps, Paula glanced back to see Ram lagging two flights above. She saw why.

Two wolves raced parallel with the stairs, sometimes vaulting close enough to strike the guardrail with their paws. With each thump, Ram hesitated, and turned, bear spray poised. One which managed to hang briefly from both paws got a snoutful of bear spray.

She flicked the sweat from her brow—her hands were wracked with tremors. For now, the wolves had no chance of leaping onto the stairs of this raised section.

"Ram." Gun in hand, Paula shouted up to him and waved him onward. "Go hard. I've got you." But added under her breath, "I hope."

Far above him she caught sight of what they feared most—a massive red wolf leapt and rolled through entire flights. The animal's sheer strength alone kept it from going into an endless tumble.

It would be on top of Ram any minute.

Paula said nothing to him but slowly took the safety off the handgun. She nudged forward a few steps to narrow the gap between them. Only one flight separated the wolf from Ram.

She watched its hind legs bend, ready to spring. Ram turned and as the animal became airborne, he aimed the bear spray—nothing came out of the empty cylinder.

Paula's first shot went wide. The second lodged squarely in its broad chest. It crashed against the railing and tumbled wildly past them to the landing below.

Ram and Paula lay sprawled where they'd stumbled backwards. She sprinted forward, crouched, and pumped another bullet into the motionless animal at close range. She rose and faltered, dizzy from the adrenaline rush. "Ra-am. I don't think I can do this."

"You just did...Arrrr." He winged the empty aerosol can toward a snout as it popped above the railing, the hollow clunk of metal on skull.

"This is crazy. We need to catch up with Julie. Stick together," Paula said. They charged forward. Far below, Julie was approaching a boardwalk section which a wolf could easily mount. "Ram. We need to hurry." She pointed, but he didn't notice.

"Where's that last bastard?" In the lead, he scanned the bushes along the stairs. "Can you see him?"

"No," she said, even though she'd been tracking the gray mass threading through nearby trees for some time. "Head for Julie. All she's got is that phony gun. And if I shout *down*, drop so I hit the wolf, not you."

Three bullets left, she thought. Enough to finish off one, maybe two wolves? Only if she was lucky. Her entire body was shaking with delayed nerves.

"Ram." She wanted him to take the gun.

But from the corner of her eye, she caught a gray blur in the air. The stairs shook as the animal landed not ten steps in front of them. It crouched, its massive white canines gleaming in the setting sun. A pulsating, guttural growl deep inside its throat raised the hairs at the back of Paula's neck.

"Down. *Now*." She lifted her quivering arm. The gun wobbled wildly. Ram dropped but immediately swept one arm up to pitch something far over the side. To her amazement, the wolf cleared the railing and leapt after it.

With the way out open, they plunged down flight after flight and soon caught up with Julie. Snatches of the road began appearing, and then they burst onto it.

As Paula handed Ram the gun, he curled his arm around her shoulders, and she was sure he could feel her trembling. Not that his pallid face didn't betray his own illusion of composure.

Julie was squatting, curled into a ball, arms encircling her head. "I'm sorry I left you guys." She choked back sobs, her voice shrill. "I heard the shots. I was sure you were both gone."

Ram tugged her into his chest and kissed the crown of her head. "You did the right thing. Exactly what I would have done."

"No, you wouldn't have." Julie pushed him away and dragged the back of her hand across her runny nose. "You wouldn't have stopped until both guns were empty and shoved down their throats."

"Julie." Paula came and wrapped her arms around her friend. "Don't give yourself a panic attack. You're fine. We all are." And then Paula's silent tears cascaded down her cheeks.

Ram grasped Julie's hand and then Paula's and started walking along the dirt road leading to the dock. "We could sure use the damn vehicle about now. At least it's still daylight."

Paula remembered the wolf at the motorhome their first night. She sniffled. "Keep the gun handy."

"Unless there's raw meat on the road, we won't need it."

She halted with a jerk to Ram's arm. "Is that what you threw off the stairs?"

He nodded.

"It wasn't a dead squirrel or something?"

"Nope. It was the prime rib they were after. Not us. I ran past another hunk of meat near the top, too. Who knows why, but someone's spending a lot of money to keep the tourists away from there."

Julie dropped Ram's hand, clenched her fists, and pumped them into a silent scream. "It's always us. We do this to them. They were only protecting their food supply." She turned to Paula. "But Ram's right. The wolves will stay up there where the easy food is."

They walked in an uncomfortable silence until Paula said under her breath, "It was a magnificent beast, wasn't it? I've never killed anything before in my life. Such a waste."

As they arrived at the dock, Paula tried to catch Ram's eye. "What do you think is going on?"

He stared ahead with the pained concentration of a scientist but ignored her. "You guys cross to the citadel. I'm going to get Claudia to phone the police. Those wolves should be destroyed before someone is killed."

"Destroy the people who fed them. There could be pups."

"Who cares," Ram said to Julie. "These aren't your rescue dogs. They're vicious animals. You saw yourself."

Paula waved a palm between them at eye level and pointed to the dock. "Look. Notice anything strange?"

"There's no rowboat," Ram said. "The kid should be on this side by now." He took a tentative step in the direction from which they'd come, then turned on his heel, an expression of dark realization. "Both of you." He gazed across the reservoir while rifling through his pockets. "Get in the motorhome and keep the doors locked."

"For what reason?" Paula asked.

He slapped the key for the ignition into Julie's palm. "I'm going for the kid."

Julie stared at it in her hand. "Wha…What's happening?"

He ignored her and strode to the motorboat. "If you see anyone, anyone at all…" He threw the mooring lines onboard. "Drive into town and find Claudia. Tell her exactly what's happened. She'll know what to do."

"And leave you here?" Julie stomped toward him, but Ram had already jumped into the stern, the outboard chugging from the dock.

"I've got the gun. See you in thirty." He slammed the gearshift into high, throwing the motor into a pitched whine before the vessel was lost in a wake of white water.

****

An hour had passed since the boat disappeared behind the citadel and still no sign of Ram. Paula, in the driver's seat, had put it off as long as she dared, not wanting to panic Julie more than necessary. "We should go find Claudia," she said under her breath.

"Damn." Julie flung her door open and stepped out. "If she's all we've got for help, we're screwed. We don't even know where that woman lives." No more than a minute later, Julie raised her head toward the water. "I hear a boat."

Ram was alone, though. He came in fast, not even throwing the fenders before jumping out and tying up.

"That citadel is goddamn big. I looked in every room. Went up the towers. Called all over the island. He's not there. Then I phoned Claudia. She agrees, the dock's not safe, either. Everyone in. We're going to her place."

Julie started to badger him for information, but all she got was "I'll explain when Claudia finds the kid."

Paula was content to ride in silence, taking in deep breaths and focusing on the soul-cleansing babble of water in a creek running down from the village. With the pension at the edge of town in sight, they turned uphill onto a steep rutted trail. After endless switchbacks through scrub, the road almost petered out in a meadow before squeezing itself between two rows of yellow birch. It led into a modest farmyard of outbuildings, each one seeming to outdo the other in disrepair.

A sway-backed horse hung its head over a railing, which butted up to a desultory showboat of a thatched cottage. Worn-out dabs of garish greens, pinks, and yellows dotted shutters and carved gables. Sunbaked pickets, too flimsy to be a bear deterrent, surrounded the yard like a fort.

Except for the satellite dish, the three of them could be entering a settlement from the Middle Ages. "Wait here. This won't take long." Ram jumped from the driver's seat.

Claudia appeared, and the two of them wandered from the yard while Claudia monitored her cell phone and finally brought it to her ear. They returned to the cottage—but stayed inside far too long for mere pleasantries with the old aunt. When they emerged, both marched to the far side of the house, even farther than before.

Paula didn't dare open her window by more than a crack because Ram and Claudia took turns eyeing the motorhome. She could make out snippets of sharp words and would have understood more had they not been shouting over top of each other.

"How could you have not known about this long ago?" Ram said at one point.

"She's not always with it. Her mind's going." Then just the last words in a sentence: "...screwed up."

"He must be the one who sent the email about the paintings, too," Ram said. "That doesn't alarm you?"

They wandered even farther from the cottage, their voices fading, only three sentences audible.

"This wasn't supposed to happen," Claudia said.

"Not much we can do now unless we take it to the police."

"Please don't," she said. "It'll finish her off. We might be worrying about nothing."

Propelling herself forward with a cane, the old aunt waddled from the cottage on a determined tangent with the motorhome. From afar, she resembled a frazzled version of Julia Child, minus the haute couture tea towel on her hip.

Paula caught "Do you feel safe? I sure don't…" This from Ram.

Claudia seemed to calm down because all her words were too soft to make out, and there was a long stretch of silence until Ram boomed, "For Christ's sake. We're the only ones that know…Don't think he won't kill again. Once we're gone, Paula could be next."

The aunt was at the passenger side window, tapping with her cane. "You lovelies," she said, after Paula lowered it. "Are you not comin' in for something to wet your whistle?"

"Hello. I'm Paula." Paula had her hand out but was staring over the woman's shoulder in the direction of the last comment by Ram. The aunt nodded, a touch irritated, and didn't shake hands.

"We only came to tell Claudia about the wolves at Poenari fortress," Julie said, straining to make herself visible from behind Paula. "They're attacking people."

The aunt cocked her head sideways at first, as if she hadn't heard properly, then reared up, her eyes narrow and fierce. "Ahh. Didn't I tell them they'd be back?"

Beyond the aunt, Claudia trotted over, one notch away from a full sprint.

"Nooo—" She tossed her head with elephantine irritation. "Wouldn't believe an old woman. I've been around these parts too long not to know what's going on."

Marching in breathless, Claudia spun her mother away from the window as soon as she arrived, but the old woman shook her off and demanded, "When was the last time I had visitors?"

"They'll be back another time, Mum. They've had a tiring day."

"So I hear. Been up to Poenari."

"We should get back to our supper." Claudia hadn't made eye contact with either Paula or Julie.

Mother and daughter toddled off, the old aunt repeatedly yanking free of her daughter's help. Almost out of earshot, the aunt turned back and fairly bellowed, "I have a photo for you...Paula, is it? Photog of the palace. Black and white, but what a beauty it is."

***

Ram slammed the driver's door, slid the key into the ignition, and sat motionless, as content as a roosting hen. "The kid's okay. Friend stopped by to go fishing. Claudia will talk to him." He popped open the glove compartment in front of Paula, tossed in another handgun, and slammed it shut.

The two women exchanged looks while he prattled on with his monologue. "She'll also call Conservation about the wolves. How about that Aunt Lisbet? Isn't she priceless?" He shifted and spoke to Julie behind him. "Goran's grandmother, the old countess, smuggled Aunt Lisbet out of communist Romania when she was just fifteen. They married her off to a gentleman sheep farmer in England. Claudia was her only child. After the guy died and Claudia was through school, Aunt Lisbet came back to Romania."

"To where? The family palace?" Julie said.

"Not likely. It wasn't under water yet, but it was a wreck. Goran's mother was still in the cottage, so that was out, too. She did what she knew, bought this sheep farm outside the village."

He pulled away from the cottage, and they were once more running alongside the yellow birch.

"What's up with you and Claudia?" Paula asked, determined not to let him off so easy.

"She can be difficult." He flashed her a shaky grin. "But can't we all."

"No problem returning to the citadel?" Julie said.

"We're good to go."

"Is that why you've brought a second handgun into this vehicle?" Paula asked.

"Oh. That. The safety's on. Claudia didn't have the proper ammo for the kid's gun."

Paula inhaled, taking her time with the conversation to follow. She'd never had to arm her home, her refuge, against anything but wildlife. She wasn't going to start.

"If we need to protect ourselves against animals, then get me a rifle. A good one could have taken out those wolves this morning one at a time from the safety of the wall. But if you're planning a shootout on my island, go somewhere else. I'm making it a handgun-free zone."

No one stirred until, "Ah. Nothing like a slice of heaven. Should we hoist the Canadian flag from the tower, too?"

"Shut it, Ram," Julie said behind him.

All was quiet while they banged side to side around

the switchbacks. As they entered the main road, Julie crouched behind her two friends, spread her arms wide, and pressed a palm to each of their shoulders, sucking the poison air into the night.

Minutes later, while they sped past the scene of their terror, an outpouring of distant howls hit the motorhome. "They're mourning the loss of the alpha, their father," Julie said, straining in the direction of Poenari's stairs.

Ram glanced over his shoulder at her. "Do you think they can still smell us down here on the road?"

"Of course they can, but if you're asking whether they'll come after us—the answer is *no*. Why would they hunt us when a defenseless rabbit is so much easier?"

"Even so," Paula said. "I'd feel better if we parked closer to the dock from now on."

Chapter Eleven

The pandemonium of rifle blasts and truncated shrieks from Poenari's wolves bounced off mountainsides and into the citadel's stone halls where Paula stood refilling the muriatic acid sprayer. The victors of this war will be taking no prisoners, she thought, lifting off her respirator hood as Julie appeared inside the feast hall.

"How long can they keep it up? It's like a war zone," Paula said.

"Long enough to kill every last one, probably." Julie pointed to the sprayer gun with an air of measured seriousness. "It must be hot inside that hood. I can do it today if you like."

Julie hadn't helped inside the citadel since taking over the time-consuming shopping trips, and Paula soon saw through her kind offer. "I'm good here, but you could start pounding in the spikes for Goran's paintings in the tavern room. That kind of racket would block out the shooting just as well as this suit.

"How's Ram taking it? Is he okay?"

"Hell, yeah," Julie said. "Him and the kid are whistling a happy tune digging the septic lines. I think Ram misses the substratum life of a geologist."

For some reason, Goran popped into Paula's head. Or rather, what he'd told her about the bribes forced on Ram's powerful Musahar family in India. "Ram needn't worry," she said, deadpan. "He'll have lots of lowlife around when he gets elected in India."

"Will ya look at you." Julie nodded with mock intensity. "Next thing, you'll be headlining for Comedy Central."

"Just being honest. I guess that's all humor is. Paying attention to what's around you." A sense of longing tugged at her heart: another relationship soon to be engulfed by time. "Since Goran, you've been my eyes and ears to the world outside my cabin back home. What am I to do, now you'll be living in India?"

"You'll have to start paying attention yourself, I'd say." Julie smiled vaguely, but Paula knew she didn't mean to smile at all.

****

Finished for the day, Paula opened the citadel's main doors and almost stumbled over a puppy dashing past.

"Grab 'im," Claudia said, racing toward her. Paula scooped up the fuzzy ball as it tried to leverage its plump backside up the grand staircase. She was rewarded with hot, wet licks over her eyes and cheeks.

Paula found Julie long-faced outside the cottage, kneeling beside a wire cage holding two more wolf pups. Inside the septic trench, Ram and his worker stood propped against the handles of their shovels.

"They're gorgeous." Julie raised her arms to receive Paula's puppy. "But I almost wish you hadn't brought them over if they're going to be euthanized." She stared at Claudia while the wolf pup lapped at the tears streaming down Julie's cheeks.

Claudia turned to Paula. "It's a litter from Poenari. You can be certain they're the alpha male's offspring."

Paula's heart sank. The pup which ran past her was a miniature version of the massive red she'd shot midair yesterday. Was it really less than twenty-four hours ago all that happened? The other two pups were gray with black outlines on their snouts, eyes, and ears.

One of those, barely half the size of the others cowered in one corner of the cage, its frail body shaking with fear.

"Did you find them up there, or...?" Paula said.

"Not me. Officers brought them to my mother's place a few hours ago. It's a temporary refuge for abandoned wolf pups."

Claudia knelt and reached into the back of the cage for the runt. "Until I find them a new home." She stood, stepped back, and put the trembling puppy down, studying it as it tried to scoot to the safety of the cage. One of its front legs was collapsed inwards, giving the continuous illusion of it stumbling into a hollow.

"This one's done, I think." She scooped it up, kissed the top of its head, and tucked it back into the cage. "If that's from something degenerative, I doubt anyone will take it."

"You mean a family?" Paula asked.

That shot Claudia onto her feet. "Over my dead body. Wolves need to range, and I don't mean down main street."

"Then...?"

"Their only hope will be as a companion for another sanctuary wolf, but these guys are too young."

The pup with the bum leg seemed to sense his fate already, squashing himself into as small a ball as possible, as if he hoped to disappear entirely. Paula knew how that felt. Like the quiet girl with the pink hearing aid and scratchy voice, in the last desk of the last row, befriended by nothing but a buffer of empty seats.

"There's no point in me taking them"—Claudia said this as if fighting her way through an old tiresome quarrel—"if I'll have to destroy them six months from now, anyway. I've already got three of my own."

"Three wolves? Where?" Paula asked. "At your property?"

"Yes, normally. But today I brought them with me. They're at the dock."

"We don't have a dock."

"Then I must have tied the boat I borrowed to a good imitation of one."

They couldn't be faulted, Claudia agreed, for not knowing the island not only had a ready-made dock but also a solid wooden staircase to it beginning in a compact stand of pines behind the cabin. There'd been no reason and no time to explore this cliff where the stairs plunged to the humpback peninsula below. They could see the strip of land from where they gathered deadfall, but not the dock on the far side of it.

As they approached the newly discovered dock, only one wolf dashed from its sunbathing. Julie crouched to receive it, but Paula and Ram froze. It bowled Julie over and licked her face until a sharp command from Claudia laid it flat, submissive. Another word and it trotted obediently back to the dock.

"He's the alpha, so he occasionally likes to remind me and the others I'm not the true master here. He's got that right." She stepped onto the dock, and a beautifully toothy grin broke from her face. "They've been with me since infancy and are quite safe under my control." It was the first time Paula noticed anything approaching tenderness in Claudia's eyes. "But I completely understand why you wouldn't think so."

Ram stayed put, but Paula inched forward.

"Come," Claudia said to her and barked another command to the wolves. They sat up and arranged themselves in a row. She handed Paula a chunk of dried meat. "Let them take it from a flat palm, like this." The first dog scooped the treat from Claudia's hand with its tongue.

Paula's terror felt palpable, to herself and possibly everyone else, including the wolves. "I don't think I can do this." She handed the treat back to Claudia, who then rewarded the other two wolves.

"I have a favor to ask," Claudia said, casually linking her arm through Paula's while they stepped from the dock. With a forced hoot which made Paula jump, she threw back her head. "You've probably figured that out by now."

Paula let herself be led but kept a vigilant eye on this appendage twining itself in the crook of her arm like bindweed.

"Will you guys take the pups for a few days while I phone my sources?" She released Paula and looked in earnest from one to the other.

Julie piped up first. "I will. We can set them up in one of the unused citadel rooms."

"Excellent idea. But I won't leave them unless everyone is okay with it."

Julie's gaze settled on Ram. "Sure. Why not?" he said.

There wasn't much of a choice, Paula thought. These pups were orphans because of her overarching fear of Poenari. "Okay."

Claudia turned on her heel. "So happens I have everything you'll need. They're only about six weeks old but eating solids already." She promptly lifted a cooler from the motorboat and slipped the handle onto Julie's forearm before striding back to haul a small bale of hay from the stern. She dropped this into Ram's arms.

"Oh. And I have the rifle I hear you want." She reached into the boat and laid it on the dock. "See you in two days," she said, climbing in after her wolves and yanking the motor to life. As if expecting something more to come, the three friends stood like statues until the craft disappeared around the citadel.

"We've gained a dock and three wolves today," Paula said, mounting the stairs and snagging the opposite side of the cooler's handle with Julie.

They trailed Ram's staggering gait up the stairs.

"So I'm not sure whether that puts us ahead."

****

In the space of two weeks, the pups went from adorable children to destructive and irritating adolescents who never stopped eating. Ram was working sunup to sundown to get the sewage lines covered before one of them chewed through something.

Julie, however, seemed happier than ever. When she wasn't meditating, she was at the pebbled beach where the pups couldn't fall into holes or cut themselves on sharp branches. She usually left the bum leg pup behind. Too much maintenance.

Paula had heard his pitiful whining and howling when he was alone but couldn't see going to him with summer having arrived and so much left to do before the fall gallery opening.

Until today.

131

It was time to dry out the feast hall's stone floor with the biggest fire possible.

She hadn't read the journal since the wolf attack. If it was the Ripper killing the villagers, then how the heck was he getting out of the tower? No sooner had she set out her lawn chair than a deluge of pitiful howls split the restful silence. Why not let him loose inside the empty hall with her?

Bummer, as she called him, dashed up and down the rectangular space in a startling show of endurance considering his awkward gait. He nosed up to the fire, then backed away and stared into her eyes as if asking for her approval—or perhaps protection. Getting no response, he flopped beside her and dozed off.

The other two wouldn't so much as enter a room with a fire going. "You're quite the explorer, aren't you, Bummer?" One eye opened, then closed. "From now on your name is Marco Polo."

Paula flipped through the journal until she found something from the last entry:

Then I asked for the day off with the qualifier I couldn't continue to function under the weight of added duties.

"Oh, bugger those village idiots," he said. "Take the rest of the week off. I refuse to disrupt my facility any longer every time a child gets lost."

I will need my wits about me for my next therapy session with Lasorov. I find myself scrutinizing my countenance in every mirror I pass for evidence of madness.

May 1, 1951

I have slept soundly on and off for the past twenty-

four hours. Feeling refreshed, I proceeded to pack my valise this morning in order to visit a school chum interned to a hospital in Prague. But it has occurred to me I could use the free time to task myself with finding Lasorov's route of escape. I managed to track down binoculars to spy on him in his cell, telling the nurse who owns them I wanted to go afield in search of birds.

While making a spectacle of this deception on the arched bridge over the moat, an orderly and nurse rowed by. They were soon forced to turn around at the wall which encircles the entire grounds. It is here where the village creek which feeds the moat enters through a submerged culvert. I remembered having asked the administrator whether this pipe could be used to escape under the wall, to which he replied: "It would be impossible for one to hold their breath long enough."

As these flat-bottomed boats are asylum property, I hopped in where they abandoned theirs. It was with no small attack of nausea I realized that due to this year's low runoff one could easily cruise through the culvert by ducking below the boats' gunwales.

Now that I knew how Lasorov escaped the facility, I needed a clear hour to inspect his cell. I went to find Elieno, the girlie magazine fan. "It's not Lasorov's turn for his weekly ablutions," I said, "but could you take him to the showers and teach the new guard the procedure the two of you will follow?"

I signed out the cell's extra key from stores, entered, and using a broom, tapped along the plaster ceiling for any weak spots which would allow someone to remove a section and descend the tower via a rope. But it was solid. How Lasorov would possibly obtain a rope, let alone one of that unthinkable length, is a matter of conjecture I base on this man's genius.

I circumambulated the room, tapping in the same manner at the stone walls, and had started along the bottom quadrant when one edge of a large stone shifted. A crowbar would have expedited nicely. Eventually by levering the broom handle, the boulder fell forward to reveal a hollow with a metal bar protruding from the floor planks. To me, it looked like the mechanism for a gallows.

I stepped back and stared at it, my heart pounding because I knew I had found what I was looking for. Whether to manipulate it? Would the section of floor where I stood give way? I had to take that chance. When pulling didn't work, I pushed and sure enough a rectangular section of planking dead center of the room fell away with the soulless rattle of an executioner's rack. A fetid gust of clammy air assaulted my senses.

The reason this trap door was so hard to discover was that the cell's bed hid one edge of it. The dim beams of my flashlight lit on what appeared as an endless chasm around which a steep stone staircase spiraled from view, most likely to the very ground the citadel stood on. I was looking at a medieval escape route used in the event of a siege but couldn't explore it further without a better flashlight and more time. Pulling the lever hoisted the trap door into position as if it had never moved in the first place.

Before leaving, the crank flashlight I'd given Lasorov caught my eye. It lay atop the book of Plato's teachings that he was apparently reading. Without the light, he would find his killing spree ponderously slow. Removing it, however, might drive him to disappear for good. I had to catch him in the act of killing.

Feeling certain Lasorov only escaped down these secret stairs at night, I returned to my tower office and in minutes found an identical trap door there. I had but a few short hours of daylight to explore this staircase and thwart his next atrocity.

Bingo for Dr. Haller!

But don't go down into that hole. She found herself shouting to him through the decades. Everybody knows what hangs out there. Transfer the Ripper, close the passage, and be done with both.

But then there wouldn't be any story. It would be *Life of Paula*—not much at all—and she could see Dr. Haller was just getting started.

Paula slipped the journal into the large pocket of her denim skirt. She found Ram's crowbar in the yard and began climbing the chanting tower.

It was time to find the secret stairs for herself.

Chapter Twelve

Paula's search inside the tower was over in mere minutes.

She looked under the wooden crate which served as Julie's altar and lifted her sitting cushion for signs of breaks or outlines in the floor, but linoleum covered the entire surface. If the trap door had ever existed, clearly, access was no longer possible.

No luck with the lever inside the wall, either. From the journal's description, it wouldn't be near the door nor at the far end of the room. She whacked one possible section so hard a chunk of joinery mortar fell free, but no secret hollow appeared.

She sank to the linoleum and continued reading for other clues.

May 2, 1951

Like the helpless little man inside Einstein's clocktower, I feel paralyzed by indecision while the rest of mankind hurtles by at the speed of light. Yesterday, after discovering the secret staircase in both towers, I borrowed a flashlight from stores and removed my gun from the safe inside my room. I found myself staring into the dark hole inside my office tower and once again questioning my judgement, if not sanity. I gingerly tested each step until I was assailed by a reek as foul as a sewage manhole. I knew then the secret staircases exited onto the moat.

At the bottom, I stood in a frightful low passage, a miasmic darkness on all sides. In the distance, my dim beam captured what must be the other staircase leading from the isolation cell.

Another much broader tunnel led away at a right angle. Intending to reach the source of the lapping water I could hear, I stepped from the final stair. I had gone no more than a few meters when my foot hit something and I tripped forward, landing on my hands and knees. The flashlight spun from my grasp across the stones. As I reached to retrieve it, illuminated in the beam was the lifeless, chalky face of a young woman, her wet tendrils twined around her neck like strangle weed.

While I had dallied at amateur sleuthing and catching up on sleep, Lasorov had killed again! The body was well into rigor mortis. I slogged doggedly until I hit ankle-deep water and came upon an aluminum boat identical to those on the moat. Furious with myself and inflamed by a desire to stop him, I discharged my gun over and over into its bottom, heedless of who might hear.

I ascended to my office in a rage, determined to disable every last one of the aluminum craft used on the moat. I found three under the bridge and was about to shoot holes in these, too, when I saw the precarious impulsivity driving me. No one, other than the guards, was allowed to have firearms within the facility. I climbed to Lasorov's peephole, satisfied myself he was there, then ordered the top guard to go out and disable all the boats, explaining I suspected them of being instruments of escape.

Now that I had the complete picture and the

woman's body as evidence, it was time to ask the warden to summon police. My watch showed after ten p.m. I expected him to have already retired. With no way for Lasorov to deliver the body to the wolves or even get into the village, could I not wait the six hours until the administrator opened his office at daybreak? Back in my chamber, I tried to at least doze, but not a bit of sleep would come as my mind spun with what else I could do.

The hour by now was approaching two a.m., so I have to question what part exhaustion played in my next irrational actions. I wanted to verify one final time that the evidence remained and the trap door functioned before calling police in a few short hours. I went up to my office and popped the trap there. Down I went yet again and was no more than halfway when, far below, a dreadful snarling and manic splashing reached me. I immediately switched off my light, lapsing into utter blackness. My fingers ached from gripping the banister, my legs quaked from despair that none of my efforts had made any difference.

The tiniest glow appeared in the flooded passage. I crept forward noiselessly as possible until I could make out a chaos of shadows swarming what I assumed was the body. A few wolves darted away, splashing deep into the water, and I soon realized what had their attention. Two wolves dragged yet another body feet first into the tunnel, their fangs deep into each ankle, streaks of blood staining the fur of their necks.

A menacing bellow reverberated, and Lasorov appeared, arms raised. The faint beams from the crank flashlight spread across the moldy ceiling to unmask the full sweep of horror. The wolves cowered in the shadows; the new body dropped from their jaws with a splash.

Lasorov waded forward, his pant legs rolled high, and threw the latest corpse over his shoulder as if it was nothing more unwieldy than a sack of potatoes. He draped it from his stairwell and returned to the badly gnawed woman's body. I saw him pick up something and raise it overhead bringing it down to chop off the hands and feet, casually throwing each aside. Then the wolves swarmed the body again, and Lasorov settled in amongst them on his haunches, ripping pieces from one of the severed feet.

Paula slapped a palm over her mouth and stopped reading. The stain of this would surely give her nightmares and remain long after. No way it was true, though. "But wolves are real and so are crimes of cannibalism," she heard herself say. At the very least Dr. Haller and the Ripper had to be real.

She remembered a past compliment from Julie: *You lack curiosity, that's why it's so easy for you to withstand cravings.* Paula agreed she had no desire to venture like her friend into the unknown corners of the globe—but a book was safe enough, wasn't it? She stuck her nose back into Dr. Haller's journal.

Lest my retching give me away, I turned and fled, using my hands to haul myself back to the safety of my office. Now I knew Lasorov had a hold on the wolves. They brought the bodies to him, not the other way around. Yet, he forced them to wait for the blood to settle and harden in the corpse so not a trace would be left behind.

All this came into focus while I trembled in my

bedchamber with a vague sense of urgency to storm the isolation chamber with a half dozen guards and gun down Lasorov and his wolves in the underground passage. Meanwhile, the plan to call the police continued to preoccupy me. I had come full circle and no longer trusted my ability to make decisions. The past forty-eight hours had taken a toll and soon enveloped me.

The next thing I was aware of was someone pounding on my door and calling. Flashes of the night before drifted into my subconscious as I jumped from the bed where I lay, fully clothed, and unbolted the door.

The warden looked me up and down. I suppose I was a sight. He wore a stern expression entirely new to me. Not one but two guards stood beside him. "What the devil happened up here last night? The staff tell me shots were fired all through the evening, and you told them to lock their doors and stay inside. Were police on the premises?"

"Yes, sir. I mean, no, sir. There were no police. I ordered security to disable all the pleasure boats on the moat because of a breach in the security wall."

"What sort of breach?"

"I've been using my time off to examine the property for possible escape routes and have concluded one can drift by boat through the culvert. The run-off is unusually low this year. I apologize, but I felt waiting until this morning could possibly mean another victim."

He stood, saying nothing, obviously weighing my actions, which is part of his even nature.

"Sir, I've been awake most of the night thinking of a solution. I recommend draining the moat immediately and cementing the culvert closed."

"Yes, the least we can do, I suppose. I'll order the backhoes today and get some crews out to restore the spring on its natural course. Make a capital good show of it. You see, doctor, another villager is missing. A woman this time."

He turned from the door but hadn't taken more than two steps when he announced, seemingly to the entire building. "I'll forward your name to the central committee in Bucharest for a commendation. Excellent work and get some sleep. You look a wreck."

I did sleep well after that, knowing Lasorov and his wolves were finally foiled, unable to scale the wall into the underground passages. I would soon transfer him to a more traditional hospital lacking secret escape routes. It grieved me, however, I had failed at the one task I'd been given, to glean something of his unknown origins, so I decided to try one last time that very afternoon.

Lasorov began by asking me what the commotion of the previous evening was about. I apologized and said I was not at liberty to discuss asylum business with patients, then went straight into it. "Lasorov, I feel we have so much in common as men of culture and education. You've heard of my upbringing with the nuns. The promise they saw in their little orphan and their determination to make a doctor out of me. Do you perchance have a similar tale to tell?"

He smiled quite warmly which I interpreted immediately as failure.

"Plato," he said, veering into another tangent, "believed art to be a corrupting imitation of what really exists. Apparently, we can become so attached to these pleasurable imposters we can't let go of life when the time comes. How wretched that must be. Hmmm?" Had

I thought he sincerely wanted a debate, and not merely to annoy me, I might have shown him a glimmer of interest. "Do you ever question whether what you're seeing is real or not, doctor?"

I felt the veins of my temples pulsating, fire burning in my cheeks. I was bone weary with this man, furious enough to grab him right there, straitjacket and all, and smash the frontal cortex of his skull against the iron bedpost. "Guards," I yelled, turning away and opening the door. "Come up here and take the patient out of his restraints. My session is complete." But Lasorov wasn't done with me quite yet.

"You know," he said, "when I was a boy fishing with my father, he told me never to go out in anything but an aluminum boat, because short of firing a shot through the hull, it would never sink."

I spun around, ready to charge at this grinning monkey, but—Horror! There, stuck between two of his upper teeth was a glistening piece of yellowish fat I knew unmistakably to be human skin! I almost collided with the guards in my haste to descend the stairs.

How could I have been so rash as to destroy the boat in the tunnel? Who else could it have been but me? Neither could I expect the most recent corpse to be of use to police since the wolves had likely already consumed it.

He was onto me, and there was no telling what evil he would have his wolves unleash during any transfer. There had to be another way to erase this scourge on humanity.

Paula was about to turn the page when she heard Julie calling from inside the staircase.

"I'm up here," she answered. "Trying to meditate."

Julie heaved herself up the final stair and gave the journal a dark look. "The pups are back in their room. Bummer, too. I heard him whining inside the feast hall."

"I've renamed him Marco Polo."

"It's better not to give homeless animals names. Harder to say goodbye."

"Goodbye? They've been here three weeks already. Claudia's leaving the coolers of raw game at the boat launch so she doesn't have to face us." It turned out the cousin did have a truck, after all. "I doubt she's made a single call to any refuge. Don't you see what she's doing?"

"Of course. But it's your call then if you want them destroyed."

Paula gaped.

"That's what I thought. You just adopted three wolf pups. In two more months, they'll be almost fully grown. Then watch them rip this place apart." Julie offered her hand and pulled Paula to her feet. "Time to get Claudia started on a wolf enclosure."

Paula had already seen how wolves could jump and dig. This would have to be one formidable fence.

****

The next time Paula heard the outboard returning with the refilled propane tanks, she headed down to help carry them up the wooden stairs and saw Claudia waving from a clearing on the peninsula. Claudia cupped her hands to her mouth: "I knew you'd want to keep the wolves." Her leathery face was lit up, transformed.

"Now. This is the perfect place." Claudia twirled a dervish move as Paula approached. "You'll only need a fence along one side to separate them from the dock and the rest of the island. There's plenty of shade and rocks to climb and fallen trees for windblock. A constant water source from the reservoir. And the occasional bird or rodent for entertainment. As wolf enclosures go, this is Disneyland.

"In return, they'll protect you. No animal is going to take on a pack of wolves needlessly."

"They are a pack, aren't they?"

"Let's get them down here for a test run, shall we?"

Let loose over the narrow kilometer-long spit of land, run they did, going on a frenzy of marking every tree they came across.

Suddenly Marco tore behind a rocky hillock, the other two in pursuit.

Paula was already running after him when she heard the three sharp shrieks she knew were his. The red wolf, more than twice Marco's size by now, had the pup pinned to the ground with a menacing growl, her yawning jaw completely enveloping Marco's head. The middle wolf in the hierarchy, named Game Boy, paced a safe distance away.

The bullying wasn't new—the other two had been taking turns driving him to the end of the line at meal time or nipping at him for no reason at all—but this attack was far more ferocious.

"Stop it. Leave him alone." Paula danced around them, a broad stick in her hand.

Claudia, too, had run over. "Never threaten these wolves with a stick," she said, yanking it from Paula's hands and throwing it aside. "They won't stand for it. You have to let this play itself out. It's a new rendezvous point. Red is only asserting herself as the alpha female. She's not misbehaving."

"Oh, Marco. Poor little guy." She felt herself shaking with rage at his pathetic whines, until Red finally wandered off, seeming bored, and Marco limped slowly away, constantly checking behind him.

Julie caught Paula's arm when she was halfway up the stairs, Marco in her arms. "Claudia is right," her friend said. "I understand how hard this is for you, but he'll be at the bottom of the pack his entire life."

They offered to let Claudia move in while she built the enclosure and put the wolves through obedience training, but she reminded them she had her own charges to feed at home. The round-the-clock responsibility Paula had taken on was starting to sink in.

****

Paula had an aunt who never tired of reliving the agony she'd felt the day her triplets left home for university. At the time, it sounded silly to Paula, but now she found herself looking at the calendar. August fifth, the day the wolves moved out of the stone citadel and down to the peninsula.

Just like her aunt, Paula's hiccup of grief was all one-sided. Even Marco, the only wolf she sometimes allowed into the kitchen while she cooked, didn't give Paula a second glance after Claudia locked the chain-link gate and he dashed off with the others.

Obedience training started the next morning with a leash. When it came to wolves, obedience was a misnomer. The wolves didn't obey her so much as co-operate as a team. She was their pack, and Red especially wanted to *train* Paula ASAP.

"You don't have to yell at her. Wolves have excellent hearing," Claudia said. "Softly, then, 'Red, let's go.' Show her the treat."

Paula tried, but instead, Red sat down and refused to budge. "It was so easy with the other two. You try."

"I really shouldn't." Claudia stood near the gate of the enclosure. Still, she took up the leash. "Watch."

Red immediately rose and strained against the leash. Claudia turned and circled back. "Red, let's go." She held out the treat and the wolf came to her. "You see how I made eye contact with her?" Red soon pulled the leash taut in that direction, and Claudia circled once again and offered the treat. After twenty minutes of this, Red understood the only way she was going anywhere was not to pull away from the leash.

Paula took it from Claudia and shook it. "Let's go, girl." Red ignored her.

"You can't hear it, but the tone of your voice hardens with Red. You don't give her as much attention as the others, either." Claudia unclipped the leash from Red and patted her head. The wolf licked her hand. "Believe me. It will come in time. She can feel your resentment, but as soon as you accept her, you'll be best of friends. Still, if you'd rather I take her away…"

"You mean, you've found—?"

"No," Claudia jumped in. "As beautiful as she is, she'll be destroyed like thousands of other abandoned wolves and hybrids. The breeders keep pumping them out, and we keep picking them up when they get too much for their owners."

"Then she stays, but I can't see ever loving her as much as Marco."

"It's personal information, but were you bullied as a child?"

Out of habit, Paula nodded, then froze. Not because of the question—but the person asking it. Their partnership had bloomed...No. Progressed was the word. You show pictures of your newborn at work. But you don't say it was *in vitro* because that would mean going into your story and leaving your guts all over the break-room floor.

If she let Claudia in, the bloom would be on the partnership. To not answer, however, would be catty.

"Legally deaf in childhood. Now I wear cochlear implants. They say whoever left me in a bassinet on the doorstep of the hospital saved my life. I was pretty banged up."

"Now you're raising three orphans of your own," Claudia said with a cocky nod.

Chapter Thirteen

The citadel kitchen was growing a field of coolers, some running off the generator humming in the kitchen courtyard.

"I hate to wake him," Paula said to Claudia. She stretched and groaned in the midst of the coolers they had just packed with the wolves' raw game. "But I'd say we need Ram to help us get the rest up here. There're all those bags of ice."

Whenever Claudia delivered meat, Paula's morning routine was to help bring it from the dock to the kitchen coolers. Since they always took a break before starting their day with the wolves, this morning, while Paula boiled coffee water in the citadel kitchen, Ram and Claudia wandered into the future tavern room.

"The room looks great," Ram said when they returned, "but you must be putting in long days to already have all those paintings mounted on the walls."

Paula stopped spooning coffee into the french press and stared at Ram. Before shoving past Claudia, she thrust the metal utensil aside so hard it skidded across the stone counter and clattered to the floor.

No, she hadn't heard wrong. There they were, hung from the spikes she herself pounded in only yesterday. Heavy with confusion, she plodded to the closest work and lifted it from the wall. Whoever had hung them had an eye for gallery symmetry. They'd used Goran's original rope loops on the backing. Still, they would have had to work through the night removing the Styrofoam she'd reapplied after the appraiser left.

"So, it wasn't you who hung them?"

Paula spun around at the sound of Ram's voice. He stood in the doorway, slowly taking in each painting as if he was seeing them for the first time. Claudia peered over his shoulder from behind with the same unmoved, poker face Paula had come to expect.

"Claudia?" Paula asked.

The woman marched into the tavern room pressing a palm to her chest. "Why would I do this when I have no claim whatsoever in what happens to this artwork?"

Ram turned to Paula. "I didn't touch them, and I can't see Julie caring what went where, either. Not with her minimalist tastes."

"Follow me, then." In the kitchen, Paula pointed into the cooler where they kept the dairy. "I guess it was the same ghost that dipped into our cheese again. We've been accusing the kid, but he hasn't been here for days."

So sure there was a simple explanation, Paula had slotted the wayward cheese at the bottom of her growing list of worries. That was before the ambulatory paintings and the dark looks sliding between the other two at this very moment.

"I don't like this," Ram said to Claudia. "Paula, at least, should know. She'll be living here."

Claudia drained her cup and slid the ceramic mug onto the countertop with such confidence that there was no doubt who was in charge. "Do it, then."

From leaning on his forearm, Ram straightened to his full height and turned to Paula, who stood with crossed arms, ready for whatever he had. "Conservation officers caught unauthorized loads of logs leaving the area. They haven't found the illegal loggers yet, but police are closing in on them. The poachers keep moving up and down the shoreline of the reservoir."

Ram stopped, seeming to wait for her to process what he'd said. "One thing is certain—that boat launch and dock we've been using is where they've been floating the log booms. Look at it like this. These thieves managed to scare the tourists away from Poenari. Then *we* turn up getting in the way of their lumber heist."

Paula was trying to match up the strange events inside the citadel with this new information. "It doesn't add up. Setting up the wolves or breaking into the citadel, maybe, but criminals fooling around with coolers of cheese, amateur paintings, and bottles of wine to scare us off?"

Claudia shrugged. Maybe not, she said, but she could think of a few locals who might for a price. Some she knew quite well.

"They probably built the dock here on the island, too," Claudia added. "I don't want to scare you, but this place is the perfect hideout, don't you think? Even if they're caught without a boat, all they'd have to do is swim from the end of the peninsula to escape into endless tracts of national forest."

That did it. Content to give Claudia the benefit of the doubt until now, she stormed around the stone counter and planted herself in front of the woman. "No. I think you *do* want to scare me." Paula raised her hand to her hip, drawing a muted cower from Claudia. "No more bullcrap. What is it you want from me? From this island?"

With the shaky hesitancy of the aged, Claudia

tucked her graying braid behind her ear and said, "You're right. I've been lying. To both of you, actually. Those men aren't harmless hoodlums. This is organized crime. The media call them the Timber Mafia." She looked to Ram as he drew near. "I regret making you culpable in this and putting everyone at risk."

She lowered her head onto arms folded atop the stone counter and gazed up into Paula's eyes. "I didn't want you to leave and jeopardize a safe and loving home for the wolves. That's all I want from you and this island."

Sour silence.

"Simple," Ram said. "We get to hell out of here. Everything's on hold until the loggers are caught."

"Not really," Paula said. Two qualities she thought Claudia incapable of—guilt and humility—still lingered in Paula's subconscious. "I can't put the wolves on hold. You and Julie should leave, but I'm staying with them."

Claudia hurtled upward. "Obviously, then, we're not going to abandon you."

Ram wheeled around and shook his head, his flat footfalls slapping across the rotunda's flagstones.

Halfway to a hug, Claudia seemed to abandon it. She gripped Paula's upper arms firmer than she probably intended. "I apologize for deceiving you. We can do horribly foolish things for love, can't we?"

Yes, I just did.

"The workmen will be here all day. Let the wolves roam at night, and nobody will bother you."

"Not unless the Timber Mafia shoots them first," Paula said.

****

At the end of the day, while Ram dropped Claudia

at her truck, Paula went up the tower for afternoon chanting and repeated to Julie everything they'd said. There had to be something more. *Once we're gone, Paula could be next.* Isn't that what they'd overheard at the aunt's house?

"It's time to visit Goran's aunt," Paula said. "I'll bet she's more with it than Claudia would have us believe."

At the end of chanting, Paula made the appearance of wanting to meditate but pulled the journal from her pocket instead as soon as Julie was gone.

May 4, 1951

Once I had my plan before me, I slept well and deeply and felt more hopeful than I had since my arrival.

I instructed the two guards to put Lasorov in his regulation straitjacket and ankle restraints for his therapy session. Instead of sitting to one side of the door on the metal stool affixed to the wall there, as was my usual habit, I positioned myself near the concealed lever as strategically and safely as possible without causing suspicion. I now knew Lasorov could easily lunge to tear flesh from bone before I was even at the exit.

"This would be an opportune time to take your supper break," I said to the new upstairs guard. "But mind," I added, so as not to appear I preferred he dally, "we expect our staff to be punctual within the thirty-minute allowance."

When the guard had gone and closed the metal door, I sank to the floor across from the foot of Lasorov's bed. "Please," I said, indicating he should slide from the bed and place himself across from me, his back against the metal footboard of his bed.

Paula raised her eyes from the page. Here she sat dead center of the doctor's former office, which was a mirror image of the isolation cell. She must be in the exact position where the Ripper sat during the interview. She continued:

It made my skin crawl to see him in an exceedingly sated and cooperative state, even thanking the guards after they had tightly cinched up his ankle restraints. I was in terror that he might be able to read my mind. When they had gone, he gave me such a chilling look of hatred, baring his ghastly incisors, that I dared not linger there for fear of catching sight of another slimy sinew.

"A villager was found strangled a few nights ago," I said, infusing it with all the banality I could muster.

"A tragedy," he said. "It's always the pretty girls that seem to go, isn't it?" He waited for me to react to this admission of murder, for how could he know who the victim was? Getting none, his eyes shone with a nauseating delight.

"I feel we understand each other quite well, Lasorov." I had planned to parley longer and enjoy baiting him, but it occurred to me I should put as much time as possible between my departure from the tower and the discovery of his escape. "So, I hope you don't mind that I have been visiting your cell while you are absent for shower privileges."

I didn't expect him to draw the meaning of this statement so perfectly, and so quickly. Immediately, his gaze shifted downwards to his place on the floor.

I had only seconds. I turned and raked the stone out of the way with one hand. Tripped the release with the other. There was the squeal of rusty hinges and a clattering as the trap door fell free. When I looked up, to my horror, across from me Lasorov had managed to loop his toes under the bed frame's iron rail. He dangled, midair over the stairwell's abyss.

I rose and for a moment was paralyzed with wonder by this seeming impossibility of human strength and agility. He flopped this way and that in the straitjacket, like a dying fish, a hideous guttural grunting helping to propel him ever upwards. My mind fought against the desire to flee the room. I frantically sought out a weapon as my gaze fell on the loose boulder.

Only the kind of terror which gripped me could allow a stout man such as myself to haul that rock across the room with such speed. When he caught sight of me raising it overhead, his grunts elevated to a macabre hawk-like screeching. There were two sharp cracks as the ankle bones of each leg disintegrated. The toes released, and he disappeared headfirst from view.

I do not know how long the unsettling silence lasted, but it seemed endless, until I heard an echoing succession of retorts like the cleaving of a blacksmith's hammer against an anvil. This I knew to be his skull caving in on itself as he tumbled.

I immediately stepped around the gap and with trembling hands pulled the lever back into position. The trap door slammed shut to blend in with the other planks as if it had never existed. If through some odious outcome he yet lived, the wolves would be of no use to him. With the water gone, it would be impossible for them to mount the citadel's vertical wall to the underground tunnel.

I couldn't descend to the guard below with my chest

heaving so. After rolling the stone into place, I lingered to marvel at whether such a simple piece of engineering invented for the gallows might have saved desperate lives in past ages.

Today, ridding Transylvania of a vile turpitude and the depraved appetites of a monster.

She flipped through the remaining pages. All blank.

Eyeing the tiles beneath her, she laid the diary aside and scooted her bottom to a safer spot.

If there was a chasm below her, she thought, absently rubbing both cheeks, did it still hold the bones of the Ripper or had they washed away into the reservoir long ago? She shook the image from her mind so completely it rattled the teeth inside her head.

How was it possible to believe in the doctor's story when nothing else held up? There was no evidence of a secret stairwell or evil wolves with a mind of their own. The only animal capable of sowing that much hatred in the minds of others…was man.

Yet, Paula thought about the doctor's words: *Once I had my plan before me, I slept well and deeply and felt more hopeful than I had since my arrival.*

She had to hand it to him. No matter what came at this guy, he didn't waver from his goal. These were not the writings of a madman but someone with the good of humanity at heart.

Chapter Fourteen

No more than a day later, Paula found herself with the perfect opportunity to slip in a secret visit to Claudia's mother, Aunt Lisbet. She was the best and maybe only source for Paula's questions about the doctor and his journal.

A collection of Goran's largest murals released from a London gallery were awaiting collection at Bucharest airport's freight terminal. A moving company could deliver the mammoth pieces to the citadel by barge and include the replacement panes for the chapel at the same time. It might turn into a three-day trip, Ram said.

How perfect is that.

"Take Claudia. She knows the language." A disingenuous blush crept up Paula's cheeks. "And use her truck. Leave the motorhome behind."

Paula delivered Ram to the village pension where Claudia waited, eyes closed, inside her tired-looking truck. "You sure we can make it to Bucharest?" Ram stood at her open window. "We can still take the motorhome and leave your truck for the ladies."

Claudia turned her face to him, slow as a tortoise on a hot rock. Her eyes fluttered open, her bottom lip ballooning. *Pffft.* "Out of the question. Get in. I drive to Bucharest all the time."

Paula and Julie waited until they were in the clear, and the truck's popping and grinding had faded before they hit the switchbacks to the aunt's place.

"Come in, come in." At the door of Aunt Lisbet's cottage, an enthusiastic hand, not a face, greeted them. Somewhere in the gloom, a television blared. She waved them in, one eye on the flickering screen which almost covered an entire wall.

"Ohhh." Knees buckling, her hands flew overhead. "Bollocks. Sneaky bugger." She pointed at the snooker game in progress on the television. "My guy'll have to send the cue ball round the angles now."

She clicked it off with a grunt. "Isn't this a treat? And no Claudia to bother us." She patted the surface of a table which seemed to be Arborite. One couldn't be sure with so much clutter and dirt. "We'll sit here."

A solitary easy chair held the spot of honor in front of the television. Unless the only other doorway led to a sitting room, and not a bedroom, the table was it for seats. More vintage vinyl and chrome.

Rrrp. Paula squinted at the floor and took another step. *Rrrp.* Whether it was honey or road tar underfoot, it was slow going to the table. The aunt spread her palms atop it for balance. "It's such a delight to have a pair of fellow Brits in my home," she said.

The two friends exchanged frowns. "We're Canadian. From British Columbia."

"Eh?" She stared at Paula, then swatted as if through a cloud of fruit flies. "Good enough. What'll you ladies have to drink?"

"Anything other than alcohol is fine." Julie would stick to her Buddhist precepts.

"Do you have any herbal tea?" Paula asked.

The aunt gave Paula an indignant grimace but saved her shock for Julie's declaration.

"I'll be right back." Aunt Lisbet snatched her cane from the back of her chair. Daylight from two smeared panes crawled across the floor to the dark, ursine recess into which she now scuttled from view. Spring hinges creaked. A door banged.

The opaque mood and low ceiling of the stuffy room was spot-on to what Paula envisioned for their tavern—minus the reek of rancid meat she suspected was coming from inside the fridge. High ledges choked with dusty knickknacks lined every wall: trophies, ceramics, china dolls with legs draped at impossible angles, and picture frames filled with indistinguishable subjects.

A stove and fridge, accented with heartbreakingly rusty fifties chrome, suffered under the weight of hammers, wrenches, and a tire iron. The appliances shoved aside any remaining suspicion this might be a brutalized dining room. "Wouldn't those look gorgeous in my cottage? Cleaned up, of course. That layer of grease is a fire hazard."

Julie yanked the cord on a floor lamp beside her. Nothing happened.

"There's the family crest again." Paula pointed to a carving above the door which depicted the same wolf-serpent motif—not a single fang, however, in the animal's benign expression of fawning kindness. Unless he carved it as a child, this one wasn't Goran's work. It was too rough and juvenile.

For the longest time, there wasn't a sound. Had the aunt gone into an outbuilding and forgotten about them?

Paula was about to investigate when someone or something kicked open the spring door. The aunt clomped in, tottering side to side with her cane. The other paw held aloft three sloshing pints of dark ale.

She skated the mugs into position on the table like props in a beer ad. "Home brew." She winked and shuffled to a broad bookcase, raking one paper after another onto the floor. "Where is that damn thing? Ohhh…here's something else I've been looking for. Well, too late now." She stuffed the promised castle photo into the one dry pocket along with a much smaller photo.

The black and white picture she handed Paula looked like it had been folded inside a wallet for a decade. In it, the palace lay along the Varges Valley, the former river nothing but a distant line.

"Here's where I slept," the aunt said. Her index finger shook from one end of the photo to the other.

"Inside the citadel?"

"Hell, no. That was for staff only." She leaned in and dug her fingertips into Paula's arm. "My brother and I were always in there, mind you. Dark hallways. Secret staircases."

Paula sat up and gaped. "There really was one?"

"Two. One in each tower. But heavens, most of the stairs would be underwater now. See, there was a trap door in the floor. Opened like this." She raised her arm and let her wrist flop. "Wouldn't go down now, but when you're a kid, everything's a dare, isn't it?" She sat back, took a long swig of beer, and drew a backhand across her mouth. "The release was inside the wall."

"Isn't that how the Ripper tried to escape? It says so in a journal I found."

"The Bucharest Ripper? He never tried to escape that I know of. 'Course I may have been in England by then. They say he was transferred to another institution. He was probably our most famous local."

Something seemed odd with the photo. "I don't see a moat or bridge," Paula finally said. "Did the institution put one in later?"

"There may have been one in medieval times."

Did the doctor, in fact, have a break with reality? Leading one life, journaling his fantasies in another?

"Was the original psychiatrist still around when you left?" Julie asked.

"Heavens, no. He hightailed out of there when the warden discovered he was drugging and raping the young boys."

Paula's mug screeched to a halt midair. "You're talking about the psychiatrist?"

"Ye-es. The Soviet soldiers weren't much better, mind you, but that warden ran a tight operation. Lord knows he would have sent the young doctor to a gulag."

Across the table, Julie batted her lids. Her sidelong air of vindication garnered only a blank stare from Paula. It would take more than the gossip of an old woman to change her mind about Dr. Haller. "The police never found him?"

Aunt Lisbet swallowed another mouthful of beer and shook her head.

"What's the other photo?" Julie pointed to the apron pocket, but the aunt had already forgotten about it. Back she went to the bookcase and picked up a frame.

"This one here? It's Claudia's grad day at Bucharest University."

Unless the institution had an odd affinity for Britain, the setting seemed elsewhere. Wearing a graduation gown and mortarboard, Claudia posed with her mother beneath a Union Jack flagpole.

"Top honors," Aunt Lisbet said. "And now she's a

teacher there herself. Cardio."

The idea of Claudia in trainers and spandex stretched Paula's face into the kind of sour grimace used to tamp down a burp. "You mean like a gym teacher."

"Nooo. I'll tell you what she does as soon as I find it." More papers drifted to the sticky floor.

"Cardio-thoracic surgery," the aunt sputtered. She returned the frame to the book shelf and headed to her chair. "Teaches those medical students. Never around much anymore."

The aunt sat and drained the last of her beer, oblivious, at first, to their mute confusion. "Oh. You mean the other photo?" She drew it out of her apron pocket and threw it onto the table. "Now there's an evil bastard, if there ever was one."

Paula picked up the colored photo of a teenaged Goran astride an Arabian horse at the door of the citadel. He stared at something beyond the camera, an odd detachment in his eyes. It wasn't the Goran of the catatonic episodes Paula knew so well. The youth on the horse was aware of his surroundings—acutely aware.

"Sent his wolves to kill his own father, didn't he?" the aunt said. "He's my blood, but I'll never forgive him for that. Same day this photo was taken, in fact. I was keeping it to show the parole board if they ever thought to let him out. Too late now."

Paula and Julie locked gazes, speechless.

"I tried to tell them about the wolves, but they let him out all the same. Showed up yesterday at that door right there, looking for money. Asked him, 'Does it look like I have a penny to spare?' He's a mean one."

The old aunt struggled to her feet, limped to the door, and tapped the wolf carving above it with her cane.

"The ancient Dacian blood runs through him strong. We all thought it was finally dead, but it just skipped a generation."

She slid the cane to the background of the carving where warriors of antiquity battled, then turned to them. "All these years, our command over the wolves has kept the northern barbarians away from our doorstep. We put the Roman legions on the run when they tried marching in. Some legends say our men became wolves themselves before the battle, but that's just silly."

More pensive, she stared at the carving once again. "The power had its place and time, but now it needs to die with Goran."

Twenty minutes later, from the iron grip Julie had on the motorhome's steering wheel, one might have thought an earthquake was taking place.

"I like that she makes her own beer," Paula said. "It wasn't half bad, was it?"

"*Oi-yoi-yoi-yoi-yoi*." Julie raked the hair from her face before slamming the stick shift into gear and driving from the farmyard.

"Some of the citadel's history was interesting, too," Paula said. "About Goran. As much as I want him to be alive, he was thirteen when his father died. I don't know who's on parole, but it's not him."

"No shit. She makes it sound like the Romans marched through here last weekend, raping and pillaging. Although…I'd believe that before the part about Claudia being a surgeon."

****

Cooped up during the laying of the septic pipes, the wolves were finally free to roam for the three-day window before the installation crews and paintings arrived from Bucharest. Minus Ram, perhaps Paula's precious friendship with Julie could also roam free a while. They could break out from the triangulation which seemed to demand one of them always be the bottom dog like Marco.

Paula knew their relationship was in for another separation as painful as the first one a decade earlier. Those were the days when Julie was holed up in a Kathmandu cottage with Ram when she wasn't chasing after stories for adventure magazines, and Paula stumbled along in Goran's wake. She'd been naive enough to think they could keep up their reunions at her cabin in Canada. Not likely the gallery would swallow her up any less.

While they strolled arm in arm throughout the citadel's main floor pointing out what was needed for the authentic feel of a medieval venue, Paula remembered Julie storming off at the hardware store weeks earlier. She bowed her head and squeezed her friend's arm. "You've forgiven me for choosing Goran's paintings over our friendship?"

Julie stopped and grinned. "Aren't you the sneaky one to remind me I'm the bad guy for moving to India. I'd be here with you if it wasn't for Ram. You know that. Right?"

Paula nodded, and they strolled on until Julie said: "What about the loggers? This place might be dangerous. And lonely."

"Not with the wolves. They'll be good company."

Julie paused and shrank from Paula as if seeing her anew. "You, Paula Douglas, are fine with basing your well-being on three unpredictable animals?"

She shrugged and smiled, if only to rein in the exact

fear of the unknown Julie spoke of. The only way to find out if she could thrive in a remote corner of a foreign country—was to try it.

When they reached the feast hall, Julie was suddenly all business. Could they join their wedding onto the gallery opening? "We're kind of running out of time. If Ram's elected chief minister of Bihar state, I'll need to be his legal wife."

"Come on. You know the answer is *yes*."

"Be right back. I'll need my cell phone to keep a record of the guest list." At the sound of the citadel's weighty oak doors creaking open, Julie bellowed, "Marco's headed your way."

No doubt he'd heard their voices echoing room to room and remembered his evenings beside the fire with Paula. When Julie returned, in came the other two. The entrance hall was empty of anything to chew on, but it didn't stop Red from marking the oak banister of the grand staircase with a pee. Paula had to resort to the cooler bait.

The three wolves flopped in the glow of the fireplace, looking like the master's exhausted hounds, in from the hunt. Julie wouldn't let up until she had Paula inserted into the iconic shot, one arm draped across the mantle, the other cupping a glass of wine.

Minutes later, while the other two wolves snoozed, Red took up a frantic scratching at the door. How right Claudia had been. What could be safer than the protection of three adult wolves? They let Red out to deal with whatever she'd heard.

Hours later, as the sun rose, Paula woke to the wolves' muted forlorn howls which usually rocked her to sleep at night. She wouldn't have given it a second thought had it not gone on for so long. Paula dressed and headed out to the far end of the peninsula where they were. Red was returning to the island, gliding like a beaver across the half-kilometer stretch of water.

On the far shore, a lone wolf paced. Red had probably been wandering off the island for weeks.

Sometime during the next night, the alpha female left the peninsula again and swam out of Paula's life forever. Marco and his brother suddenly lived in peace as equals—Paula's problem solved.

****

"This is a miracle," Claudia said, when she heard about Red. "We couldn't hope for a better outcome."

Fresh from Bucharest, she set down the cooler of meat on the dock and straightened to stare in the direction of the enclosure. Though smiling, her face was hot with tears. "Godspeed, my sweet girl. Let him teach you all that he knows."

When she pivoted to see Paula gaping at her, wide-eyed, Claudia gasped and scoured her cheeks with her palms. "I'm anxious to get home. Let's get the last of this meat up to the coolers."

"Red wasn't the only event while you guys were away," Paula said after everything was unloaded. "Can you spare a few more minutes to hear about it?"

Ram scrambled from the boat. "Don't tell me someone came onto the island again."

"No," Paula said, and suggested they sit with her on the stairs. She started by offering to build Aunt Lisbet a new house.

"You went to see her?" Claudia chuckled. Ram, too, bore a shadow of humor.

"Goran left more than enough for his aunt," Ram

said.

"Thanks for your concern about my mum. Truly. But she refuses to take it. She told me: 'If I don't think the house is good enough, I don't have to stay there.' "

The answer made sense. Paula allowed them that one but drew in a long breath. "She gave me a photo of Goran. Said he came to the door looking for money a few days ago."

That wiped the merriment off both their faces.

Claudia pinched her bottom lip, her mind somewhere else, before catching Ram's eye. "It's the kid. He's always bumming money. I guess he's finding out working isn't much fun."

Ram bobbed his chin up and down in agreement, too over-enthusiastic to convince Paula he really believed it. If they thought that was all she had, they were wrong.

"Your mother thinks Goran sent wolves to kill his father. Is that why she doesn't want his money?"

A quick arch of one eyebrow and Claudia took in Paula with an edged stare off the tip of her nose. "Who knows what she thinks most of the time. She went into all those delusions about Dacian wolves, did she?"

"You don't think it's possible to control the minds of wolves?" Paula herself didn't believe it, of course, the question was only meant to uncover Claudia's dubious intentions.

But amusement sprang up once more. "It's a longstanding myth; however, if I did, I doubt my boss at Bucharest University Hospital would be very impressed."

"Wh-what? A hospital?" With arms like rubber, she felt for the railing to steady herself. Her gaze glommed on to Claudia's outfit.

"This?" Claudia crowed and splayed the ends of her outlandish vest. "I only wear this garb up here during summer break and weekends. Made it myself. The tourists lap it up. They'd be disappointed to find out I wear scrubs at work and jeans at my house in Bucharest. I'm a cardio-thoracic surgeon."

With the memory of Claudia that first misty morning seeming to levitate among her advance guard of wolves, the corners of Paula's mouth lifted with anticipation. If the old aunt got that one right, what else might be true? Goran's appearance at her door? Surely not Dr. Haller's sick appetites? She told Claudia she'd see her in the morning, then headed up the stairs to the cottage.

"Wait." Remembering the most critical question of all, she turned and sprinted back to the dock. "If Goran's father wasn't killed by wolves," Paula yelled above the churning outboard, "how did he die?"

For such a straightforward question, the air fairly crackled as Claudia and Ram exchanged tense looks inside the boat. "He was shot by vandals ransacking the ruined chapel." Claudia said it in an even clinical tone. "No one was arrested for his murder."

"Ram?" He nodded at Paula and stared out at the water. Blindsided once more, Paula hung her head while Ram gunned the motorboat away from the dock.

Goran had carried his father's murder alone, not even allowing someone who loved him deeply to share his grief. Pressing her fingertips into her temples, she tried to uproot this image of Goran's tender adolescent heart aching for endless hours of the night.

A glance at the departing boat instantly yanked her back into the moment. There it was again. Claudia had swung around to face Ram in the stern, their heads bent together like wilting flowers. Whatever this cousin was still up to, the only man Paula trusted with her life appeared to be part of it.

Chapter Fifteen

The wolves versus the plumbers.

Fueled by voodoo-type stories handed down through the generations, Paula couldn't tell who was more terrified of whom. The men averted their eyes from the enclosure as they passed, and the wolves shied away from the plumbers coming and going from the dock, choosing to hang out at the far end of the peninsula where Red had escaped with the lone wolf.

For the first two weeks of September, glass installers and restoration crews streamed in and out of the citadel. The chapel doves were forced to set up house elsewhere and daylight penetrated the rotunda's stained glass for the first time, perhaps, in a millennium. Goran's depressing murals, while not a dramatic improvement, clothed the naked and cheerless stone walls in funeral shades of gray.

But it was the plumbers who brought the civility of running water to Paula's island. Ram finally had to admit he had the knowledge but not the equipment to sink a line to the depths of the reservoir and pump water into the cottage and citadel.

Paula peered into the trench running between the cottage and fortress. "You're not thinking of taking that line under the citadel, are you? There could be a tunnel down there."

The oldest of the three Romanian workers,

appearing long past his ditch-digging days, leaned heavily on his shovel. "No. We take the water along the side, over there, to the kitchen. Then inside. I work here with my father when it is a hospital. I know every part very well. We did the maintenance."

What were the chances of running across someone as knowledgeable on the citadel's history as he was lucid? Paula squatted near the edge of the ditch. "I've been hearing about this patient called the Bucharest Ripper. Do you know about him?"

"Yes. Very famous. By his real name. Only asylum workers call him the Ripper."

"Well, no wonder I couldn't find him on the internet. Did he ever escape?"

The old guy shrugged and turned his palms up. "One day—gone. They always move him quickly in the night. Not to make excitement. People want to see what he looks like."

"And the secret stairs in the towers. Did you ever see those?"

He shook his head but paused to reconsider. "Maybe because of our first job. The warden order us to cover the floor with tiles."

"For what reason?"

"To stop vapors coming inside." He made a face and shook his head. "Such bad smells all day we work. We only cover this tower here. The other one, no."

Bad smells? That would make sense. Especially if Dr. Haller had managed to stop the Ripper's last killing spree. If the locked tower still had the original planks with the trap door, she could find the secret stairs and underground passageway. Probably the Ripper's corpse, too.

Julie would have to suck up her disbelief and declare Paula right.

****

The next morning, when Paula delivered the meat inside the enclosure, Game Boy didn't appear. Marco's downcast expression in the direction of the water told her Red and the lone wolf had also snared Game Boy.

That evening, on the farthest shore of the wolf enclosure, Marco snuggled between Paula's legs and watched the other wolves pacing on the opposite side of the narrow strip of water, sending their piercing howls into the valleys.

The orphaned wolf, alone once more, whined constantly, but it wasn't only Marco who was going through a life-changing event—the decision Paula feared most had also come and gone with barely a whimper.

Paula couldn't help but notice the date—the first school day after the summer holidays. When Paula's students opened their books today, she wouldn't be there. To think this was how the final chapter of her teaching life would end.

Giving up her classroom wasn't supposed to be this easy, but the gallery, Marco, and citadel island felt like the do-overs in life everyone wants but never gets. She could tutor by satellite. With her parents gone and Julie living in India, what was back there, anyway? A remote forest in Canada or Romania, it was all the same.

Even Ram, with his memories of his best friend before the illness swamped Goran, seemed happier here than anywhere else. The hub which connected the three friends was no longer Paula's childhood home—but Goran's.

Since her first day on the island, Goran had been

trying to contact her. She wasn't about to leave and give up on him so quickly this time.

"We're going to find you another mate," she said to Marco, ruffling the short gray fur between his ears. "A girlfriend this time. Won't that be nice?" *But not until the spring. You're mine until then.* Of the three, he was the most obedient and least intimidating because of his small stature. Once the opening day was over, the two of them would have the whole property to themselves. No enclosure for Marco all winter.

During the wolf's first night alone, she left the gate open for him to wander and found he dutifully followed her to the door of the citadel. She hadn't even reached the grand staircase when his pitiful whines started outside. Claudia would have reprimanded her, but Paula opened the door and in he scooted straight for the feast hall—the one room she didn't want him in anymore.

"No." At the sound of her voice, firm but calm, he trotted by her side into the former pups' room. Still in a chaos of chewed branches and hay, this was the site of his loneliest moments, and his downcast eyes quickly told her that.

The plank frame and air mattress she'd set up as a temporary bed upstairs was easily dismantled and carried to the wolf's room. What was she doing moving into a stinking, filthy space? One night only, she thought, but of course, that became two, then three, then many more.

The week of the grand opening, Paula must have forgotten to pull the door tight on the hall where she slept with Marco. Julie stormed into the citadel kitchen and demanded to know why Paula's bed was there.

"Marco can't run loose from his enclosure the week Ram's son is with us," Julie said. "He's only six."

Paula didn't dare look her friend in the face but continued to carry armfuls of vegetables from their coolers to the bottom crisper of the new propane-powered fridge. In the shuffle of the opening and wedding, she'd counted on them not noticing Marco's whereabouts.

"Better he get used to being alone now, than howl all night." Julie hovered over Paula's bent back. "Paula?"

Paula straightened, turned to the new ceramic sink beside the fridge, and opened the cold-water tap. "Did you ever think we'd have running water in here, or what?"

The lame attempt at small talk was a bust. Paula cranked off the water. "He'll only be out of the enclosure at night. If I leave him down there, how do I know he won't swim off like the other two?"

"I knew that's what this was about," Julie said. "He's not going to attempt it with his useless front leg." She laid a hand on Paula's shoulder. "Please. If Alana sees a wolf loose, that'll be the end of their visit. Who knows when Ram can see his son again."

****

It was hard for Paula to think of Marco as anything but a dog. Not only would he be her ears, eyes, and nose all winter, but her only companion. Ram and Julie's overnight trip to Bucharest to collect the Stockholm group for the wedding was an opportunity to test him inside the cottage.

The loft was already out of bounds due to it being a winter storage space for Goran's smaller paintings. She tucked her friends' things inside the pantry and sat down at her desk beside the woodstove to see if Marco would behave himself with the new bed and couch on the

173

ground floor.

Her laptop was where she imagined herself all winter, video tutoring her deaf students while Marco snoozed at her feet. The new satellite internet at the cottage was spotty but no worse than her cabin at home—adequately crappy, however, to force her favorite estate planners to take over the entire online art auction.

She checked wedding emails and lists for anything forgotten. Poenari pension's catering was in place, as was the guest houseboat shuttle across the reservoir donated by a patron Ram knew in India.

Not once did the wolf jump onto the couch, or atop the kitchen table, which was more than she could have said of the other two if the kitchen door happened to be open. That night she indulged him to snuggle beside her on top of the bed. A training no-no.

Out of the chaos of Goran's suicide had come the companionship she needed, but what would he think of her living on his citadel island?

Only once during the night did she wake to find Marco at the kitchen door, not wanting out, but sniffing, pacing, whimpering. She knew at once it wasn't a bear in the yard—he was hearing the lone wolf and his siblings across the water, hunting in the forest.

"We'll get you a playmate soon, sweetie," Paula said, her face buried in the dense winter coat of his neck. She never imagined she could love an animal so much. The chicken coop she had tried once only attracted the kind of animals she didn't want. In the end, she had decided it would be unfair to leave a dog alone so much while she was in town at the school.

With Ram's young son now on the island in the

lead-up to the wedding, Claudia echoed Julie's concern the boy not go inside the enclosure, even accompanied. One time only, perhaps. "You've forgotten Marco's roots as a wild animal, haven't you? Children are less intimidating. Often the same size as prey. All it takes is one confusing incident, and Marco could revert to instinct."

It was inevitable the boy would be fascinated with the wolf. "Can I pet him?" Ram Jr. asked Paula the first time he saw Marco. Marco stood back, apprehensive with this miniature version of people. But after a few minutes his tail whipped wildly. He wanted the touch as much as the boy.

Marco could revert to instinct.

"Sorry, honey. He's not a dog. If we're not busy, you can come visit him anytime you want from outside the gate, though."

Chapter Sixteen

The longer Paula stared at the guest list for their grand opening-slash-wedding, the more uneasy she felt. It was a sense of impending grief like the moment the two-headed sheep materializes inside the cloning lab's test tube.

Near the bottom end of the social ladder was Julie's constellation of aged aunts, uncles, and cousins on her father's side, Italian immigrant orchardists. They'd left Europe after the "Scorched Earth War" and weren't interested in returning to the continent even for a wedding.

Of the surviving members of Julie's immediate family, her sister and brother-in-law, a property developer, declined until they found out the entire trip would be gratis, then they tacked in-laws onto the tab, too.

Julie's older brother and his wife desperately wanted to attend and so did her late mother's sister, Aunt Dot, but neither would travel without their spouses. The brother had a good ten years left on his manslaughter sentence. As for Aunt Dot's husband, he was so opposed to multicultural pairings, Ram had left the only family dinner he'd ever attended with a bloody nose and black eye.

Certainly, the patrons of Goran's art would stick together harmoniously enough—not exchanging the names of reasonably priced handymen or the best all-inclusive deals, but rather, favorite tax havens and solid hedge-fund managers. Paula had arrived at a place of ambivalence with these "robber barons" when she came across how much they were forking over for Goran's paintings.

At one point, she would have relinquished everything and lived anywhere with him, even in a hovel like Aunt Lisbet's, if only he would have taken his medication.

The problem for Paula, and it was a daunting one, was never being able to decipher his art. She'd sat with it when he wasn't around, trying to find the optical illusion everyone else but her could see embedded in the lines and circles.

No, she didn't get it, she said. Why pluck out the dark corners of one's mind and say that benefits man's existence. Go live in the light, then, he told her. Settle for a bogus life.

He stirred her and stirred her until the jealousy and resentment she'd never let anyone else see rose to the top. By the time Paula's mother asked her, *What has he done to you?* Paula knew the question could easily have been, *What have you done to him? Is this how people live together these days?*

Yes, Paula said, theirs was a typical relationship.

They lived in hotel suites, changing countries with no more thought than the lines of a subway grid. Could he not find a permanent warehouse loft somewhere, perhaps build one on her rural property in Canada?

Not likely.

The morning after a bash, he'd start his droning epic of someone he'd met the night before, repeating every tedious detail, tailing her from the en-suite bathroom to the galley kitchen to the laundry room. Sometimes down the hotel hall as she left.

They were *wild,* he'd said, *a helluva great guy*, but the smudge of their existence stuck to his index finger like the soft grit from carbon paper—easily rubbed off, completely gone by the end of the day.

In the beginning, his naive enthusiasm had endeared him to her, so lacking in confidence he depended on these servile dogs to continually reinvent himself. The time she'd grabbed his wrist midsentence shocked her as much as it did him. It took her most of their three years together to figure out Goran wasn't the mind reader she'd hoped.

At the time, she missed the peaceful hum of her cabin's forest. "Is that the *bogus* life you're talking about?" she once demanded. Those harsh words on the beach in Madagascar were the ones she remembered. They were her last with him.

****

The morning of Ram and Julie's wedding, catering staff streamed between the dock and citadel kitchen like opposing lines of working ants.

Aunt Lisbet, their so-called patron of honor, insisted on being the first to ride the houseboat shuttle over and *receive her guests*. It wouldn't be that kind of event, Paula said. More mingle and mix.

Catching her breath on the wooden staircase, Aunt Lisbet stuck out an aggrieved hand against an armload of paper cups and plates. "Hold on, lad. What's this? Disposable?"

Paula waved the startled catering worker onward.

The last time Aunt Lisbet had set foot inside the

citadel at age fifteen, the place had an industrial kitchen and scores of staff. It wasn't her wedding day nor her gallery opening, but how depressing it must be to have a load of strangers on the land your ancestors once occupied and no one even curious who you are.

A crooked arch of the eyebrows greeted Countess Lisbet each time Paula presented her as the heir of Vlakia Palace. "Sounds awesome. Where is it located?"

These monied high-tech wizards of the world were there to view the paintings found in the tower and put in their online bids. The old woman in the flowered retro house dress and her obscure castle were of no more urbane interest than a giant ground sloth wiped out during Earth's last mass extinction.

Like, who needs a palace drawing room when you can have an internet chat room, or a recital hall instead of iTunes…?

As wedding guests streamed in, Paula found Aunt Lisbet inside the wolf pups' former playroom, standing like a statue, her back to the door.

Sandwiched between the kitchen and chapel, the gloomy room had a solitary window. It was open, but even with the debris gone, the sting of wolf urine still clung to Paula's nostrils as she ambled in, her heels clicking across the stone floor. "Are you lost, Aunt?"

She glanced over her shoulder at Paula. "If I ever forget *this* room, you'll know I'm ready for the loony bin. Ha. Ha…this *was* the loony bin. One guard taught me to shoot snooker here. Oh Lord, was he a dandy kisser, too." She slid a tender pinkie across her lips. "Such a lovely name he had. Elieno. He smuggled my mother and me out of here and got sent to the gulag for his trouble. 'Course, that's what everyone assumed happened if you disappeared in the night.

"Tibor. That was my brother. We had our share of laughs, though. Didn't mind living in the stables, not like our parents. In the loft where we slept, we kept some hay that still smelled like our ponies."

The gleeful, arch expression of a prankster came over the old woman. "This one night we're up there and in marches our mother. She's wet, see, up to her armpits from scrubbing in the scullery." Aunt Lisbet chuckled and handed Paula her cane. "She stands in front of our father, hands on hips like this…'Your fifteen-year-old daughter,' meaning me, 'has been drinking with the guards in the citadel's snooker hall. Until all hours of the night.'

"The old codger reaches over and turns the radio down. Probably wondered which part was the problem. None of us were allowed in the citadel where the other staff lived and ate in the cafeteria.

" 'The Americans are giving the commies a run in Korea. That bastard Stalin is next.' That's all he says to her. While we worked, he sat in front of that bloody radio waiting for America to rescue his palace. Paid for his idleness with my mother's hidden jewelry, too."

The aunt took her cane back and leaned on it heavily, gazing into a far corner of the room. "Those ponies? A guard told me they went to a meat factory."

"Aww." Paula tried to embrace the old woman, but she waved her off.

"It doesn't matter."

"Of course, it does."

"You know…I told that guard if he said anything to Tibor, I'd kick him in the nuts."

"Good for you." Paula chuckled.

180

Aunt Lisbet had no interest in visiting the crypt where her father and brother were buried. She linked her arm through Paula's. Was there time before the wedding ceremony to see the stone steps to the beach, though?

As a sailor might search for a landmark, Aunt Lisbet stood on the top step and squinted along the flooded valley. From the lowest reaches of the reservoir where the broad new highway spanned the dam and climbed from sight, a blinding arc of midday sun bounced off a vehicle.

This spot, above all, was where she wanted to be while wedding guests filtered in.

"Is it very sad for you to be here today, Aunt?" Paula asked.

"What do you think?" she said, with a random flick of the wrist. "I've lived thirty minutes away for almost twenty years, yet I haven't returned until today." She tapped her temple. "It's all up here."

"What is? The palace?"

"No, sir. Romania was a lost cause. Even I knew that. I wasn't going to become no bloody countess." The aunt swung her cane at something only she could see. "Of what? Broken windows and piles of bricks?"

She jammed the butt end near her foot. "This patch of dirt is where I said goodbye to my brother. 'Course, he didn't know it was goodbye. Nobody did. Never saw Tibor's sweet face again. I cursed my mother for leaving him behind with that stupid bastard. We were a family." She balled up her fist and shook it at the reservoir. "That's what I want back. Those people and that time.

"Arrr...The place is cursed," she said under her breath.

Paula tried tugging the old woman from the brink of

what would surely be another rant, but the island seemed to have suddenly cast a net of lucidity over her. "Goran watched his own mother jump from that tower over there. And poor Tibor. Shot in the face by a greedy thief."

She turned abruptly, and in the minutes it took the old woman to reach the doors of the citadel, her clarity had snuck off once again. "Let's go see your paintings," she said. "Will any of the artists be here today?"

Chapter Seventeen

There couldn't have been more than twenty-five guests milling around the citadel rotunda's staircase where Julie and Ram said their vows at noon under the sunlight from the overhead cupola. Their original location on the knoll couldn't compete with the citadel's kaleidoscope of gothic skylights. Afterward, it was as if a wind tunnel had blown everyone out of the hall while the caterers set up the buffet tables.

A soft glow from the gallery fireplaces flickered across Goran's paintings, and in the arcades, strings of temporary wall sconces lit the way. Paula managed to find a dim corner for a breather until the guests for the gallery opening started to flood in. While slumped at a row of vinyl folding chairs outside the future tavern, a middle-aged Indian man in a pristine white Nehru tunic and dress jeans approached.

Across the room, Ram watched. *Oh, no. It was a setup.* He hated matchmaking, all the rigid *do-si-do and promenade your partner* stuff from weddings in India. Yet, here on his own day, he grinned from a safe distance, looking happier than a dog rolling in squirrel guts.

"I was just thinking," the Indian man said, "you have the loveliest complexion."

She wiped the scowl from her face. "Thank you. So do you." Where did that come from, she thought?

But did he ever. With skin radiant as a burnished chestnut, the man had the kind of square jawline framing dusty-rose lips you knew many a red-lacquered fingertip had caressed. Deep-set eyes simmered with amusement.

She felt herself being pulled to the edge, tipping and plunging, helpless to halt her rapid-fire chuckle, the two of them playing off each other to a simultaneous climax of laughter.

It was the wonky laugh Goran had said made him fall instantly in love with her, right after he pressed his lips to the hand she offered. A decade of living later, and Goran's kissed fingers routine wouldn't rate anything today but an eye roll.

But this man simply offered his open palm. "I am Ram's uncle. Benny."

She shook it. "Paula." So, this was the childless playboy uncle she'd heard about. The one Ram revered as an example of a life well-lived. He had Ram's stature and the messy bangs and ducktail which only the most cosmopolitan of men could get away with.

Without so much as a *May I?* he pulled over the closest chair. Here was a true twenty-first-century gentleman—someone who expected Paula to have the wherewithal to blow him off gently, without feigning a run for the powder room.

"I owe you an apology, then, for not sending out an invitation."

"Ah. Singles always get lost in the shuffle." The amused twinkle was back. He knew as much about her as she knew about him and the violent end of the Musahar clan in India. Paula had been using the goat-milk soap his multinational company produced long before she met Ram. Hence, the *lovely complexion* comment.

"Thank goodness for phones," he said.

She reached over and squeezed one of the hands in his lap. The man sitting before her was the last of his generation. Every other member of Ram's family had died as a victim of terrorism or a recruit within its ranks.

His eyes softened, straying to her touch, and for a moment the warmth of this embrace said what words of empathy could not.

"Thank you for coming. For Ram."

He could have minimized his feelings with *Oh well, I had a meeting in Switzerland, anyway.* Or *If only Ram's father could be here. He was twice the man I am.* Or *Ram's all I've got now.*

He didn't.

"I have been to see your wolf," he said, folding her hand between the two of his and leaning in as if to whisper something tender. "Beautiful animal. I know a few things about goats if you ever want to get that going."

"Wouldn't they be a nice appetizer for the wild animals around here?"

A tandem chuckle broke between them.

"Wildlife is shrinking in India, but our worst predators are the terrorists." Whether he'd meant to say this or it slipped, he fixed his eyes on Paula and refused to let go, his intoxicating gaze finally arousing her in the same way Goran's had.

Who knows where the conversation would have gone had Ram Jr. not bounced up and jerked his uncle's hands from hers. "Uncle Benny. Please. Can we go to the wolf now? You promised to take me."

"Why don't you come with us?" He stood off-kilter

as the boy pulled on one arm.

"Love to." Paula shrugged and spread her arms. "But it looks like I'm the hostess all day."

"Here then." Benny dug deep into a pocket with his free hand, flipped open his wallet, transferred it to under his chin, and pinched out a card. "My apologies. I'll have to catch the next shuttle out from down there, but…My personal cell and email." Ram Jr. grabbed on with both hands like a water skier and let himself be dragged a step or two while Benny handed her the card. "We have our soap in Bucharest health-food shops. I can always find the time to fly in and admire it on the shelves."

He tucked the wallet into his pocket and twisted awkwardly to wave at Ram, who hadn't moved from his spot at the far end of the arcade. Benny's final smile for her. Gorgeous. Sweet. Authentic.

"You never know." Paula hoped her grin was as dazzling as his.

Bhimrao "Benny" Musahar, the card said. No company title or address. Just a global toll-free phone number and email which she was sure few had in their contact lists. Bottom center was a rough caricature of a goat in a top hat. A nod to the dairy and soap conglomerate he'd founded with Ram's late father. She suspected this attempt at cartooning was his own, so as not to forget his low-caste beginnings in a slum.

A humble, but not servile, breed of man. Or was she trying to give him more depth than he deserved? Goran constantly accused her of doing that. Turning everything into a drama.

There was the cooking experiment, after all. Paula loved to cook and eat healthy. Goran loved to eat, period. "Don't muck it up, love. It's perfect," he said when she'd suggested they share the cooking whenever he wasn't involved in a commission. For the next three months, she white-knuckled it, ate Goran's take-out, and only caved when she started to imagine migraines from monosodium glutamate overload. They turned out to be stress-graines.

She hadn't wanted Goran to cook, only to tell her how well *she* could. He never ate another meal of hers without saying so.

It was Goran at his most frustratingly attentive self, but never could she get her mother's sympathy. "He's all excited about this Skype thing everybody's using. He says I can go back to what I love. Just like that. Teach my deaf students from anywhere. Oh Mum, he can be so infantile about life's problems."

What should she do with this card in her hand? Was Benny the normal guy she continually begged Goran to be? "I can be like that," Goran had said. "But it's not what you want, so why should I bother?"

From what she'd seen so far from Benny—ten minutes of his wardrobe—his attitudes to money fit exactly with hers. She could join her millions with his millions and create something…

Horrendous! Was that not how the aristocracy protected their entitlement, or what? Better that she take her money back to Cedarwood and marry one of the sawmill workers. Perhaps someone she went to school with. A normal guy.

Or file this card somewhere in her room and think about staying single.

****

From her bedroom window, Paula caught sight of the houseboat already loading gallery guests across the

187

reservoir. A few art collectors had caught the early wedding shuttle over, but the motherlode would be at the citadel's doors in a mere twenty minutes. She jammed Benny's card into a pocket of her backpack, the edge peeking out where she could see it.

About to head down the grand staircase, she noticed a middle-aged woman at the far end of the second floor, peering up the bottom stairs of the meditation tower. The woman, in heels and a smartly tailored suit, backed away from the tower doorway when she saw Paula. A brilliant red crept into her cheeks.

"Can I help you with something?"

"Oh. I'm probably not supposed to be up here."

"No problem. The wedding guests have the run of the place until the gallery reception starts. From your accent, you must be another one of Goran's cousins. I had no idea how many there were until they showed up with Claudia."

Paula extended her hand, but the woman was slow to take it. "You're very kind, but I must be honest. I'm from Bucharest.

"No," the woman said, when Paula's face lit up. "Not that wealthy family of art lovers…although…we did run in the same circles in the past. I'm a crasher—I think that's the term, isn't it? Wedding crasher. My name is…is…Haller." The self-declared crasher opened the space between them, almost imperceptibly, and flinched as if someone else entirely had said her name. "There was a news story about the gallery opening. I didn't know it was invitation only."

No doubt Claudia again.

Paula wracked her brain for who she knew in Bucharest. A friend from Claudia's university? Maybe someone inside the firm which shipped the paintings?

"My uncle spent a lot of time here when it was a hospital. I've always been curious to see it. The tower, that is. He loved being in there."

It was as if the woman couldn't decide whether to pour on the charm or soldier on—shamelessly sheepish for some reason. Haller. Of course—the doctor. Oh hell. Julie was right after all? If he'd snuck off in disgrace, no wonder she was nervous.

"Could I go up and take a look at the room?"

"Yes, yes. Of course."

At the top, the woman's whole body seemed to exhale, but not from the climb.

"That's a shrine over there. We meditate here sometimes."

"What a wonderful idea. Despite everything that happened, my uncle had a family like anyone else. He wasn't always...Well, my father suffered terribly. They were brothers, after all."

She circled the room, wide-eyed, her bottom lip quivering. "I don't know how many times he reread the old letters my uncle wrote from here. You wouldn't think it possible, but they were full of love for us and had a lot of wisdom in them."

She crossed to one of the narrow windows and paused to stare out. "Our family's story is similar to the Vlakias. We eventually lost everything. Before that, the two brothers trained as classical musicians. A lot of people around my uncle had no idea he used to play the violin in a symphony. Papa is gone, but I told him if ever I could see the tower, I would."

The Haller woman ran one hand along the curvature of the stones. "It's like a child's playroom, isn't it? Safe, cozy." Still far inside her thoughts, she stared out the battlement slit once more. "Beautiful views of the mountains. Sunrise, too, I bet. I never knew my uncle, but yes, from what my father told me, I can see his brother here, content for once."

Yeah. Especially when the young men came for their therapy sessions. Paula snorted, but Dr. Haller's descendant appeared not to notice such a visceral reaction.

"Psychiatry still doesn't know why it happens," the woman said. "If it's genetics or something triggers it. Probably a bit of both. Like a bomb waiting for a spark."

The niece rested her palm against the stone, not long, but with the same reverence and love of a priest at an infant's baptism. Paula stared at the spot, a stale taste in her mouth. Had this patched hole in the mortar held the anchor for the Ripper's bed? The place where he reveled in his dreams of cannibalism?

The time for polite smiles had passed. "I-I think that's the houseboat arriving with the guests for the grand opening," Paula said.

"Yes. Of course." The woman jerked her hand away, snapping from her trance, all business. "I'll hurry down to catch it back to the landing. Goodbye."

This tower room had given Paula the discovery of Goran's paintings, the rejuvenation of chanting, and peaceful meditations. Today, it also held the inexplicably sad essence of a third person, listening in and watching. One of Julie's hungry ghosts?

Paula fled on the Haller woman's heels.

She circled down the endless stairs, remembering this tower had also given her the doctor's journal and its gruesome fantasies. Since her time with the wolves, she was quite ashamed she had once believed these reclusive animals could attack for no reason other than evil intent.

The journal…Instead of burning it, this niece should have it. Paula opened her mouth to shout but snapped it closed. Dr. Haller was obviously out of his mind when he'd written it. Had he even been aware of committing serial rape? What useful purpose could the rantings of a madman serve?

Chapter Eighteen

The day after the wedding, rapt outside the gate of the wolf enclosure, his overnight bag beside him, Ram's young son barely acknowledged his mother's tears dockside.

The one person Paula had been most excited to meet at the wedding was Ram's ex-wife, Alana, whose Indian descendants had moved to Sweden three generations ago. *Pleasant, polite, genuinely kind*, were Julie's words for her. Perhaps an unenlightened society did not yet have accurate words for the rare woman who readily admits to seducing a fellow female's partner for the sole purpose of having a child. But her plan had backfired when Ram insisted on marriage and raising the boy.

Of course, Ram's six-year-old male issue was also a charmer, well-mannered, and as fluent in English as his mother, a former translator for the United Nations. A mini-Ram, he could do no wrong in Paula's eyes.

Alana's amenability, however, stopped at her only child. A few days before the wedding, she'd set foot on the citadel dock, scrutinized the shoreline as only a mother could, and declared the island "an accident waiting to happen." Its most worrisome surprise had yet to show itself.

"Good God, is that a wolf I see?" Alana peered past Ram to where Marco paced inside the enclosure's fence line, sniffing the newcomers in the air, while Paula and

Ram Jr. stood nearby.

How did they plan to keep her son clean all week? Ram spread his arms before the reservoir in a grand gesture. "There's water everywhere and high time Ram Jr. lives rough for a while."

Oh, the mischievous lies Ram was capable of when it came to ex-wives. The island's occupants had been taking hot bubble baths for over a week.

"You can't possibly think this unsanitary place is suitable for children. There must be treacherous stairways like that everywhere." Alana scowled at the wooden stairs, blissfully unaware they were the best of the bunch.

Remarkably apt perceptions, Paula thought, considering what little Ram's ex-wife had seen of the island prior to the wedding. But Alana folded under his options: he could see his son here in Romania or use his visitation days later in India. Alana detested India, a country she'd never been to, and hoped her son never would either.

As soon as Ram disappeared in the outboard to deliver Alana and her new husband to a car rental for their European vacation, Julie said to Paula, "*Eff-it*, Ram can't be blamed for taking his son up the tower if he isn't here."

****

"They shot their arrows at enemies from these windows." Julie held her stepson up to peer out one of the tower's windows.

As she set the boy down, he pointed to a small frame on her altar. "Who are those people?"

"This one," Julie said, crouching beside him and picking up the photo of Ram's parents and two older

193

brothers as children prior to his birth, "is your papa's family from India. Your grandparents and uncles."

"This little boy is my uncle?"

"Yes, but he would be a man now. Even older than your papa."

"Why aren't they here, like us?"

Julie stopped cold; the joy children awaken with their innocence gone from her eyes.

"Because they aren't alive anymore," Paula said, picking up the thread.

He turned to her. "Why not?"

Oh boy. Paula knew that question was surely next. How she would love to fathom the brutal volleys men launched on each other, constantly trying to even the score but never succeeding. Good thing children lived in the moment. "Your papa might tell you someday."

From the altar, Paula scooped up the photo of Goran which came from Aunt Lisbet. "A long time ago, this man was your father's best friend. I'll bet you have one, too."

Ram Jr. nodded vehemently.

****

Except for the mounds of used bottles, cans, and plastic left from the reception, the citadel kitchen was barren once more, an echo chamber of clangs and clinks every time Julie and Paula dashed something into a recycling bin. Perhaps that's why they didn't notice that out in the rotunda, the thuds from Ram Jr.'s soccer ball had gone silent.

The whir of an outboard motor skipped across the reservoir. "That was fast." Paula glanced at her watch. "Didn't he say the car rental was at least an hour away?"

Julie chucked another beer can into the bin. "Once a

speeder, always a speeder."

At first, they couldn't hear the boy's screams above the wind—only Marco's barking. As Paula opened the french doors to the kitchen courtyard and hoisted a crate of empty wine bottles outside, she heard the muted barks. *The lone wolf was back.* In Paula's mind was always the fear he could entice Marco away, too.

"I should go down." She gave Julie an apologetic shrug and walked out to the citadel's yard. From the wolf enclosure below came a cascade of desperate screams cut with snarls and growls. The chilling *crack* of a gun. A sharp *yip.* And silence.

Marco! Ram shot Marco.

Chapter Nineteen

Paula took the cliff to the wolf enclosure, not the stairs. "No. Don't shoot him." She shrieked as she slid. "Please."

At the bottom, other than the pitched wail of a departing outboard, all was silent. An idea was taking shape in Paula's mind, but Julie had already figured it out. Paula turned to the sound of her flying down the stairs with the rifle from Paula's bedroom.

The enclosure gate swung wide; no movement inside.

Dribbles of blood led off into the densest bush. "Ram Jr." She screamed it loud enough to be heard across the peninsula. "Where are you? Are you hurt?"

Panting from the descent, Julie handed Paula the rifle. "Ram. Answer if you can. Please." She turned to Paula. "I saw the boat from your window. The boy wasn't in it."

There was soft crying and a trembling voice said, "I'm hiding over here, Julie. Is the man gone?"

"Thank God."

"Yes, he left, sweetie."

Ram Jr. crept forward and ran into Julie's arms while Paula peered around, the rifle ready at her hip.

"Are you okay?"

Ram Jr. nodded, his words gushing forth. "I was outside the wolf gate. I promise I didn't go in. I was outside, and this man came in a boat and grabbed me and tried to drag me to the dock. But I got away, and then I tried to lock the wolf gate from inside, but he still came in and chased me again. Then Marco bit his leg, and he shot him. He had a gun, Julie. He shot Marco."

"Noooo." Paula wailed, "Ma-ar-co." She called again and again, before crouching in front of the boy. "Where did he go?"

"I-I don't know. I was hiding. Maybe there." He pointed down the peninsula in the direction of the blood trail.

"Whoa. Whoa." Julie caught Paula's arm as she stepped away. "Where're you going?"

"To find him."

"You can't leave us unprotected. Whoever shot him might return."

"Marco could be dying." Paula paced, her chest heaving under jagged breaths.

"Keep it together, girl. He's still moving. When fighting didn't work, he's taken flight." Still holding Ram Jr.'s hand, Julie turned to the stairs. "I'm taking him to the cottage and bolting the door. Spot us until the top. When you hear me fire the blank gun, it means we're inside safely."

She paced, waiting for the blast, then ran along a disjointed path streaked with blood. "Ma-ar-co. Marco."

At the grassy shoreline where Red had crossed to the mainland, the blood stopped—but Marco wasn't there. Had he tried to cross and drowned from his injuries? Or did he make it to the other side and was bleeding to death that very moment?

"Oh, God." She sat in the wild grass, the rifle across her lap and screamed his name, and it bounced back to her from across the water. If she had to sit there all night for him, she would. Setting the gun aside, she rose and immediately heard a halting whimper.

It was the gun. Today wasn't Marco's first encounter with guns, and he wasn't going to show himself as long as she held one. She imagined the three pups huddled inside their den against the endless rifle shots and death shrieks of their pack members.

A blood-stained front paw inched from under the bush beside her. "Marco? Oh no. Let me see you." She crouched but didn't reach for him in case he bolted.

He dragged himself forward on his belly, the bloodied paw held aloft. Head down and submissive, until he was close enough to lick the hand she offered, his red-rimmed eyes pleaded with her not to hurt him. She ran her trembling fingers along the side of his belly where she could see blood, and it came away dry.

"Let me have a look at you." She gently prodded him to stand. He hesitated, then stuck out his deformed leg at its collapsed angle; the limb vibrated as he tried to raise himself halfway. Dammit, the gunshot wound was to his good leg. The bullet hit just above the paw.

At this time of year, the sun plunged from sight so quickly the chill of evening frost was already creeping into her bones. If she abandoned the injured wolf in the open, he might lapse into shock and die.

Until Ram returned, Paula was on her own.

She strode forward to an overhanging oak and squinted through the soupy shadows of dusk. Could she visualize herself carrying him to the shelter?

Paula crouched, wrapped her arms around him and tried to stand, tears rolling off her chin and onto his fur. Although the runt, Marco still had to be fifty pounds.

Carrying him was out of the question, and Marco seemed to know that only too well. With nothing to stabilize him at front, he lurched up into a faltering gait. If the bone was shattered, he would be walking on a broken leg the full kilometer to the shelter hut.

"I know, baby. It hurts, but I can't leave you here." After a few more staggering steps, he stopped and collapsed. She did likewise, sniffling between clenched teeth.

"All right, let's try this." She stripped off her bulky sweater; an icy wind whipped across her bare back. After checking the rifle's safety, she jammed the butt end into the back of her wide waistband. With the sweater slung under his torso and his useless front legs raised out of the way, he waddled forward on his sturdy back legs, so fast she could barely keep up.

After ten minutes of her bent back taking all his weight, though, unbearable cramps throbbed up and down her spine. She let the sling drop, but an emboldened Marco continued hopping upright on his hind quarters, circus-like, until he reached an area chocked with rotting logs and boulders. Not slowing, when he glanced back to see her still watching him, he settled onto his bum leg and began a three-legged scramble across the log blocking his way.

"No, Marco. It's too much."

In the instant she rushed forward, his weak leg collapsed, he tumbled, slamming full-weight onto his shattered bone. Even Julie must have heard the shrieking howl.

After that, he lay motionless on his side and refused to go on. Paula tucked her sweater around him and curled herself at his back, the winter coat at his neck dense and warm against her cheek. Whitecaps rolled across the reservoir in the twilight. If she hauled some leafy branches around them, could they survive the night this way? He shivered continuously, stealing the odd glance at her, obviously ashamed he couldn't continue. Was he going into shock?

In the distance, the outline of a dome glowed in the twilight. If it was the straw-bale wolf shelter, it couldn't be more than a block away. She slipped on her sweater and propped the rifle against one of the tallest oaks. Bending deeply to hug him to her chest, she began her plodding march.

Within a few meters of the hut, she couldn't go on. Her legs gave way; she laid him on the ground and rolled onto her back. He licked the tears rolling off her chin, and she knew he was grateful and telling her they were both going to be okay.

It was dark when she crawled through the tight opening into a confined space gamy with the smell of damp hay and wolf sweat. She pulled Marco in after her, into the warmth of the straw, and he drank from the pail they used to fill the trough with game. By the time she'd hollowed a space for it near him, his airy breaths rose and fell in the stillness. He was asleep. There was nothing more to do until Ram arrived with the boat.

Clinging to the possibility that Julie had finally reached him by text through their iffy cellular connection, she hustled to retrieve the rifle and climb the wooden stairs to the cottage.

Chapter Twenty

Outside the cottage's kitchen door, the place seemed all but deserted. "It's me," Paula said.

Inside, the bolt clicked and eased aside. "I've cut all the lights." Julie pressed the wooden door closed behind Paula. "We're in the pantry. The generator is off, too, so we can hear if anyone is on the island."

In the safety of the windowless pantry, Julie raised the flashlight and stifled a gasp. "You're exhausted." She scooped a heavy wool blanket from the floor to gather around Paula. "I heard—"

"He's alive." Paula smiled down at Ram Jr. and kissed the top of his head while the Nintendo game in his hand gave off spurts of lyrical sounds.

"Is Marco okay?" he said, wide-eyed but calm.

"Yes, sweetie. I found him. He has a little cut on his paw, but he's in his wolf house sleeping." Paula caught Julie's eye and cocked her head at the pantry exit. "Ram. We're just going into the kitchen a minute."

"What happened?" Julie asked, when they were alone.

"The bullet hit his front leg—the good one. He tried—" She closed her eyes and felt the ground shifting beneath her.

"Here. Sit down." Julie held her while she collapsed into one of the nearby chairs.

"I had to carry him." The warmth of her friend's

arms encircled her.

"He's going to be fine."

She could see the boy's face illuminated by the flickering screen. "What does he think is happening?"

"A game of hiding from Papa."

"Nothing from Ram, then?"

Julie gave a flat wag of her chin. "I tried an email and text to Claudia, too, but our new satellite is pretty useless in this wind." She massaged her eyes with her fingertips. "I'm trying to understand why these log poachers would grab a kid and bring even more heat on themselves."

"I know. There are easier ways to drive us out of here than that."

"Do you think they're waiting for Ram at the boat launch?" Julie said.

This was the kind of question it was best not to answer truthfully, if at all. "I think the best place to be right now is probably in the citadel. We can see the boat launch from my room, and the cell phone signal is better."

Julie told the boy they would hide in the castle instead, then the three of them crept from shadow to shadow around the base of the hillock.

Inside the rotunda, Paula slid the wrought-iron bar across both doors. "There. To get in you'd need one of those bombs SWAT teams use."

"I like hiding in a castle," Ram Jr. said as they entered Paula's bedroom. He climbed onto one of the alcove's benches to unclip the window shutters.

"No, honey. Don't open those, or your papa will see our flashlights."

Minutes later, Julie clawed her phone out of her

daypack as soon as it dinged and studied the screen. "It's finally Ram." She leapt to the door, ready to slide the bolt, but Paula gripped her arm.

"Not so quick. Show me the text."

Julie raised the screen to Paula's eye level.

—Where the fuck are you guys? The cottage is dark and empty. Are you inside the citadel? I'm at the main doors waiting for you to unlock them.—

"How do we know the loggers haven't taken over his phone?" Paula said.

"And if it really is him? We leave him out there while we're safe in here?"

"Don't respond. Let's see what happens."

Within minutes came the faint but unmistakable rattle of a metal ladder scraping against the kitchen courtyard's stone wall, followed by what they both agreed was the metal shower rod collapsing and the french doors being kicked in.

"Only Ram would know—" Julie started to say.

"Put your phone on mute. Hurry." Paula strode to Ram Jr. to place a finger against her lips. She sidestepped to the fireplace mantel where the rifle lay, pointed to Julie's flashlight, and clicked off her own.

The frantic footsteps up the stone staircase were those of someone who knew the citadel well, but that didn't mean they weren't plotting with Claudia. Paula wasn't yet a hundred percent onside with the wolf trainer and so-called surgeon. How well could Ram know her after so many years?

At the landing, the thuds echoed along the mezzanine in a direct path to Paula's bedroom door. A dim border of light spread along its underside. The nineteenth-century glass knob began to turn. They backed away as someone booted the door, then ran at it with their shoulder. But it barely budged against the iron latch.

Seeing Julie shifting foot to foot and thinking she might say something, Paula sliced her hand across her throat.

Outside the door, a metallic clank rang from the flagstones, and the light blinked out. "Oh, shit."

"Papa," Ram Jr. screeched. "You finally found us."

"If you want to know what's going on…" Julie deftly relocked the door once Ram was inside. "Then read the text I sent to you hours ago. No. Wait. Try Claudia's number first."

"No signal," he said, looking up from the screen of his satellite phone, his face contorted. "Your message came in while I was crossing the reservoir. I didn't see the point by then since I was so close."

"Go on, read it," Paula said, wanting to monitor whether he would pile on another layer to whatever story he was still spinning with Claudia.

When finished, he didn't stomp around nor call Claudia names for manipulating them into staying on the island. As expected, he dashed to sweep his son into his arms and scrutinized the boy. "You're sure you're okay?"

Ram Jr. nodded. "Why did your best friend chase me?"

"What do you mean?"

"The man on the white horse," the boy said.

"I have Goran's photo on my altar. The one his aunt gave me." Julie crouched in front of Ram Jr. "Was it the man you played badminton with? Remember? On the beach during the wedding." Turned out the kid helping

Ram, despite being a serial daydreamer, had a way with bona fide kids.

"No." Ram Jr. shook his head and glared at the insinuation he didn't know one person from another. "It was the man in the photo, but older."

Was this not validation enough that Goran was alive? The others seemed to have finally warmed to the idea, too. Julie stood motionless at the news, her eyes round and shining in the flashlight's glare. Ram was pinching the bridge of his nose as if trying to squeeze out a toxin.

Unfortunately, the witness was six years old. But if this *was* Goran, it was not the one she wanted to be alive. *The power we hold over the wolves had its place and time, but now it must die with Goran,* the old aunt had said. She thought of Marco, vulnerable and dependent on her, a killing machine in the wild but no match for the brutality of man's own machines. *Whoever attacked Ram's son did not command wolves, or they wouldn't have had to shoot Marco.*

Paula steered Ram to the far corner near the fireplace and whispered, "I can't see these timber poachers pulling a kidnap just to scare us away, can you?"

He glanced at Ram Jr., still engrossed with his game in the alcove, then motioned for Julie to join them.

"Goran has a brother four years older. He's in prison for killing a cop. Or he was up until a month ago. Yes…" He acknowledged Julie's slack jaw. "Don't react. Just listen until I'm done. Goran channeled the pain of his mental illness into art. This guy likes killing. And lots of money. Like the million from the hydro company which he thinks should be his now that Goran is gone.

"He also killed his own father when the man tried to stop him from ransacking the chapel downstairs."

At the same instant, Paula gasped and reached for Ram's arm, he glanced over his shoulder at his son.

"Goran and I heard a gunshot and collided with the brother on his way out. I went for help. Goran stayed with his father while he lay there bleeding to death. We were thirteen but made a pact to never speak about what we'd seen. The thought of his brother running around loose, with what we knew, terrified us.

"Then the guy started poaching trees from public land around the palace. Technically, he was right to claim they were his, since Romania never returned the Vlakia land. But the law didn't see it that way when he killed a conservation officer and got put away for life."

"Why…" Paula threw back her head and sighed. "…did Goran never tell me about this murderous brother?"

"Once the guy was locked up for life, I think we both just wanted to put it behind us. I eventually told Claudia. Goran told his mother but…"

Julie stepped forward. "For God's sake, Goran's been gone seven years."

"I know." Ram shrank from their gazes. "Despite what he said, Goran did care what people thought of him. His fans. But especially you, Paula."

Paula gaped. "None of this would have mattered to me. I loved him." She hung her head and squeezed her eyes closed, the despair of knowing he didn't trust her with his secret ripped open the old guilt.

"You were dealing with his schizophrenia. He thought it was enough. But if you ask me, I think he kept quiet out of respect for his mother. It must have seemed like an echo of the past."

Paula was picturing Goran's distraught mother perched atop the tower above them, looking down for the last time at her ruined life. She turned to Ram. "An echo?"

"Yeah. Her sister apparently killed their parents with an ax while they slept. The girl was fourteen."

Paula had hit her limit. She stood, unblinking, numb.

"When Goran's brother killed his own father, it did a number on Aunt Lisbet, too. In her dementia, she's convinced herself wolves killed her brother, Tibor. Now she's excised Goran's jailbird brother from her mind so well that he and Goran are one and the same."

Ram fell silent, the only sound in the room a whoop from Ram Jr. at a move on his game.

"No illegal loggers, then?" Paula said.

"There are, and it's possible the brother is back with them. I'll bet it was the cousins who fooled the parole board. Point is, he's coming for the money and likely me, too, since I'm the only witness who can put him away for murdering his own father."

"I can't believe you've been sitting on this for God only knows how long," Julie whispered. She backed Ram into a corner to hiss, "You brought your son here knowing the threat from this maniac."

"Hell, no. I knew about the parole hearing the day the wolves attacked us. That's why I was so freaked out about the kid, but when I phoned the prison from Aunt Lisbet's, whoever I talked to said the hearing was for show, there was no chance for early release. So I put it out of my mind." He glanced over Paula's shoulder at Ram Jr. "It was only today while I was in town that I heard the brother had been released. I was coming back to move us out of here.

"But you're right," he said. "I shouldn't have listened to Claudia that day at Aunt Lisbet's. I wanted to go to the police. Make sure the brother stayed in jail. But she begged me not to for the sake of her mother. Claudia would rather risk her own life than force Aunt Lisbet to unravel her fantasy world. For years, Claudia spread the rumor she used the money for a yacht. Someone must have told the brother I had the money and was building this gallery."

"The kid?" Paula said.

"That's what I think," Ram said. "Maybe not intentionally."

In the silence that followed, the three drifted apart.

Julie stopped in her tracks. "I say we wait for help. Even if Claudia is in Bucharest, she must have my email or text by now. The local police are likely on their way."

Ram pulled out his satellite phone, went to the window, opened the shutters, and extended the antenna. "Still no signal. I wouldn't depend on Claudia. She doesn't carry her personal phone into the operating theater. We can't assume she's even seen our emails." Ram glanced at his son.

Whatever they did, Paula knew, would center on keeping the boy safe. "If the brother wants the money, let's give it to him. When Claudia phones, we'll ask her to be the intermediary."

"Yeah. I doubt he'll stop at that." Ram lowered his voice. "More than anything, he probably wants me silenced. What good is money when you're in jail? He does the kidnap, gets the money, and...my expiry date comes due. The guy is psycho."

He lowered his voice further and leaned toward

Paula. "He'll come in here with lots of firepower. They'll circle the citadel and find the easiest way in—my ladder to the kitchen courtyard or one of the tavern windows. That door will be down in no time.

"We need to leave this island. Quietly and quickly."

Chapter Twenty-One

The main door was too obvious, the outboard too noisy. Not only that, the dock was likely where the brother and his gang were waiting to ambush them, Ram said.

"I doubt the outboard is still there, anyway," Julie said. "That's the only reason I can think of why they let you onto the island. With what you knew, would you have docked with a strange boat tied up?"

Ram pondered that. "With nothing more than a piece of driftwood to defend myself? No. I would have stayed on the reservoir until I got through to you or the police."

"I've got my doubts about the rowboat, too," Paula said. "Maybe that's why the kid went down to the beach to play badminton the day of the wedding. They sent him to see if it was still stored under the trees for winter."

Ram wasn't willing to take his son from the safety of the citadel without knowing for certain. He could squeeze through the tavern window, which opened meters from the stairs to the beach.

"The rifle and satellite phone stay here." He pulled the phone from its holster and handed it to Paula. "You'll need them if I don't return."

"But—" Paula glanced at Julie who was biting her upper lip and trying to distract herself with Ram's son.

Ram held up his industrial flashlight. "This is all I need, although…I don't plan to turn it on."

"If you see anything suspicious, turn around and come back. Right away." Paula gave him a quick but tight hug.

Ram's lower lip quivered as he crouched and drew his son into him. "Papa's going downstairs for a few minutes. While I'm away, listen to everything Julie and Paula tell you."

"I *always* do." The boy forced his mouth into a pout.

"You do. Don't you?" Ram's eyes glistened with tenderness before he kissed his son's forehead and marched to the door where Julie stood, her chest heaving.

She wrapped her arms around his waist. "Don't make me a widow forty-eight hours after our wedding." She landed a hard kiss on him. "See you in a few minutes. Okay?" He gave her a shaky nod before slipping into the dark hallway.

His footsteps faded, followed by the sharp squeal of a metallic hinge.

Of course, it seemed much longer, but within ten minutes they heard someone jogging up the stairs.

"It's there," he said, gasping for air inside the bedroom. "The three of us will have to carry it well into the water. Avoid scraping it along the gravel."

"Brrr." Julie hunched her shoulders.

Paula started jamming every piece of warm clothing she had into a backpack. T-shirts were still enough when the sun was shining, but the nights were dropping almost to freezing. Ram would have to use one of her Mexican ponchos.

Ram lifted his son from the bench. "We're going down to hide inside the rowboat. No talking. Okay?" The boy gave him a tight-lipped nod.

"At the stairs, climb onto my back."

211

****

The wind had died down, and except for the gentle dip and dribble of the oars, they coasted without a word across the reservoir's flat silence. At the bow, Paula stared over her shoulder at the receding island. A flashlight, left to confuse the brother into thinking they were still on the island, flickered inside her bedroom, but otherwise, from afar the citadel seemed like a half-dead sea creature, floating through clouds of shifting debris.

While Ram rowed, Paula sat up front with the flashlight, scanning the path ahead. The dock was nothing but a white smudge in the distance.

She clicked off the light. "Stop rowing," she said, the command hushed but sharp. "Everyone. Not a word. Someone is out there heading to the island."

Minutes later, the vague outline of a craft approached, low in the water. When it was parallel, no more than six meters away, Paula's pulse quickened: it had the same shape and motion as the surfboard she'd seen from her window.

"It's Goran," Paula said, urgent but soft at first. Ram turned and lunged at her, but too late. "Goran. Stop." She waved her arms at the craft.

"Shut up," Julie hissed. She stumbled past Ram to pull Paula out of sight and clamp a palm over her mouth. "Stop struggling, or we'll all end up in the water."

The other boat drifted a moment, then turned in an arc, its light scanning the water.

"Down off the seats." Ram dipped the oars. "Son. Come sit between my legs."

"It's gaining," Julie said.

"I see that. Fire the rifle to slow him down. Paula? Now."

The rifle lay under her at the bow. They wanted her to shoot at Goran. Was she the only one thinking straight?

"Out of the way, Paula. Ram? How does this work?"

"Same as the mock gun. Fire above your head." Ram reached behind to click off the safety, but Paula held up her hand. "Hold on." Ahead, she could see lights moving on shore. "Someone's at the dock."

Ram kept rowing. "Police?"

"Probably not," Paula said. "They're outside the motorhome with flashlights. We shouldn't give ourselves away." She twisted and scanned their wake for Goran's light, but it was off, the surfboard out of sight.

Between pulls, Ram glanced over his shoulder to shore, then back in the direction of the mystery craft. "Dammit," he said, while Julie slid the gun under his seat.

Paula squinted at the shoreline. "Aim for the right side of the dock. Where the bushes are. The motorhome will hide us from their line of sight."

Ram stopped rowing and twisted for a look ahead. "This isn't good."

He was right. Not only was the boat headed for the wrong side of the dock, it was coming in too fast.

Ram thrust the flat of the paddle against the current. The bow jackknifed to the right, slowed, and corrected. He unhooked both oars, turned, and, meters from running aground, thrust the butt end of one against the first piling he came to. The rowboat bucked and ricocheted off the pilings under the dock. All three clawed at any nearby surface to keep the boat still.

Finally, Ram's oar hit bottom. He slid them under the dock.

"What was that?" a male voice on shore said.

From where Paula sat, she could see the bottom half of two horses and their riders' legs. One swung down from his horse. "Idiot. It's deadwood under the dock. Are we going to torch this camper or stand around?"

Only feet away, a high-pitched grating came from the opposite side of the dock. No more than a dim outline, this sleek craft was not a surfboard but a kayak, the paddler already out.

"I wouldn't waste your time with that, boys." The familiar voice hit Paula in the gut. "Not unless those draft horses can outrun a cop car." It was Claudia's.

Using the paddle again, Ram nudged the boat closer to the action.

Claudia stood in a wetsuit, pointing a handgun and powerful flashlight at the same two strange men they'd run into the night their rowboat was stolen. The bearded one held a gas can, and both of them squinted against the beam.

"You still poaching trees, cousin? You'll go to jail this time. Put the petrol down, and get back on your horse." Claudia stepped forward and quickly switched her aim to the second man still on his horse. "I wouldn't. I'll blow your head off before you can get hold of it."

The man with the gas can released it and mounted his horse.

"Now. I'm going to shoot into that petrol. I wouldn't want to be under it." She aimed. There was a dull pop, a dribbling, and the fading sound of hooves pounding through underbrush. At the same instant, Claudia dove behind the motorhome as shots from across the road pinged and whizzed into its front.

"You dumb shit." Claudia struggled to her feet at the

rear. "Punching a hole in a can of petrol won't make it explode. But now you've given away your position, haven't you? Think I didn't see you hiding back there?"

A string of Romanian sentences came from the hillside at the back of the clearing. More shots riddled the van.

"Still don't know bugger all about English?" Claudia asked. "Yeah, that's not the only thing Goran beat you at." There was no response.

She scanned left to right and back again. "If you're here for Goran's money, you're out of luck. I already spent it." The van was raked with even more bullets. "How were you going to get it? Kill us all? Me, my mother? Until you're the only one left? Like you killed your own father for a gold angel? Such irony. You're a real poet."

Claudia peered through the darkness at the ramp, then shifted her gaze around her feet. Gasoline from both the can and the motorhome's damaged gas tank spilled down the gravel launch to pool at the water's edge.

A bluish sheen lapped at the base of the pilings and sides of the rowboat.

Claudia backstepped into the water. "You might as well end it here tonight. Either that or die in a cell." Submerged up to her waist, she dipped from sight and resurfaced at the stern of her kayak, tugging it from the shore.

Something in the shape of a running shoe, a flame sprouting from inside it, landed short of the launch. A roar of shots made it jump, but didn't send it any closer to the gas-soaked slope.

Frantic to get out from under the dock, Ram was already jamming the butt end of an oar against the pilings when the first shoe hit. The bow swiveled free. He slammed the oars back into the gunwales and used his powerful biceps to slice them deep into the water.

But nothing moved. The push to free the bow had wedged the stern between two pilings.

"No. No. No." Paula flopped onto her back and booted one piling as hard as she could. The boat drifted free.

A second *thud* of rubber on metal…Tumbling.

They knew what came next.

Ram got in one powerful surge from the oars when a *whoosh* like the lighting of a giant gas burner threw a wave of heat and light at them.

A layer of solid flame sped across the launch to explode under the motorhome. The eruption rocked the boat and lit up the shoreline like a blood-red spotlight. Flames roared up each side of the vehicle, blowing out the windows as they went, before jumping to the dock.

Ram rowed straight out into the reservoir, then stopped, and lifted his shrieking son into his chest. The boy's shoulders lurched in rhythm with his sobs. "Shh, shh, you're okay now."

"I'll row." Paula's voice cracked; her body tingled and throbbed from the detonation's shockwave.

Ram slid to the bench at the stern and slipped his free arm around Julie, her head still cranked to the scarlet cyclone enveloping the dock. "Oh. Fuck," she said.

"Don't assume he can't see you from there." Someone was shouting to be heard above the crackling blaze. It was Claudia, her kayak bobbing farther along the shoreline. Paula turned the boat and sprinted to come alongside her.

With so much to say, no one seemed to know where

to start until the faint peal of police sirens reached them.

"Good God, Claudia," Ram said. "You're lucky we didn't shoot you."

"We'd all be out of luck, then, wouldn't we?"

Paula squirmed under her gaze. She'd obviously heard her calling Goran's name, and for once Paula welcomed a dose of the woman's caustic judgement. Surely, that was the least she deserved for putting Ram's son and her friends' lives at risk. She was an utter ass. Just inches away, Ram's glare pierced right through her.

Still, in Claudia's eyes was only pity.

"You got our emails?" Julie asked.

"Uh-huh. I was already up here at my mother's, but they didn't come into my phone until I got in the truck to go into Poenari. I called the police and came down here right away with the kayak. My truck's a few minutes away at a launch the locals use."

On the road above, flashing lights and sirens screamed past. "The police won't let you return to the citadel tonight," Claudia said, bringing her attention back to them.

"We'd have to be crazy to want to," Ram said.

"What about Marco?"

Claudia pulled her kayak hand over hand along the gunwale until she was close enough to pat Paula's knee. "The police will help me get him to a vet tonight. That's the first thing I'll do after I take you guys to the village pension."

Paula squeezed Claudia's hand warmly.

"I won't go back there with my son until they've caught everyone."

"Nor should you." Claudia turned to Ram. "The police will be all over this place at first light. They'll send someone to patrol the island."

A heaviness lay over their boat but not from the fire's smoke and eerie glow. It was the dregs of fear. Confusion.

Claudia batted at the chunks of burning dock which had started to fly past like sleet. "Goran's brother won't get far in bare feet...if he's still alive by morning." She glanced at Ram's still-quaking boy.

****

Police investigators had come and gone the next morning when Claudia burst into the pension's homey basement dining hall. Within the cluster of long oak tables and benches, she positioned herself squarely in front of Ram and a pile of dirty breakfast dishes.

"They found the brother's body. And...and..." She leaned in. "Alana called my cell this morning. Got the number from police."

Ram squeezed his eyes shut and moaned. Beside him, Paula's eyebrows all but flew off her forehead.

"You're not taking her calls?" Claudia asked.

"Not yet. I was thinking about what my story would be. They're touring outside Romania, aren't they?"

"Yeah, but she saw the news footage of the burnt-out dock and motorhome. The citadel in the background."

"Oh Lord."

"Conservationists are livid they paroled a cop killer and notorious poacher of old-growth timber." As Julie walked in with Ram Jr., she cut her narrative off and bent to the boy. "How would you like to see Marco? He's in the back of my truck." She turned to Paula. "You can open the cage. He won't go far."

Paula bolted from her seat and extended her hand.

"Come on. Let's go see him."

"By the way," Claudia called after Paula. "He can stay at our farm until you're home. I mean, back at the island."

Marco caught their scent and started to whine the minute they stepped outside. When Paula dropped the tailgate, he struggled to stand before giving up, wan-eyed, his tail thumping out metallic bangs inside the narrow cage. His injured leg was the shape of a caveman's club swathed in bandages.

The diagnosis by phone the night before—the bullet had grazed the wolf's wrist. They'd removed the bone fragments, but until it healed, the leg would be extremely painful to stand on.

****

Within days, the last of the Timber Mafia were in custody. The airport limo was already out front of Poenari pension's picket fence and loading the suitcases when Claudia drove up to tell Paula and Ram, "The lawyer has convinced my dense cousin to plead guilty to timber poaching, attempted arson, and email fraud. Yup, the *cvlakia* email was his invention, but he's adamant he never trespassed into the citadel. I guess the wine and cheese thief has moved on to the next cocktail hour."

The smug quip sent a chill through Paula which Claudia immediately sensed.

"I didn't mean Goran. It's just a joke, albeit not a very good one." She held her vehicle keys out to Paula. "I actually came over to give you my truck. It's time I bought a new one in the city."

Before Paula could hug her, Claudia's hand shot out. "Deal?"

"Deal." Paula grinned. Just how many tactics did

this woman have for evading hugs? The vehicle meant she and Marco could return to the island.

With Alana and her son reunited, the limo would drop off the Stockholm group, Ram, and Julie at the airport, then deliver Claudia to the door of her Bucharest townhouse.

"Call me anytime—anytime—you need to talk." Ram hugged Paula and held her longer than normal. "If you can get that damn satellite phone working, that is."

He slouched to stare into Paula's eyes. He still had a few inches on her. "Final words? Questions?"

Her eyes as round and glassy as Ram's, she managed a feeble grin. "That sounds kind of morbid." She knew her question, had been thinking about it since learning of Goran's brother, but feared the answer.

"It's not going to be easy to get Goran out of your mind this winter," he said. A somber air settled around them.

Already on the far side of the limo, she took him by the arm and led him farther still. "Tell me—honestly— do you think Goran's brother had someone murder him in India?"

"No." The answer burst out of him. "I've had seven years to reflect. No. You think a shit-for-brains hitman could track Goran's movements? Goran himself didn't know where he was headed most of the time. I never worried about my own safety because I was either, literally, in Outer Mongolia or surrounded with the oil refineries' security."

It was the answer she wanted—a gift. The landscape of her hectic lifestyle with Goran flashed before her eyes, and she stared into her hands until Ram took them into his own.

"Goran moved around on purpose." He whispered this like a fact held back inside a confessional.

Her head jerked up.

"Is that the reason he refused to stay at my cabin?" She tore her hands from his, her voice that of an exhausted child. "He thought someone might kill me?"

Ram shrugged. "Just the possibility of his brother's violence took a toll. Didn't matter if he was locked up or not."

Past accusations rampaged across her mind. While Goran had been afflicted with paranoia, a real-life threat played out. "What have I done to him?" Paula said through hands cupped across her lips.

Ram's face appeared close to hers. "Goran's suicide is not your fault. Okay? How could it be? He gave you one option. Which was to leave. He was proud of you for that. 'I never thought she had it in her.' That's what he said to me. 'She never looked more powerful. What a beauty I had.' "

The revelation of Goran's secret protectiveness wrapped her in silent tears.

"It was simply his time, you know," Ram said. "Time to walk away while he was ahead."

Chapter Twenty-Two

Within two weeks, Marco was chugging down the stairs to the peninsula and running from one end of it to the other in his usual lopsided hippity-hop. That's where he wanted to stay most nights now, inside the strawbale igloo, emerging only to catapult his forlorn howls into the valleys beyond the water.

Paula never heard any response from the shoreline, but this fantasy of Marco sleeping soundly beside the fire all winter was perhaps too ambitious.

Getting him a companion wolf had more to do with Marco's happiness than her own safety. He was the child she would never have; she had become the fawning aunt with the triplets, after all.

A weekend in mid-October dawned with a rare heat wave. It shimmered across the reservoir with the promise of new beginnings rather than the grim reality of the dark months ahead. Paula climbed aboard the motorboat, intending to ask Claudia to begin the search for Marco's female companion.

The satellite phone Ram left with her always grabbed a signal on the open water. As she cut the motor to check her messages, a low-flying float plane roared into view from behind. Claudia would know if it was conservation officers looking for more timber poachers. Before she could finish dialing Claudia's number, the phone rang. An Indian prefix. Likely Julie checking in with her new number.

"Hey, girl," Paula said, answering.

"Have I reached Ram Musahar's satellite phone?"

"Uh, yes. Sorry. He's at another number now. I can give it to you if you'd like." The man had an Indian accent.

"Paula? It's Benny. I am in the country and wondering if I can drop by."

*Benny...Drop by...*Overhead, the strange plane's erratic flybys had her attention. Neither was there any official insignia. It banked sharply and dove straight for her outboard. This was no government plane. The timber poachers were back to clear the reservoir of any obstacles, including her. She had to get off the water—now.

"Paula. Are you still there?"

She stuffed the phone into the bag at her feet, Benny's voice reduced to a jumble of spits and pops. Over and over, she yanked at the motor. *Damn, damn.* Why hadn't she cleaned the carburetor like she'd planned? Behind, the plane touched down, shooting a plume of water into the air. It would be on her in less than a minute.

The truck was closer than the citadel and her rifle. She jammed the emergency oars into the gunwales but hadn't taken a stroke when the plane overtook the boat and cut her off.

A man flung open the cockpit hatch. "Does this mean you will not join me for lunch on the Danube?"

"Benny. For goodness' sake. Why didn't you say it was you?"

"I said I would drop in. That's what I just did."

His naughty smirk left her no choice but to cock her

head and stifle a smile. "You really had me scared."

"Of what?"

"The loggers. Didn't Ram tell you?"

"Yeah, but those rowdies will not be back. Engine not turning over?"

She shook her head.

"Try again," he said, and on the third pull it churned to life.

"I will meet you at the citadel dock. I heard about Marco. Poor guy."

****

How odd it happened when the sun was at its highest and brightest.

From the dock, at first it sounded like the howling inside the enclosure was centered around the feeding trough. Her fear that a bear or other wild animal would swim to the peninsula was stronger now that Marco was alone.

She waited until Benny was close enough to see her enter the enclosure, then she followed Marco's barks to the same spot he'd taken refuge after being shot. He paced frantically while on the opposite shore the lone wolf, Red, and Game Boy sat howling. When Marco saw her, he trotted to her side, whimpering.

She could go for her rifle. One shot into the air would scatter the new wolf pack, hopefully forever, but it might scatter Marco, too. She didn't expect him to ever lose his terror of gun blasts. "Come on, boy. Let's go." She marched in the direction of the dock and Benny's voice. He followed no more than five minutes, halted, and turned abruptly to return the howls which had become ever more insistent.

"I'm here." Paula waved when she caught sight of

Benny teetering atop a log. Almost a month since the wedding, she braced herself for his downcast eyes and perhaps the inevitable "Why didn't you call?" Neither of them made any move to hug, yet his face was as mirthful as the last time. A web of laugh lines broke across it when Marco pounced and lapped Benny's cheek.

"Marco. No. Down," Paula said.

Just before the wolf obeyed, Benny examined the shaved leg of bristly hair. "He has definitely recovered." He massaged Marco's ears while Paula patted the wolf's neck, their eyes sparkling in the shared enjoyment of the wolf.

Benny slid his hand toward hers but paused, his eyes suddenly narrow, hesitant.

"Sorry, but I'm not going to be much fun today," Paula said. "I've got a situation with Marco." Benny's arrival was fortuitous but only because it alerted her to the return of the shore pack. The trick would be to let him help her distract Marco from his siblings without encouraging the man. Or was she making more of his invitation than it deserved? It wasn't a candlelight dinner on a Danube cruise boat. He wanted to *do lunch*. Grab a burger.

No. He wanted to get her in his private plane. Fly to the most romantic river on earth for a dockside lunch. And no doubt seduce her with free-flowing vintage wine. What made this flyboy think he could appear without so much as a call and she would drop everything to keep him entertained?

"Marco's siblings have turned up again to lure him off the island. You must hear the howling."

"I will help in any way I can," Benny said. "I am not expected back in Athens."

225

"Marco, sit." The wolf continued pacing and whining until she pulled a treat from her pocket and sat on her haunches to pop it into his mouth. "Athens?"

"My jet lands there from India. I always use the seaplane for quick trips around the Mediterranean. Life is too short to waste it inside chaotic airports. I do love that little plane." He pointed skyward. "Up there, it is easy to see what is worth fighting for and what is not. Three days to myself and the wings to go anywhere."

She stared at him, askance. "What makes you think that's enough time to accomplish what you've got planned?"

"Aha. You have caught me in my deception of self-importance." He grinned, enjoying her caustic quip for some strange reason. Or was he too full of himself to catch it? "In fact, there is no need for me at any of the meetings. My junior assistants are quite capable."

"That's—not what I meant."

He blinked a few times, the lines of his brow suddenly revealing his age. "Is there anything I can do to help you?" This open-ended offering could mean anything. He knew it and so did she.

"Let's see if we can get Marco away from the pack and inside my cabin." Her hand lighted on Benny's shoulder before she could stop herself.

"Marco. Let's go." Paula strode forward and turned. The wolf searched her face but didn't move. Not until Benny joined Paula did Marco trot between them. They walked in silence but continually slowed to let him catch up.

Marco soon fell farther and farther behind until Paula looked back and he wasn't there at all. "Marco? Marco?" She dashed over the ground they'd just covered until she saw him up ahead, already back to the shoreline—the pack waiting, but silent.

Such a desolate howl slid over the reservoir from his puckered mouth. She moved closer to crouch a few meters away and called tenderly.

"Come home, baby. It's going to be cold soon." Her voice was shaky and tight because she was feeling it, too. Something had shifted. "No, sweetie. Please. Let's go." Tears streamed across her cheeks. The warmth of Benny's hand lighted on her shoulder.

Marco stepped forward into the glowing orb of an October sun. With the water washing over his front paws, he raised his proud curved snout, the one she'd washed, kissed, rubbed playfully, and patted. A howl erupted, not so much sad but edged, decisive, lifting into sharp yelps.

God help her, but she needed him.

He stood motionless, then pivoted to face her, his deep amber eyes locked with hers as if he had decided once and for all—he belonged on the island.

But it was only goodbye. Marco plunged into the water and swam as best he could for the far shore.

"No. No. Marco." Paula would have splashed in after him had Benny not held her back.

"Let him go, Paula. Let him go where he belongs."

"Marco. I love you." Paula fell to her knees, bent double, the sight of him shrinking from view felt like a giant hook to the heart, ripping through, shredding off, to lay strewn between them on the very ground where she had carried him to safety: where he redeemed her and put the pieces of her together again.

"Don't leave me." Why are you leaving? *I can save you. Not like...Goran, forgive me. Oh, God, but I wanted to help you.*

Or the faceless person who changed Paula's diaper, wrapped her in a freshly laundered blanket. Pink, like the new baby bonnet she wore. Tucked her in one last time and left the bassinet under the bright lights of the hospital's staff entrance.

All this at once pushed her to the ground and held her there. When she raised her head, Marco was a mere dot in the water, bobbing in and out of view.

"He's sinking." Paula rose, shoving the wet strands of hair off her face. His front legs were weak—the water cold. "He's not going to make it."

"He is. Look. The red wolf is swimming to get him."

A streak of tawny fur and chevron wake reached Marco. It paused, turned, and swam back, hauling the gray mass to shore. She pulled him, mane first, across the gravel, and lapped at his face. It took Marco a few minutes before he struggled up, shook the water from himself with a satisfied fury, and joined in the reunion. Red's new mate, taller but disturbingly gaunt, stood back but eventually moved into the prancing round to sniff the new kid. Only now did it occur to Paula that her wolves' halcyon days of ready-made raw game were over.

They trotted into the trees and disappeared.

Marco didn't even glance back. No, he didn't. "Go where you belong, sweetheart," Paula whispered.

She stayed long after dark, watching the hoarfrost creep into a weedy field at the shore…and wondered. Benny fetched Paula's flashlight, down coat, and a blanket from the cabin. Marco's scent lingered on them, which in the past would have been a comfort.

When Benny wrapped a sheepskin throw from the plane around her, his icy fingers grazed her cheek. "This is nothing more than a windbreaker," she said, pinching the sleeve of his thin leather trench coat. There's no need for both of us here. Go and warm yourself in the cabin."

He took the flashlight from beside her and wheeled around, his footsteps fading on the stairs. No more than a half hour later he was back. "I have a fire going and water on for tea. Do you realize neither one of us has eaten since this morning?"

Shrugging the blankets off, Paula pushed herself to her feet and scanned the black strip of water. Seeing nothing but the memory of Marco's head sinking in and out of view, she turned and pressed her face to Benny's chest, trying to squeeze the image from her mind.

"I am so sorry he is not returning." He cradled the back of her head in his palms. "Not tonight, at least."

Chapter Twenty-Three

Inside Paula's cottage, Benny spread the wool throws and blankets along the window alcove in the way someone lays out a sleeping spot. Paula put a pot of leftover borscht on her new gas range and began sawing chunks from the crispy sourdough loaves she'd baked in the wood-fired ovens in the citadel.

The mundane familiarity of the spongy loaves soaked up some of the sorrow of losing Marco just hours before. Benny nudged past a few times with armloads of firewood from the stacks outside the kitchen door.

"That's thoughtful of you to keep the fire going. You seem to know what you're doing." How aloof and inhospitable her words sounded.

He didn't flash one of his toothy grins as he squeezed by but merely rubbed her upper back in a brief, soothing touch before crouching to feed kindling into the potbelly woodstove behind her. "I haven't lit that one since last spring," Paula said. "It's going to be real toasty in here tonight."

In the same instant she reached behind her to give his shoulder a grateful squeeze, he rose and collided with her outstretched arm, almost pulling Paula on top of him as he toppled sideways.

Benny clambered up, brushing his pants with erratic flicks. "Sorry."

"Sorry." Awkward silence.

"I better get out of your way while you cook. Do you mind if I sit here? Or I could get the wine out of the plane."

He was trying ever so hard, a slight erratic edge to his serene demeanor.

"I have a rule never to drink when I'm sad," she said.

"Smart. Oh. The soap. I brought you a box of my goat soap. I should bring that up."

With him halfway out of his chair, she laid her hand across his. "Thank you, but...it's such a long way down there in the dark. Just relax. Anyway, the soup is ready. I hope you like beets."

They ate in a weighty silence broken only when Benny said, "This is absolutely delicious. Goran told me what a good cook you were, but I just thought it was what every husband is expected to say of their spouse's cooking. I would love to return the favor, but I am afraid all I can cook is curry."

She had no doubt this enigmatic man could cook. She put down her spoon and closed her eyes, imagining the exotic aroma of cinnamon and ginger wafting from a pot on a stove where a man stood with a wooden spoon, but when he turned to smile at her—it was Goran.

"Benny. I'm not myself tonight. I'm sorry."

They exchanged fleeting smiles and finished their meal in silence. It was only when he insisted on doing the dishes and began filling the sink with water she asked, "How is it you know Goran?"

"Ram's father took Goran into our family like a son. You knew that, didn't you?"

Paula nodded from her seat at the table.

"I had the dairy and factory to run, but we sometimes hung out when he was in India and Ram was away working."

She threw her head back and sighed. Of course. From everything she'd heard, why wouldn't Goran and Ram's womanizing uncle be two of a kind. "Yeah. I can see it." Paula chucked a piece of wood into the firebox so hard it hit the brick backing. "Two handsome bachelors with money to burn." She slammed the iron door shut. "That was before me, so it's none of my business, I suppose."

The dirty soup pot dropped from Benny's hands into the brackish water with a splash as he turned to her, wiping his dripping fingers on his jeans. "I am here because I am attracted to you so, yes, it is your business. I know what people say about me. Some of it is true…or used to be. Most of it is not. May I set the record straight?"

A crushing weariness took hold of her. This same refrain from Goran never worked because the paparazzi's technicolor *record* was everywhere. His women were social climbers, always "using him." As if he wasn't using them.

Before long, in addition to Goran's sex addiction, she had to forebear the loathsome stares of other women. "If you're going to fuck them," she'd told him, "have a thought for me and at least do it between four solid walls where cameras can't reach."

"I'm listening."

Benny slid into the chair opposite Paula. His hands, clasped as they were to within an inch of her own, felt more like a gesture of desperation than the *bended knee* illusion of respect he likely intended.

"I was single and only in my late twenties when the money started to come in," Benny said. "I could not get enough of the women and parties. I thought, why not? I figured we would soon lose everything and end up back where we started in the slum. But that was before I knew how much baksheesh we were paying. After Ram's father was murdered, those corrupt cronies came to my door instead.

"Yes, I was a party boy but nowhere on the level of Goran. My idea of fun was not to numb myself on drugs and act like a wild beast in heat on a beach somewhere. I never joined those groups."

She couldn't look Benny in the face, and he seemed to know why. Paula *had* joined the group sex in her first year with Goran—more times than she wanted to admit. All to please him.

"By the time Goran met you, our wild fun consisted of riding horses near the dairy. Playing scrabble in the evenings. I rarely saw him after that." A touch both cautious and ardent, he slid his hands forward to cup hers, sending a jolt of warmth into her loins, no less insistent than the day of the wedding.

"Forgive me." He removed his hands to reach for the woodpile behind him. "Perhaps it is not fair to talk about dead men who have no chance to defend themselves."

"Goran isn't dead," Paula said.

Clunk. The piece of firewood slipped from his hand back into the pile. He looked at her, his face pinched with confusion.

"I can prove it, too. There's a fresco of me in the chapel that Goran could only have painted after he disappeared."

Benny stared into his lap a moment, then his head snapped in the direction of the citadel. "Can I see it?"

"You mean tonight?"

He rose and grabbed the flashlight from atop the fridge. "Right now."

****

When the life-size image of Paula spread from the darkness like a pool of mercury, Benny crouched and pressed his palm to her cheek, as if to brush away the sand memorialized there in oil. It may have been the dead air or how the shadows set his eyes into bottomless pits, but the way his fingers slithered along the painting to where the perspiration bubbled at the swell of her breasts made her scalp crawl.

"This is why it's not going to work," Paula said. "It's been so long since I've been with anyone except Goran that…" That what? Where *was* she going with this missive on the benefits of celibacy?

Benny rose and to his credit bounced the flashlight's white lightning off the ceiling instead, erasing the interrogation-cell mood from the subterranean space.

"I've grieved that man for seven years. Here I come to finally be done with him, and this is what I find. Goran couldn't have done this before he disappeared because we were never apart. He painted this knowing I would find it."

That seemed to utterly baffle Benny. "And do what?" he said.

"Wait for him to show up."

"You would return to him?"

"Not in the way you're thinking but as a kind of…support. I can't abandon him for the second time."

Benny stared at the fresco and said nothing.

"You must have known Goran had mental health struggles," Paula finally said. "That's the reason I left, not because I stopped loving him. You see that, don't you?"

He paused at first. "Yeah, I see it." He handed the flashlight to her and groped his way up the crypt's dark stairs.

She followed close behind, lighting a path for him until they were outside the citadel, and he turned to her. "I can take the boat to your vehicle and stay at Poenari's pension for tonight."

"At this hour? I'm not going to turn you out like that."

He strode up the hillock ahead of her. "Then I'm ready for sleep."

****

As Paula crept forward to feed the fire a final time before bed, Benny stirred in his alcove and shifted onto his side. The flames licked the edges of the open door, casting the muscles of his broad back into the virile sheen of a man much younger and more indestructible than his fifty-two years.

She changed into her usual wool long johns and lay awake in the dark, a sense of panic pecking at her insides—a distant image of someone lying in this same spot for years to come, the skin on their bony limbs growing translucent and wrinkly in the threadbare patches of men's underwear.

"Benny? You still awake?"

"Hmmm."

"Do you think I'm searching for something that doesn't exist? With Goran, I mean. Am I acting like some old woman in black mourning clothes? Putting in time until she joins her husband."

"I cannot answer that." A short, brittle silence fell between them until…"But if so, you are not alone."

235

It wasn't clear which one of them fell asleep first. Either way, it took a long time.

Chapter Twenty-Four

Paula woke. *Plink, plink, plink*. Frantic bursts of ice pellets were slamming into the windowpane above her. Inside the bay window, his blankets lay folded into a neat pile. No sign of Benny. Under the soothing white noise of the hail, she'd overslept.

This couldn't be how they'd part.

She dragged herself out of bed, tugged her skirt and sloppy sweater over her long johns, and slipped into the first boots she could find, then clomped outside with them untied. Halfway down the stairs to the dock, the edge of the plane appeared with Benny inside the cockpit. "Benny. Benny." Not likely he could hear her above the metallic din of the hail, so she waved her arms in a broad arc above her until he lifted the hatch to indicate he was waiting.

He climbed to the bottom of the drop-down stairs and stood patiently in the downpour while she clambered into the cockpit passenger side. Now they were both dripping.

"You were leaving without saying goodbye?" Paula said.

His eyes flew open. "Of course not. I was doing my preflight checks." He looked her up and down, a boyish pucker forming at the side of his mouth. "You look good in here."

Paula flung her soaked mop of auburn hair from her

eyes, horrified to see the wet folds of her long johns pooled in the gap between her skirt and the flopping tongues of her lowcut boots.

"Like hell I do." They both laughed until she caught sight of a photograph taped above his altimeter. "Is that—?" She reached over and pinched one loose corner between her thumb and finger. "This is the photo Goran copied inside the crypt." She twisted to face him. "Where did you find it?"

"Goran gave it to me. Said he used it for a painting and did not need it anymore. When I saw you at the wedding, I realized the woman was much more than one of his random dates. I knew then why he wanted me to have it."

"I don't understand." She spoke to the photo in a voice so frail Benny couldn't have heard her above the hail. "When did he…?"

Benny shifted to face her and shook his head. "I must confess. The wedding was not my first time here. For the past seven years, I have been stalking you. Or the painting, I should say. I flew all over this world trying to find it. Galleries, collectors' homes, anywhere which housed his work. I even came here once and looked from one end of this island to the other. But not inside the crypt."

The hail's deafening drumming began to burn itself out, leaving the sealed cockpit in utter silence and each of them lost to their own thoughts. "Why this painting?" she asked.

"Why is anyone obsessed with a particular work of art? The only thing I can come up with is the childlike glee in your eyes. It was like looking into…" A pained grimace gripped him. "The face of an emotional virgin."

"Virgin! Believe me, Goran was not my first disappointment in life. Not at all."

"No. No. Of course not. It was my own interpretation. A craving for the idyllic childhood I never had."

"I expect you'll want to set up house in the crypt now and live out your childhood fantasies."

Benny chuckled, taking up Paula's hand and kissing her palm as he did so, before releasing it. "The woman in that mural no longer exists. Not in body. Not in mind. The wedding and this visit have given me a real dose of reality—you see, I too have been searching for someone who no longer exists."

She slumped and turned away from his smiling face. *Oh...that hurt.* More than she expected. Benny, the only man since Goran who had managed to crack open the door to her heart, had taken one startled look and slammed it shut. *Of course, what else should I expect? "This is why it's not going to work." I said that last night. Didn't I? DIDN'T I?*

"Paula?" She started at Benny's hand on her knee and found herself pinching the bridge of her nose so hard it hurt. Exactly how long had she been muttering to herself?

"Are you okay?" he said.

"You're saying Goran isn't alive, is that it?"

He sighed, bringing his chin to his chest. "My flight checks take twenty minutes. The rest of the morning I have sat here trying to think of a way not to hurt you. You would not want me to lie, though, would you?"

Ha. Why not? Brutal honesty hadn't worked for them so far. Her energy and patience were dissipating. "Just tell me when he gave you the photo."

"During his last weeks in India, he came to my dairy and asked if I could fly him here to do some painting inside the citadel. I did not think anything of it. It made sense he would want to be somewhere familiar after the break-up. We used the jet. I dropped him and his paints here using my seaplane and returned a few days later. We were not gone from India much more than four or five days."

She sat frozen to the spot while, within her soul a mash-up of assumptions and reality duked it out.

Benny reached for her but quickly drew back. "I came so very close to telling you last night. Forgive me."

She waved his apology aside, the heat rising in her cheeks. *Wouldn't Goran have a laugh over this, the mother of all dramas, my embellishments and paranoia nothing but a fantasy.*

"I'm sorry I wasted so much of your time," Paula said, still avoiding his eyes. "Truly, I mean it. You're a busy man." Feeling utterly lost and with nothing else to say, she motioned to the door on his side. "Can you let me out?"

"Already?"

"Grieving is time-consuming." Paula looked past him to the dock. "I've got Marco, and Goran, for the second time I might add, and—" She stopped short of including Benny on the list. He swung the door wide, climbed to the dock, and stepped aside to let her pass. At the last minute, she swiveled and extended her palm. "Have a safe flight."

He left her hand suspended for the longest time as if observing a strange ritual of a lost tribe. Instead of shaking it, he cradled it between both of his. "I…Well, you too. Stay safe."

She felt his eyes on her as she tramped up the stairs to her cabin. Only when she heard his door slam and the plane's engine turn over did she stop and look. The plane puttered out of view behind the citadel. The engine revved into a pitched wail, the chop and slap of waves reached her, but still, she couldn't see it.

In the yard, she climbed the hillock for a better view and felt the earth under her shake as his plane came from behind, buzzing past her towers and climbing. She raised her arm and as she did so Benny banked the seaplane over the hydro dam and down the Varges Valley toward Bucharest. How incredible it must be to see the dam's soaring walls and her citadel from the air. She watched the plane until it was nothing but a dot.

She had never been in a seaplane. Would she ever get the chance again?

****

Paula spent a lot of time on the mainland behind the citadel that fall, collecting more winter wood than necessary since there was always a chance Marco might return to her. Red circled with her pups one spring day, but Marco never appeared again.

It was too painful to speculate what may have happened to him.

Chapter Twenty-Five

They started with one, Paula's treat. Then agreed to another. By the time Aunt Lisbet slammed the third stein of overproof stout in front of Paula, the old woman was glowing. Whether from winning the second game of pool or outright drunkenness didn't much matter. Neither of them would be trying to drive home.

A month after Marco's departure, Paula found herself inside the pension's dining hall, waylaid once again by Aunt Lisbet's taste for beer—a crate of the homebrew she sold to them regularly and which Paula had helped her haul in.

Too pricey for locals, the pension's dining hall was the closest the village came to having a pub for tourists. With mess-hall dining tables and a pool table in one corner, it doubled as a games room for guests. On this gray, slushy November day before the snow, a mammoth fire blazed in its glassed-in woodstove.

Claudia had suggested she stay with them for the weekend, and Paula admitted she found the old aunt's company…invigorating.

The woman toddled from the toilets and paused to unpin something from the dining hall's bulletin board. It was the kind of cork wall which operated like an archeological dig, layer upon inevitable layer: signed beer coasters of supposedly famous people; paper money from around the world; a car rental flyer; amateur photos of Poenari fortress which Paula always avoided; a notice of a lost—probably dead—parrot from the previous winter; and a mug shot of someone she had tried to plaster over with a photo of her citadel.

"Would you look at this." Aunt Lisbet slammed the piece of yellowed newsprint onto the table in front of Paula. "The Ripper's obit." She whispered even though, along with Claudia, they were the only ones present.

Someone had scrawled: *Bucharest Ripper, 2009*, in one corner of the rectangular clipping.

Albert Haller, a serial murderer known for a killing spree in Bucharest during the 1940s, died yesterday of heart failure at a Bucharest institution for the criminally insane. He was 84. From 1946 to 1950, he strangled 12 women and cannibalized their hands and feet. During the first 30 years of his incarceration, he was held at a Soviet-era asylum in the Varges Valley where he participated in trials of the first pharmaceuticals for psychosis.

That's as far as Paula got. Despite the fog upstairs, she was sure the doctor was called Haller in the journal.

"What was his psychiatrist's name? Do you remember?"

"You bet I do," Aunt Lisbet said. "I was in charge of laundering the staff uniforms. I had to fold them and take them to their rooms. His name was embroidered on the inside of the collar—Dr. R. Lasorov."

The journal had been written—not by the doctor—but the Ripper himself.

Paula gripped the edge of the heavy table, scenes replaying inside her head: the Haller woman's timid curiosity with the tower of her notorious uncle's happiest incarceration. What to make of the journal now she knew it was penned by the Ripper? It's daring vigilante justice had spurred her to take on the wolves, protect Goran's legacy, face the threat from the loggers, and so many other things which had wrinkled the flat plane of her benign existence.

If a depraved soul pens a heroic tale, does that then make them more likeable? After all, she'd judged Goran's creations and found him guilty based on the same reasoning. Good thing she hadn't tossed the journal into the fire yet. It was more valuable than she'd thought.

****

From the vantage point of Aunt Lisbet's cottage, the clapboard outbuilding Claudia lived in when not teaching resembled a barn.

"You don't think I torture myself with nonstop snooker tournaments, do you?" Claudia caught Paula's confusion and held the weathered door open for her. "I reached an impasse with my mother. This is where I stay on weekends."

Other than Claudia's wrap-around granite breakfast counter, stainless steel appliances, and Italian leather sofa in front of a wood-burning stove, inside reminded Paula of the rustic loft she'd shared with two other students while attending the University of British Columbia.

"I drive up from Bucharest to unplug from the world. No internet. No phone. And definitely no television. You may not have noticed, but Mum does have a satellite phone if she needs to reach me." Claudia spoke over her shoulder from a short hallway. "I have to catch her early morning before the competitions start or she won't answer it…Back here's the bathroom. That sofa makes into my bed."

She headed up a steep set of stairs. "You can sleep up here in the loft on the studio's daybed."

At the top, watercolors of wolves in their natural habitat lined the walls. They lounged in the sun by a river, sated, a consumed carcass in the background. None of the vicious facial expressions of the chapel.

Paula was immediately drawn to the portrait of a gray wolf, still propped on an easel. "Is this…?"

"Yes, I've been painting him since Red left. I knew it was only a matter of time until you lost him."

Paula's eyes, wide and glassy, roamed to Claudia and back to the painting. She ran a finger around the dark outline of Marco's ear, and a single tear rolled down her cheek.

"It's yours whenever you want it…When you're ready. It hasn't even been a month."

Paula wandered painting to painting, a chronic tightness in her chest easing. Claudia had captured on canvas what Paula couldn't explain—the budding love and respect in her heart for the noble wolf. "If I lost my dog, people would understand. But a wolf? All I get is silence on the phone. It's hard to take."

"You can't blame them," Claudia said. "We've demonized wolves for hundreds of years—now we want to turn them into lap dogs. It might be worse. They're the stealth bombers of the forest, but it doesn't define them any more than combat is the sum of a man."

Paula moved under the largest mural: wolves weaning their young, the pups ambushing each other in mock attacks. "I'd like to cover Goran's mural in the chapel with some of these. Would that be okay?"

Claudia didn't think long. "No. That wouldn't be right." She quickly added, "For what purpose?"

"This is the reality of wolves, not that...ugliness."

"Wolves still snatch babies from their cradles in India to this day. There's no wild game left. Try telling those parents that Goran's painting isn't reality."

"But when I stand in the middle of these, I feel...content."

"You don't think Goran painted for the same relief? To help him make sense of his world? What else is art for?"

****

The next morning, Claudia walked Paula to her former truck and patted the hood. "I'm half thinking to trade you the new jeep."

Was she serious? On the far side of the chocolate brown wreck sat Claudia's classic Ford Bronco SUV.

"Once your crew gets the new dock up, I suppose it would only be a target for thieves. Then you'd be back to square one." She patted the hood twice. "Bye, bye, Little Turd."

"Speaking of human waste."

The comment knit Claudia's brow.

Now that Paula knew the secret staircase below the isolation cell was real, she remembered the putrid "vapors" the plumber had described. Someone had to be down there. If it wasn't the Ripper, then might it be Aunt Lisbet's former boyfriend, the one who guarded the Ripper and was apparently snatched during the night and sent to a gulag. Elieno may not have got out of the citadel at all.

"I was wondering if you had the key to unlock the second tower."

246

"N-n-no. My nefarious cousin might know, but his lawyer has wisely barred me from contact with the imbecile. Why do you ask?"

"I could lie and say I want it open for the public. Truth is—there might be a body in there. I mean, in the hidden staircase. I'd rather get rid of it."

Claudia's lips curled with unholy delight. "Wait right here." She disappeared into a shack but soon trotted back with an electric drill holding the mightiest bit Paula had ever seen.

"This will do it for you." She hoisted it level with Paula's line of sight. "Drill out the keyhole and the whole deadbolt will come loose."

Neither woman moved.

"I was wondering…if you want to come with me? I mean. Only if you have time on your schedule today."

The Claudia Paula remembered during their first meeting suddenly emerged. She threw back her head and cackled. "There's nothing on my schedule that can trump a desiccated skeleton in a stinking stairwell."

Chapter Twenty-Six

Claudia and Paula climbed the tower where Paula had peered out the broken window at Poenari's mannequins. After drilling through the metal door's deadbolt, they used a wedge to pry out the wall's boulder and pushed on the lever. *Thud.* The hatch dropped cleanly without a single creak of the hinges.

Claudia couldn't get into the dark hole fast enough. "I've been hearing about this for so long. I can't believe I'm here." She hung over the opening with one of Ram's powerful flashlights.

The beam of light settled on a spiral staircase much like the tower but with a hollow cavity at its center. A frail-looking wrought-iron banister was the only barrier keeping one from going into an endless fall.

"Nothing? Right?" Paula said, standing with her own flashlight and not feeling quite as brave as she'd expected. It was one thing to idealize the secret stairways inside the journal—another to be hit with a chilly rush of mold-laced air when the trap dropped open.

"I'm going down."

Before Paula could argue, Claudia had turned and popped from sight. She left a metallic *clatter* and *creak* in her wake, until all Paula could see was a bouncing glow far below.

"Don't go too far." On her knees and hunched over the pitch black, Paula yelled, "Are you okay?"

A faint echo, elongated and shaky. "Fine."

When it had been far too long since that response, Paula struggled to her feet with an urge to do something—other than dive in herself.

Bang, bang, bang. The familiar retort broke the silence, but Paula couldn't tell whether the sound was fading or growing. The next time Paula looked down, a face entered her beam and Claudia boosted herself from the opening. She was wet from the knees down.

"There is one fuck of a lot of water down there. No wonder it stinks."

"Anything...floating? You know."

"Nobody—alive *or* dead. A passage branches off. Must slope all the way to the reservoir because it's filled with water. I could still make out a bit of daylight at the far end of it."

Paula exhaled all the oxygen from her lungs and slid down to rest against one of the walls.

"How's this for clever?" Claudia was pointing at the trap. "The metal bar that holds that door in place looks like it can be manipulated by hand from inside the stairs...Put the boulder over there back, climb in, close the hatch behind you, and you could vanish from this room without anyone knowing."

The wet footprints. Paula's jaw dropped. "Could someone get in and out of the citadel through here?"

"They'd have to really want to sneak in. The loggers are gone, but you may want to think about art thieves. I'd alarm that door."

Someone else entirely was on Paula's mind. The Ripper's moat may have been a fiction of his imagination, but the secret staircase was real. He never escaped—but he could have.

"How about the other tower?" Claudia said.

Paula knew what Claudia wanted but wished she didn't. "It's all closed up. The boulder is cemented in permanently."

The light in Claudia's eyes began to dance, and she whistled, long and low. "Nothing's permanent...We'll need the hammers and wedges you use for log splitting and a crowbar."

Inside the second tower, while Paula pried the floor tiles from where the trap door should be, Claudia hammered the wedge into the mortar surrounding the stones. "We're making enough goddamn noise to wake the dead. *Hee hee hee hee.*"

"*Ha,*" Paula responded. She peeled back one corner of a tile to see a sliver of an indentation between two planks. "I think I've found it."

That was encouragement enough. Once the entire trap door was exposed, Claudia drove the mallet and wedge into the mortar so hard Paula feared a trio of stones would let loose and crush the lever.

Soon enough, a single boulder fell out, revealing the release bar. Claudia slid it forward and a rusty creak of hinges opened the cavity below.

No horrific smell of rotting flesh, Paula thought, remembering what the old plumber told her.

Again, after they'd trained both flashlights into the hole, appearing to throw caution aside, Claudia hopped into the darkness and out of Paula's view. *Bang, bang, bang...*then nothing. And more silence.

Paula scrambled from her cross-legged posture and leaned over the hole. "Claudia? Claudia? You okay?" There was no way she was already out of earshot. Then again, she hadn't heard any crashes which would mean the stairs gave way. They could have ended abruptly, though, with Claudia stepping into nothing but space.

Paula placed her foot on the first step. Then two more. "Claudia?"

Her beam picked up dark cloths spaced at random along the cylindrical staircase, like an armful of laundry thrown down basement stairs. She descended only to see it was a pair of khaki type pants. A few steps farther, she passed a long-sleeved shirt of the same color, hung up on the wrought-iron banister. A black work boot lay nearby.

She'd been so caught up with following the trail of clothes, by the time she looked above her, the trap door opening was no more than a smudge of light.

Cheep, cheep. Squ-eak.

She whipped the flashlight to shoulder height and scoured the black-streaked ledges, inches from her face. The next step down—another squeak behind her. She jerked the light over her shoulder, heart pounding, expecting the clipped ears and fangs she knew so well. This dark, dripping passage, its entrance a mere slit, was a perfect breeding ground for bats.

She saw her dad goading her on into the murky water, already up to her waist, the sharp stalactites overhead ready to split her skull asunder. The buzzing colossus of bats vibrated as one against the ceiling. Any minute they could engulf her entire head, nibble her lips and ears to bloody pulp, peck out her eyeballs.

"Look over there," her dad said, pointing to a six-inch-wide spider hanging from a translucent spindle. "It's just like Genevieve, isn't it?" It was every bit as beautiful as her pet spider, Paula thought, her pulse slowing.

According to Paula's mum, he'd done exactly what

he vowed at the adoption agency: "You can have your girl," he told her at the time, "but she'll always be my boy just the same."

Her dad had tried to convince her inside the cave. "Paula, the bats have no interest in you. They'll stay up there where they live."

Oh no, they won't. She still had the scar to prove it.

"Remember what I taught you about the submarine's sonar? The bats' sonar is on right now. They're more scared of running into you, than you are of them."

That was a lie, too. The one on the floor of her dark bedroom wasn't scared of her at all. And that's why it sank its teeth into her arm when she tried to lift it, mistaking it for a stray sock. Older now, she understood rabid animals.

The next step down, she fell against the wrought iron—*squeak, squeak, squeak*. No bats, just the banister settling against her weight. She tried again. "Claudia?"

"I'm down here," came a surprisingly clear reply. Paula headed to the white corduroy jacket Claudia wore atop her jeans, tourist season long over. Now that she knew the stairs and Claudia were both safe, it took only a minute to reach the spot where Claudia was bent forward examining something.

"Claudia?" Paula placed her hand against the woman's shoulder. A skeletal torso collapsed into her legs; its hollow-eyed skull snapped back. She shrieked and stumbled backward up the steps but missed one. Down she tumbled into the remains. *Crr—unch*. Like the snap of branches underfoot.

"Don't, for Christ's sake, fall off this thing." Claudia clambered up the final steps to Paula. "Or we'll end up with three corpses instead of two."

"Wha—"

She propped herself against the banister, panting. "Yup, another body down there. I figured the clothes had to belong to someone. The skeleton down there is only wearing boxer shorts and an ID lanyard around his neck. Name's Elieno. No straitjacket or leg manacles like this guy. But one side of his skull is missing."

Paula ran her flashlight up and down the skeleton near her foot. In addition to the straitjacket, it was dressed in white cotton pants and one leather shoe. It was then Paula noticed a band of cloth protruding between its teeth.

"He's a bit more mangled since you fell on him, but he looked fine to me except for a broken leg. Probably starved to death."

Claudia pulled out a corner of the visible white collar. "It looks like here lies Dr. R. Lasorov."

Chapter Twenty-Seven

Doctor Lasorov did die of starvation, the coroner's report said. Aunt Lisbet's old boyfriend, of blunt trauma to the head, probably from the rusty flashlight police had found in the watery passage below.

Since both men were listed as missing, Paula went with Claudia to the police station in the next city over and brought the journal for whatever use it might be. They speculated Albert Haller had used the guard's uniform to catch the doctor by surprise.

"The Ripper could have easily escaped at any time by wearing it."

Claudia translated Paula's comment. The cop said something and shrugged. "He thinks Albert Haller must have liked the place. A lot more than he liked the doctor. He wonders if he was one of Dr. Lasorov's rape victims."

Paula shuddered. Who would sexually assault a known mass murderer and cannibal?

She set Claudia to tracking down the Haller woman's phone number or email. It might comfort the Ripper's descendant to know her uncle didn't escape when he had the chance, perhaps knowing incarceration was the best place for him. There was a measure of vigilante justice to his final two victims, his mind likely anchored securely in reality.

Within hours of sending Alberta Haller an email from the cottage laptop, the woman had emailed back.

Not only did she want the diary, but she'd attached a scanned letter her infamous uncle had written to her when she was only a child.

Your Uncle Albert, November, 1963
To My Beloved Niece, Alberta Haller
You will have the news stories, the police reports, the memories of Gustav, and perhaps even the psychiatric assessments, if they ever release them. I wanted you to know the story in my own words.

In 1946, the year I landed my first job as second violin in Bucharest's symphony, someone accused me of "being on the rag"—so I strangled them. It was my first kill and an odd episode since I'm a man and she was a woman.

I tell you this at the top because everybody wants to know "why." The only answer I have is through the "how." She was a coworker, a fellow violinist, giving me a ride home, and probably thought that was a safe insult to use on a man, even humorous.

Back then, I was the kind of killer I have since found repugnant. I didn't plan ahead. In the alley next to my flat, I reached over and wrapped my hands around her neck, and when she was dead, I hauled her body to the trunk in full view of the building, then pushed the vehicle into a marshy pond I knew would soon freeze over. After that, I anticipated my killings with the surgical precision I would need to start collecting hands and feet.

She had the ugliest hands and feet, anyway—meaty and stubby like one of our perpetually angry uncles, an alcoholic bricklayer. The emphasis here on "angry," not bricklayer or alcoholic. I've known alcoholics who started as some of the finest humans you could hope for.

My mother, for one.

When did my hatred of women start? That's what this new doctor wants to know. He's a very kind young man from Bucharest who tells me I'm a misogynist with severe dysphoria, although the woman I sent to the bottom of that pond in 1946 would call me "bat-shit psycho."

All this is true. To the degree I hate women—Frida and my mother hated men.

Frida was a skyscraper of a dark Saxon beauty with elegant hands and feet. A hellish governess who arrived after my drunken mother dropped me on my head, so the story goes. Frida eventually skedaddled back to Denmark eight years later, but by then the damage from this sadistic bitch's childcare was done.

Yes, I include the obligatory depraved childhood here so look away, niece, if you don't wish to know about the grandmother you never met or her lover.

Like my mother, Frida was a flapper from the jaded twenties, a drinking companion and fellow cock-tease to the rash of young lords around the palace. In the early bloom of my hatred against women, that's what I thought of my mother and Frida.

Otherwise, these two untethered women couldn't have been more different. My mother, dumpy and abandoned by my father in favor of his hunting lodge, was like a dying dwarf star pulled into the spinning galaxy which was Frida. Looking to this governess for her salvation was like opening a parched mouth in a downpour only to find sulfuric acid raining down.

I continue my story with how Frida held me upside down from my ankles while I screamed—one of the earliest torments before things escalated—then immediately shift to an incident which stalks my daydreams. Not for its depraved cinematic nature, but because of what I saw in my young brother's eyes.

Like any three-year-old, Gustav dirtied his pants and tried to ignore it. Not until I caught a whiff and looked at him in horror did he run, but Frida caught him and yanked his pants down. "Aha, Master Gustav. And now it is your turn."

The smell of my brother's feces left me long ago, but not the vile gleam in Frida's eyes. It plunged Gustav into a kind of self-propelled seizure, his skinny arms and legs pumping like pistons, eyes bulging, mouth slack, already inside the torture before it had even begun.

"I'll take it." I scooted along the tiled floor of our playroom to where Gustav continued to beat his heels. "Whatever it is."

Frida studied me off the tip of her weasel-like nose as one woman might covet the pearls of another. She admired my idea so much she upped the ante the next time. We had two choices from now on: be the victim or the tormentor.

Our governess did have a patient side after all; she could sit and smoke for hours waiting for my brother to press the lit end into my bare buttocks. Gustav, the tender-hearted piano player, never got used to inflicting pain no matter how dreadful I said the waiting was.

By the time my father caught wind of what was happening, I was already eight years old. He rushed in from his hunting lodge, but it was too late. Frida had escaped home to Denmark, my mother left swinging from her noose in the palace cellar.

Too late for me and Gustav, too.

Now it's my doctor's turn to speculate why I eat

women's body parts. It's no surprise I inherited my mother's depression and came into the orbit of a monster, but it's the childhood head trauma, he says, which seems to seal the deal for psychopaths. He's my second doctor here in the tower, and I trust him. So, I agreed to be part of a clinical trial of a new type of medicine which he says could leave me happy—or dead. "Since I don't know anything about either of those," I told him, "it makes no difference to me."

When he asks, I say there is only one regret. Gustav used to be known as Romania's greatest pianist. People's minds gravitate to darkness, and for this reason he will forever be remembered as the brother of Romania's most notorious serial murderer.

Stay in the light, my dear niece. I don't know why your father did and I didn't. If only I could be like Gustav, neither the victim nor tormentor of my story— but the hero.

In a second file was a recording as scratchy and melancholic as a Victrola. The two young brothers played a lofty duet of Franz Schubert's "Ave Maria," the Ripper's mournful violin swaying and dipping against his brother's piano.

At the end of it, Paula went to the cottage bookcase and patted along the upper shelf where she'd left the journal for the next fire. The journal was merely the fantasy of a disturbed mind but written by a man desperate to be the hero of his own story.

Not only did Alberta Haller want it, but Paula reasoned the tourists might like it, too.

If she had the stairs inspected, could the secret passage be part of a tour all its own? They could pass out wetsuits and flashlights before the visitors began their descent into hell. Plaques and news clippings inside the former cell could tell the story of the Bucharest Ripper and his imprisonment there—that this was the site where he disposed of his final victims.

This was a possibility she needed to sleep on a night or two.

****

The Ripper's mental illness wasn't a joke, Paula decided a month later. Nor was it entertainment. She would not turn her meditation tower into a freak show and undo all the spiritual energy generated.

All summer the two friends had built a bridge of loving kindness to speed the island's hungry ghosts on their way: the doctor, the Bucharest Ripper, Goran himself, and his parents. And now she could add one more—Goran's brother.

The altar was gone, but perhaps she could find a way to heat the room and continue what Julie had started—prop up Goran's photo alongside his brother's mugshot and send both her unconditional love.

It had become *Goran's* tower, after all, long after the hospital packed up. Here, in his first studio, she imagined him piling the losses of his life onto canvas one layer at a time, no doubt unable to make sense of the schizophrenia from which all the other disasters sprang. He did end up with the family curse, but not the one Aunt Lisbet thought.

Despite the island's unsavory past, it was the only permanent residence Goran had known. He'd sent her here, and now she knew why. It wasn't just to collect the paintings in the tower.

He wanted her to have his home. The stability he

couldn't give while alive.

Paula's start in life had been rough, but Goran's existence in the midst of his illness? It was the kind of unbearable life few expect until it's sprung on them like a practical joke.

She thought of her own father. As long as he could go spelunking, descend into dark caverns, the wheels of his life kept turning as they always had. Inside the hospice house, as soon as her mum had left the room to get coffee, he yanked Paula close and whispered, "I can't walk," as if it was a terrible secret he'd just heard about.

He'd known the cancer was headed for his brain, but that morning, somewhere between his bed and the toilet, two meters away, his reason for living evaporated. Soon, her mother's only motivation would be gone, too.

Inside the former meditation tower, Paula wiped her hands on her fleece-lined work coveralls and threw the metal spatula into the bucket of leftover patching mortar. The trap door's loose boulder was once again part of the wall, as permanent as humanly possible. In the spring, she would lay the new tile.

She grabbed the bucket and headed down the worn steps, chanting to the tower ghosts swirling in her wake:

"The pure-hearted one. Being free from all sense desires.

Is not born again into this world."

She stripped off her coveralls and left everything inside the citadel kitchen, walking through to the feast hall where she'd be spending hours this winter stoking the fires to keep Goran's art safe from frost and humidity. The afternoon sun had bathed it in a striped pattern of amber rays. As she moved down the line, nodding to each painting, there on the stone floor was a trail of muddy paw prints.

Marco?

She raced down the arcade to where they crossed the rotunda to the double doors. They were ajar. This time, fortunately, there were no human footprints.

If it was Marco, he would be waiting either outside her cabin or inside the straw bale shelter she hadn't had the heart to dismantle yet. Perhaps some of the shoreline was freezing overnight and shortening the distance to the island.

At the top of the knoll, she halted at the sight of the cabin below. A light was on in the main room. No, never would she leave on a light during the day and waste energy in the generator's battery. Neither could it be Claudia, who was in Bucharest, teaching.

She backtracked off the rise, squinting into the shadows for movement, then turned and cut a wide path to the cabin behind the beech trees bordering the courtyard. Crouching in the bushes at the cabin's back door, she edged closer and peeked into the kitchen but still couldn't see movement in the lighted main room beyond.

Whoever had come onto the island while she made her repairs atop the tower might have had a dog with them and already left. She stepped back and sat on a stump, half thinking to still go down to the wolf shelter.

The main problem: her rifle was inside the cabin. What to do next? *Oh.* She pulled her head in between her knees, a familiar longing rising in her gut. *Sorry, Marco. I'm going to have to find your replacement sooner rather than later.*

Before she could raise her head and jump to her feet, the kitchen door flew open. An animal shot out into the shadows.

Chapter Twenty-Eight

"Grab 'im," Claudia's voice said. She stood in the kitchen doorway, silhouetted in her kayak wetsuit. The escaped pup gnawed Paula's boot while another squirmed in Claudia's arms.

Paula scooped up the furry ball and stepped inside. It had been too long since she'd felt the delight of an animal's warm fur against her cheek. "Aren't you the squirmy worms." She managed a peck on its head before it struggled and flopped out of her arms to the kitchen floor.

"Oh yeah," Claudia said, shoving the door closed with the edge of her dive boots. "I'm supposed to say *surprise*." She lowered her pup to the floor, and it tore off into the sitting room after Paula's.

When Paula embraced her, Claudia went stiff, arms at her sides. "You're harder to get a hold of than the pups."

Red in the face, Claudia merely shrugged. "The doctor and I will set up the wolf hall with straw from below, and then I've got to get back to Bucharest."

"Doctor?" From the kitchen sink, where Paula was lathered up to her elbows in soap, she turned to see a thin, middle-aged man with a gray ponytail show his face in the doorway between the kitchen and sitting room.

"Hello." He extended his hand, but Paula grinned and held up her soapy arms. "I'm a retired vet. From

Canada, actually. The animals are medium to high-content Arctic wolf dogs. Confiscated from a breeder in British Columbia. Pups this young don't travel well, so I was hired to accompany them here and monitor their vitals."

"That cooler over there has their food," Claudia added. "They're already eating solids. Eight weeks old, I'd say." She scooped up two bomber jackets from the kitchen chairs. "Just going to the wolf hut for the straw."

The scene was a repeat of the day Marco arrived on the island—except for the doctor.

On her way out, Claudia twisted and gave a parting wriggle of her eyebrows before closing the kitchen door. Only later did Paula realize the cheeky eyebrows were for her—and another dark figure sitting in the bay window of the main room.

"It's good to see you again, Benny." Paula leaned against the door frame, trying to look casual with crossed ankles. Their two-month separation felt much longer, yet, from where he sat, she feared he could sense her racing pulse.

He was slumped, nonchalant, feet tucked under him inside the bay window—a natural tongue-and-groove harmony with whatever space he found himself in.

She settled herself on the floor so the wolf pups could get used to her smell. Their amber eyes against the brilliant white fur pierced to her very being, and for a moment she doubted herself. Was she up for the inevitable heartbreak of owning another pet?

"I didn't hear your plane arrive."

"Touched down up reservoir and floated with the current. I always carry paddles in case of engine failure…Or surprises." The same impish grin as before cut through the final remnants of tension still hanging between them.

"Your idea, then?" She walked to the shoe rack at the door, pulled off her boots, and lifted her chin over her shoulder. "It's a long way for them."

He shrugged, a nervous tic kind of movement, and said the mother wolf was found chained and lying in her own urine, so traumatized she killed four out of six pups after the birth.

"Oh." Julie turned her cheek from him as if she'd been slapped.

"I have upset you again." He shoved off the window seat and dropped to his knees in front of her.

"No, no," Paula said. "I need to know this. Everyone does."

"Obviously, I have no idea how to talk to women anymore, much less impress them. Especially one who deserves an apology."

Benny's poker face was no help as to what this meant. She brought the pup to her cheek and moaned into the delicate musky smell of its downy fur—and that's when a few silent tears broke.

"Oh gosh." She lifted the rambunctious ball to the floor and flicked at the tears with her knuckles. "I'm not the mountain hermit I thought. It's been a hard winter so far without the wolves. But this is the best present I've ever got."

To her surprise and Benny's too, it seemed, she leaned forward without warning from her crossed-leg position and pressed her lips to his.

Afterwards, he drew in a shaky breath. "I do not know what it is you want from life, Paula."

Yet, he appeared frustrated with no one but himself.

"Perhaps you yourself do not know. But I never asked you, and that is something I need to rectify. Forgive me. In desperation, I went to Julie to understand what went so wrong last time. I told her about my childish obsession with the painting, and I repeated word for word what I said to you.

"Well...She hit me over the head with one of her sandals and called me a lovestruck ass. It was rather unpleasant because the *chappals* were dusty with cow dung."

She'd been staring at her lap to this point but couldn't resist a peek at his face.

Still kneeling before her, he wriggled forward far enough to wedge his knees against her crossed ankles. "Goran's painting is nothing more to me than a cardboard fantasy. It is the woman you have become whom I am falling in love with. That is what I wanted you to know."

Certainly, she didn't expect Benny to come circling back with such determination. Not with the way she'd rejected him because of her festering guilt over Goran's suicide. But neither had she foreseen Goran's money, or a castle in Romania, her gallery...or so many other events.

Perhaps fearing he was losing her, Benny grasped her upper arms, firmly enough to deter her from rising. "I am not Goran, but even if I was before, that is over. I always move forward because this is the only way to forgive. Maybe you would like to join me?"

Benny was offering her another chance at love. Or was it forgiveness? Of Goran? Herself? What Paula heard was Claudia at the brink of the chasm—"*Nothing's permanent*." Even her strange new friend knew change was inevitable and that one had better get used to it.

"You sure you're up for this?" She cocked her head. "I might hold you to your word."

Benny scrambled off his knees, panicked, but it had nothing to do with their future relationship. At the shoe rack behind her, he grabbed each pup in turn by the scruff like a mother wolf, Paula's leather boots falling from their jaws. "These guys are going to have to stay in the cage while you cook dinner."

"Cook dinner? I thought you were flying me out to the Danube."

Benny paused, his eyebrows climbing to the very extremity of his brow. "W-we would have to stay the night. What about the wolf pups? We cannot abandon them here until tomorrow."

Paula considered this detail. "If your doctor is still on the payroll, make him work for it while we enjoy ourselves."

At the docked seaplane, out came the vet's overnight bag and in went Paula's. Claudia had changed her mind. She didn't have any early morning rounds and felt it best to stay overnight at the cabin and assist the doctor.

Paula knew exactly what the cardio-thoracic surgeon would be assisting with.

House lights were coming on up and down the slopes of Poenari village when they lifted from the reservoir and turned south. Within the black patch of Dracula's ruins, a thrill-seeker's light twinkled. Citadel island, which had burned so brightly in her imagination since arriving, looked deceptively inconsequential.

But the snow-laden summits of the Carpathian range—they sparkled at day's end like roses on a blue silk kimono and snatched her breath away. From this angle, her life was so much fuller and more meaningful for having embraced the unknown.

A pair of mating eagles sped past the climbing seaplane to cartwheel from sight into the cavernous mouth of the hydro dam. Benny winked at her and did likewise, dipping the seaplane over the crest of whitewater surging from one of its turbines. Paula's hand flew to her throat. She looked over at him and laughed.

Reviled by some, this awe-inspiring structure was lifting Romania from the quaint inertia of its history, just as surely as Goran's fortune had prodded her into adventures unimagined.

The way for her, as Romania, was into that future.

Thank you for purchasing
this publication of The Wild Rose Press, Inc.

For questions or more information
contact us at
info@thewildrosepress.com.

The Wild Rose Press, Inc.
www.thewildrosepress.com